BIBLE TALES

FOR AGES 18 AND UP

G. RICHARD BOZARTH

SEE SHARP PRESS ♦ TUCSON, ARIZONA

For information contact:

See Sharp Press
P.O. Box 1731
Tucson, AZ 85702

www.seesharppress.com

Bozarth, G. Richard.

Bible tales for ages 18 and up : the Terminally Ill Sea Scrolls / by Richard Bozarth – Tucson, Ariz. : See Sharp Press, 2014.

Contents : Introduction -- Creation Scroll -- Noah Scroll -- Ham Scroll -- Abram Scroll -- Tamar Scroll -- Exodus Scroll -- Elisha Scroll.

225 p. ; 23cm.
ISBN   978-1-937276-68-3

1. Bible stories, English – Humor. 2. Bible stories – Humor. 3. Bible. Old Testament – Humor.
                    817.54

Cover and interior design by Chaz Bufe.

CONTENTS

NOTE: I want to thank Dr. William Harwood for his unusual generosity regarding use of his *The Protestant Bible Correctly Translated* (World Audience, Inc., 2010). On the copyright page he announces that "scholars, commentators and public benefactors are free to quote and reproduce unlimited passages, provided the source is properly acknowledged." I have taken advantage of his generosity, and highly recommend Dr. Harwood's translation as better than even the best modern church-sponsored translations. I should also note that one verse quoted in the "Tamar Scroll," Tobit 4:15 (the "Silver" version of the Golden Rule), comes from Dr. Harwood's *Biblical Apocrypha: Books Excluded from the King James Version* (World Audience, Inc., 2009).

—GRB

INTRODUCTION

April 1, 2015

My Dear G.,

Your profound interest in my mostly ignored research has been a constant source of pleasure and encouragement to me. As I perhaps have mentioned previously, my wife constantly nags me to give up my life's work for research that is more lucrative, such as translating Babylonian pornography. I refuse, of course, since I am a serious scholar and not another Carl Sagan who forsakes the lonely purity of true research to lust after the corrupting glory of being a mere celebrity. I am a *man of science*, not a television science buffoon. However, if glory should happen to come my way without prostituting my professional standards, I would gladly accept it. Therefore, I am highly receptive to your suggestion that I permit you to endeavor to publish some of my translations of the Terminally Ill Sea Scrolls.

I am acting on this suggestion by offering for American publication some of my most favorite translations. These are the ones I feel will be the most profoundly received by serious theologians as well as the ones likely to also have popular appeal with the masses, though I assure you I am in no way pandering to the masses! I am hoping your abilities as an agent prove equal to this grand opportunity. Of course, you cannot expect the usual ten percent, since you are not a professional and also, though I mean this as no insult, just merely an unfortunate fact of your life, not, as I am sure you will be the first to admit, educated any higher than secondary school. With that in mind, and being the generous person I am well known throughout my family to be, I think five percent should be more than fair.

However, and I must stress this strenuously, I insist on acting as my own agent when negotiating the movie rights. I *must* have creative control and final say on the casting! My only concern is with the integrity of the artistic interpretation of these precious, most fascinating scrolls, but I am sure you hardly need reminding of that.

As you know, the unjustly ignored Terminally Ill Sea Scrolls were found in a cave at Wadi Cumhard by accident, though I can assure you that had I had any reason to believe they existed, they would not have eluded deliberate discovery by my cunning analysis of the evidence, had there been any evidence. I will now tell you the specific details of the discovery now that I am confident you are an ally and not one of these tabloid exploiters who want to spread sensational lies and half-truths merely to make money entertaining the ignorant, unscientific masses. What happened was two shepherd boys intended to use the cave to violate the virtue of one of their flock. I fortunately was then doing my first season of field research after being awarded my Ph.D., and my subject was the sexual behavior of Arab shepherd boys, hoping to prove how they perniciously influenced British policy in the Middle East during the days of the Empire. I was permitted to accompany the lads in order to witness their activities, thus I was present when one of the young fellows stumbled over one of the large clay jugs containing leather and papyrus manuscripts. I immediately recognized the Paleo-Hebraic seals on the jug as identifying it to have belonged to a minor Hebraic religious sect known as the Misprisionees. My scholarly fate was, if I may make a bold pun here, sealed.

This was in 1947, and I feel the discovery was shamelessly overlooked while all the collected fools in my discipline and related disciplines, not to mention every idiot associated with the commercial media, were making bigger fools of themselves over the much-inferior discovery of the Dead Sea Scrolls in that same month. With your help, I hope to see them all embarrassed and will, I assure you, accept their apologies as graciously as possible.

The Terminally Ill Sea lies only a few kilometers from the Dead Sea, and it was here the Misprisionees built a cave community. Little is known about their laws and doctrines, and I have yet to find a scroll shedding light on this intriguing question. From the graffiti on the cave walls, I have been able to learn that they were convinced Yahweh intended them to restore the Nation of Israel to the full glory of global empire, or, to use their term, "New World Order." They also were convinced Yahweh had revealed the secret to unlimited prosperity for the Nation of Israel. The secret was reducing the taxation inflicted on the rich while simultaneously increasing military spending and slashing aid to the poor. Evidently the poor were supposed to be sustained by the economic activity of the rich, who were expected to continually pursue greater and greater riches, which would mean jobs created for every Hebrew willing to work hard and play by the rules. One interesting saying they had is "Don't be anxious about your spirit, or what you're going to eat, or what you're going to drink, or about your body, or what you're going to wear. Isn't the spirit more than food, and the body more than clothing? So don't worry, asking, 'What are we going to eat? What are we going to drink? What are we going to wear?' For those are all the things the humanists seek. Your father in the sky knows that you need all those things. Set your hearts on getting a job first and then being a good servant, and all these other things will be earned by you as well." The only other thing I have been able to learn from the fascinating graffiti is that some woman named Hephzibah evidently had no morals.

The language of both the Scrolls and the graffiti is an esoteric dialect of Aramaic the Misprisionees developed to prevent unholy eyes from reading their holy texts. They called it New World Order Hebrew. They were, in my unquestionably expert opinion, writing the Holy Book that would serve the Nation of Israel as the One True Tanakh after the global empire was established, when the Misprisionees would be recognized as the True Levites; that is, if you do not already know (and may not, being merely a high school graduate), they would be the theocratic aristocracy of the Nation of Israel. Fortunately one of the first scrolls I analyzed was a dictionary used to translate Aramaic, Hebrew, Greek, and Latin into the secret dialect. This, I assure you, merely saved me time in my labors, for, had no such dictionary existed, their secret dialect would not have withstood my scholarly powers.

Unfortunately they destroyed the ancient texts they possessed as they were translated into their secret dialect, but I am sure a sect so concerned with holy truth would not lie about their ancient texts being more ancient than any known texts of what we call the Old Testament. I assure you, if that claim was a falsehood, my skills as a scholar would have by now penetrated such a lie. There is another form of verification, that of the noble tradition of Hebraic plagiarism, of which the Bible offers numerous instances. One such instance is Psalm 53 being almost identical to the more famous Psalm 14. Another is the 16th chapter of 1 Chronicles, which uses extracts from Psalms 105, 96, and 106 to make the song of praise claimed to be authored by David. Similarly, extracts from various Psalms are to be found in my magnificent Terminally Ill Sea Scrolls, though usually not identical to the Psalms as they exist in the Bible. Also there are numerous proverbs that are very similar to those of the Bible (however, I am proud to assert, there are many more proverbs in my Scrolls entirely unknown until now, and to regain their wisdom for all humans is yet another reason why my tireless and dauntless labors deserve the fame and fortune they have for too long been denied). There are as well lines of dialogue that are identical or very nearly identical to those existing in the Bible. Therefore, though lacking the kind of evidence lesser minds among my peers would require to achieve what I have achieved, I can assure you these texts are derived from the most authentic Biblical texts ever to have existed. That is, of course, not a claim the so-called "experts," reaping unjust fame and honors with their Dork Sea Scrolls, can make while they possess what few shreds of scholarly integrity they still have.

◆ ◆ ◆

NOTE FROM GRB: Dr. Piafraus's first example of what he calls "Hebraic plagiarism" is in what I have called the Introduction. (Dr. Piafraus basically insisted that this book be presented in the way he presented it to me, though he did permit me to break it up into traditional chapters — and was willing to tolerate this note from me since it allowed him to elaborate on his translation technique.)

That quotation about getting a job struck me as being much like the version of Matthew 6:25–34 in *The Protestant Bible Correctly Translated* (PBCT), which was published by World Audience, Inc., in 2010. As I read the letter, the other parts that are "Hebraic plagiarism" turned out to be exactly like or very close to the PBCT translation of the plagiarized texts (for examples, Elisha's cry to Heaven in the "Elisha Scroll" is almost exactly PBCT's version of Psalm 64:1–4, and Gabriel's lament in the "Creation Scroll" is PBCT's Psalm 13 modified). Another excellent example is Zadok's lament about his lost wealth in the "Tamar Scroll"; it's mostly a mix of quotes from PBCT's version of Job (3:11–13, 17–19, 24–25; 7:2; and 23:2–7). I naturally asked Dr. Piafraus about this and he replied:

"Very good, my dear G, that you who have such limited formal education should be so perceptive. Yes, the Hebraic plagiarisms I discovered in my Terminally Ill Sea Scrolls are presented to the reader using *The Protestant Bible Correctly Translated* when its translations are close enough to be of service (though I kept the traditional names of people and places, deeming its translations too outré for common readers, such as yourself). These are usually not precisely identical since the Misprisionees usually didn't plagiarize precisely, and I am obligated to respect the differences between the texts being translated, especially since my Terminally Ill Sea Scrolls are unquestionably the most authentic texts. I chose to do this for two very excellent and unquestionably ethical reasons.

"The first reason is that I wish to honor *The Protestant Bible Correctly Translated*'s translator, Dr. William Harwood, for the excellence of his work, which could only have been better if he had utilized my unequalled powers of translation. Alas, he chose to ignore the sublime and supreme contributions I could have made, yet nevertheless managed to produce a translation that is worthy of my acknowledgment. I also desire, by honoring his work with inclusion in what will become documents at least equal in importance to the Bible itself, to show that I hold no grudge for having been unjustly snubbed by him. No doubt it was the undeserved obscurity that has been inflicted upon me by my envious peers that persuaded him that I could not possibly possess the superior powers of translation which, in fact, I fully possess even though my Ph.D. did not come from a university as prestigious as it should have been for a scholar of my intelligence and abilities.

"My second reason is to present to the discerning reader a direct comparison of my powers of translation with those of Dr. Harwood and thereby prove beyond all possible doubt the indisputable superiority of my powers.

"Yes, once you have accomplished the publishing of my Terminally Ill Sea Scrolls, those foolish enough to esteem themselves my peers and indeed all the world, or at least those sufficiently intelligent to appreciate the sublime quality of my work, will weep because the Bible has not yet been glorified by the translation of it I could provide. However, that is not work I am seeking with the publication of these first Terminally Ill Sea Scrolls. I am content to humbly continue translating the most important ancient documents that have ever been discovered, knowing the invaluable contribution I am making by eventually giving to all the world a magnificent book that will surely be equal to the Bible in importance and quite possibly even exceed it. Soon I will, like Einstein, Darwin, and Newton, be known simply as Piafraus, ever shining as an example of intellectual excellence and achievement that all will envy and only the very fewest possible will approach near to."

Well, I hope he's right, because it wouldn't hurt my feelings if I got a chunk, even if a small one, of the money.

CREATION SCROLL

(from Cave V)

MY FIRST SELECTION concerns the greatest moment in human history, that being, naturally, the Creation. Genesis fails to give a satisfactory account, and the Dope Sea Scrolls offer no better! My magnificent Terminally Ill Sea Scrolls take us to the very throne of Yahweh when he was moved to create the known universe and Earth and all the living things, including humans. (Forgive me for not using the scholastically, theologically, and philosophically correct term "Man," but, alas, my wife calls me a male chauvinist pig if I do so and used to refuse, during the decades when I enjoyed physical virility that was, I assure you without bragging, well above average, to give me what, after all, should have been my rights as her husband, so, I must confess, I do bend my professional integrity here out of habit formed when I believed it was, I am sure you will agree, better to be politically correct than to burn.) You will soon be aware that in the future the most important question to be answered by scholars of Judaism's and Christianity's holy scriptures will be: Why were the writers and redactors who produced Genesis unaware of the much more authentic and believable account of Yahweh's creation process that my glorious Terminally Ill Sea Scrolls record? What a blessing it will be when Creationists and Evolutionists can embrace each other as friends, each knowing that the other is right in their own peculiar way. Even a man of your limited education can appreciate the fact that the "Creation Scroll" will cause theological and scientific earthquakes once it is published and on the bestseller lists. Then, yes, then the laughter that has been my cross to bear will die on the stunned lips of my unjust and erroneous detractors.

◆ ◆ ◆

IN THE BEGINNING Yahweh created Heaven and the angels. After so much time passed as to be incomprehensible to mere humans, Yahweh sat on his throne enduring yet more eons of continuous worship from the assembled angels.

There were millions and millions of them, because Yahweh wasn't the kind of God who'd settle for unimpressive thousands. Most were ordinary angels. The rest seraphim, cherubim, and numerous other kinds of mysterious special forces. All were in formation, endlessly, dutifully worshipping Yahweh. Striding in front of the awesomely glorious formation was Archangel Michael, a lightning bolt in his hand serving as a swagger stick, his relentless eyes scanning his troops.

"All right, girls, keep it tight, keep it loud," he boomed. "Don't get loose on me!"

Michael's executive officer, Archangel Gabriel, having nothing to do because Michael had a problem with delegating authority, was blowing his horn. Archangels Raphael and Uriel, who dealt with the troops, moved among the radiant, worshipping units, aggressively inspecting for flaws in appearance or performance. Occasionally one or the other would bark, "Drop and give me twenty, maggot!" at an angel not worshipping loudly enough, having a ruffled wing feather, or just because they were in the mood to make some poor innocent suffer.

Archangel Satan lounged near the throne of Yahweh and looked upon the worshipping army with amused contempt. He was not required to worship Yahweh. His job was to provide Yahweh with interesting conversation. Yahweh often regretted creating the smart ass, but at least he wasn't boring.

And that was Yahweh's problem in eternity. He groaned, "This is boring!"

Satan chuckled. "Zombies you wanted, zombies you got! Why don't you give them the gift of speaking in tongues? That would be interesting for a while."

Michael glared at Satan and snapped, "These're the finest troops I ever had the privilege to lead!"

Satan laughed. "Get real, lifer. They're the *only* troops you've ever led."

"I'm still bored," Yahweh grumbled.

"Yeah, me too," Satan confessed. "I've been thinking about that."

"I'm listening."

"Well, what we need is a show without an end. I mean, you should create a herd of beings that are loose and undisciplined and rowdy and irrational. You would have to make their wills free enough so they'd do their own thing and could even disobey you. They'd be even more undisciplined than I am, and a lot more amusing. It'd be an endless variety show. It'd never be boring."

"Why would I want to do that? About half the time I regret I ever created *you*, so why would I want to create a bunch of uppity beings who could disobey me, their creator? I am who I am!"

Satan grinned. "Come on, boss, I'm just saying a bunch of beings without an obedience compulsion would be a lot more fun to watch than this herd of zombies. Think about it. Do you want to be obeyed by everything you create, or be amused?"

Yahweh watched the humongous army of loudly worshipping angels until he realized Satan had a good idea. His creative juices flowing again, Yahweh pondered many eons until he figured out in all its glorious details precisely the kind of living theater that would amuse him until the end of time, which, of course, he had no intention of ending.

Yahweh went to that part of Heaven that was still a formless void. Satan accompanied him and so did Michael, whose curiosity about what Yahweh was going to create was so great that he actually handed command of the army of angels over to Gabriel in order to accompany Yahweh. Since there was no worshipping to be done while Yahweh was creating, Gabriel put the troops through close order drill. He thought a parade was a more glorious form of worship than singing hymns, but unfortunately Michael didn't agree, perhaps because not many angels could sing hymns and march at the same time.

Thinking on his miseries made Gabriel lament, "How long are you going to ignore me, Yahweh? Forever? How long are you going to turn your face from me? How long must I tolerate disrespect of my rank and sorrow in my heart on a daily basis? How long is my commander going to triumph over me? Pay attention and listen to me, Yahweh my Commander in Chief!" However, his nearly silent muttering went unheard. Yahweh, of course, could have heard, but he was too busy creating.

Michael looked into the void until his eyes hurt, then said, "That's without a doubt *definitive* black!"

"That's night," Yahweh answered. "Now watch this! LET THERE BE LIGHT!" Immediately the black void became filled with the most beautiful, soft, romantic light there ever was. "I call that day," Yahweh bragged. "Not too shabby, eh?"

"Outstanding, sir!" Michael barked with authentic awe.

"Where's the night gone?" Satan asked.

"The day destroys the night, and night divides the day," Yahweh replied mysteriously.

"Ohhh-kay," Satan responded.

Michael wisely said nothing, and nodded his head to imply he understood Yahweh's bizarre comment.

Yahweh commenced to create. First came water and then a vault to divide the water, half of it for the void that he now was calling the universe, and half of it for Heaven. Satan and Michael smelled and touched and tasted the new stuff. When asked what it was for, Yahweh merely said he would teach them how to swim later. He had more creating to do.

He gathered a small amount of the water contained in the universe into a flat square and caused dry land to appear. He called the dry land "earth" and next pronounced dramatically, "Let the earth produce vegetation!" Instantly, every species of plant life appeared all over just about every square inch of the dry land and over vast areas of the continental shelf under the water. Yahweh described how plants worked to the archangels. While doing this, time passed on the earth, and the plants began to wilt and wither.

"This is not good," Yahweh grumbled. One glance at the two archangels told him they concurred.

"It's the light," Satan pointed out. "It's pretty, sure, but it's too weak for photosynthesis the way you set it up to work. Make the light brighter. You want the creatures you're going to create to see what they're doing, don't you?"

"I like the light the way it is now, sir," Michael said promptly.

"We can have both," Yahweh declared and created the sun to give very bright light and the moon to provide much paler light that he pronounced good.

Yahweh and the archangels looked upon the new, tiny geocentric system. It was not impressive. It was very small. The flat, square earth looked silly. The solid dome covering it that contained its atmosphere was not very imaginative. Even the lowest ranking angel could cross this entire universe with one flap of his wings. Michael and Satan exchanged uncomfortable looks, neither being willing to say what they thought of the lame universe Yahweh had created.

Fortunately, Yahweh didn't need their criticism to realize how he had failed to create as omni-excellently as he could. "It's been too long since I created. I'm rusty. If I can't do better than this, I ought to promote one of you to be God and start singing your praises forever and ever and ever."

Satan sighed with relief, "Well, I didn't want to say it, boss, but I would have, you know."

"Yeah, yeah, I know. I am who I am, and you are who you are."

Yahweh decided his original plan of making the sun and moon orbit a flat, square earth just didn't turn him on. He kept the moon orbiting the earth and made the earth orbit the sun. The flat earth in motion about the sun looked too silly to endure, so he turned it into a sphere and vastly increased its size until it looked like something to brag about. To make the new solar system look better, Yahweh increased the size of the sun and moon and moved the earth and its moon much farther away from the humongous sun, which required the universe to be simultaneously enlarged. He pronounced it good, though the expression on his awesome face suggested some lingering doubts.

Next, Yahweh had to ensure that all the plants got their fair share of sunlight. He solved that problem by making the earth rotate. He tilted the planet's axis in relationship to the sun and made its orbit elliptical to cause the seasons and all sorts of entertaining weather phenomena. He added precession to the earth's rotation, explaining that figuring it out would drive the creatures he was about to create bonkers.

As soon as the idea came to him, he ensured the same

half of the moon would always face the earth. Another prank on the creatures he would create shortly. Satan naturally approved, but Michael thought it was a little undignified for an omnipotent god to play such a prank. Naturally, he didn't say that out loud.

Soon it was obvious the sunlight was just what the plants needed. As water evaporated and filled the atmosphere around the earth, wind, clouds, lighting and thunder appeared. It was an impressive display. Instead of watching it for a day, Yahweh and the two archangels watched it for a thousand years.

Finally, Michael said, "Meaning no disrespect, sir, but it looks kind of doofus with just that sun and the earth and the moon and that humongous glob of water in the universe."

"Yeah, it spoils the effect," Yahweh admitted.

"Create a bunch of planets," Satan suggested, "and make them reflect sunlight like the moon. That would probably be more beautiful than just the light."

"Sure, that's the trick! Every now and then you make me glad I created you, smart ass."

Yahweh again expanded the size of the universe and created seven more planets, all of them identical to the earth. Yahweh and the two archangels looked at them for another thousand years.

Finally Yahweh asked, "Well, guys, what do you think? Be honest."

"Hey, I'm always honest, boss!" Satan protested, pretending to be highly offended.

Michael said, "I have to say, sir, it could look better."

"Yeah, I agree," Satan said. "Why don't you really show off what you can do, boss?"

"Stand back for some serious creating!" Yahweh declared in an impressive baritone that was heard throughout Heaven.

Yahweh first enlarged the universe again. Leaving the

earth alone, he changed the seven other planets. He gave most of the altered planets moons, some of them lots and lots of moons. He gave a few planets beautiful rings. He created an asteroid belt between the fourth and fifth planet, and also clusters of asteroids in the fifth planet's orbit that precede or trail it. Beyond the eighth planet he created an enormous number of objects, some of them as big as moons and a few almost big enough to be called planets. To one of the largest of these objects he gave a highly peculiar orbit, unlike that of any of the planets.

Pointing to this strangely behaving large object, Yahweh said, "I did that to see if any of the creatures I'll be creating will be stupid enough to call it a planet." Yahweh then chuckled, but Satan and Michael exchanged questioning looks again; the entertainment value of this didn't impress them at all.

"Ah, another brilliant idea!" Yahweh declared and created comets. "When one of these is seen from the earth, it'll terrify and mystify everybody." He noticed the two archangels' skeptical expressions. "OK, don't believe me, but you'll see I'm right after I've created humans! Oh, I'm on a roll! Watch this!"

Yahweh created thousands of fifth-planet-size suns and placed them to surround the solar system two trillion six hundred forty billion cubits beyond the object in the solar system that was farthest from the sun. They were all the same distance from each other. He called them stars and made them the sources of the light he had first created. It was beautiful, but Yahweh didn't get job satisfaction from it.

Again he asked his archangels, "So, what do you think? Be honest."

Michael immediately said, "Sir, it's real pretty and all, but it's, well, kind of small scale. It really doesn't show what an awesome and mighty God you are."

Satan promptly said, perhaps more provocatively than

necessary, "Mike's right, boss. If there was another God, would you brag about this to him?"

"I probably wouldn't. OK, I can do better. I will do better!"

A tsunami of inspiration came over Yahweh. He expanded the size of the universe so that it would take light two hundred billion earth years to travel the entire diameter of it. He dispersed the stars he had created throughout a much smaller volume that light could cross in only fifty billion earth years. They were not nearly numerous enough, so Yahweh created trillions and trillions of stars. Still not satisfied, Yahweh changed the nature of the stars so that they were not all like the sun. As soon as he spoke the words, the universe became decorated with a vast variety of stars in different sizes and colors. Some weren't even stars any longer; they were black holes that even Satan thought he wouldn't want to get close to.

All the water still in the universe was put to use making all kinds of different solar systems. Then he decided it was more interesting to make vast, dazzlingly colorful gas clouds. Next he set the whole thing in motion. He created natural processes that would create new stars and solar systems without him having to do any work, and that would eventually destroy them in spectacular manner.

Satan and Michael wanted to see how the stars would eventually die, so Yahweh sped up the process for a few billion stars. Both were impressed and praised Yahweh highly. Satan came up with the idea of temporarily speeding up the light coming from the destroyed stars so that supernovas would occasionally be seen from the earth. Yahweh liked that idea and said, "Make it so!" He also altered the ages of trillions of stars so that there would be constant spectacular displays of stellar destruction throughout the universe.

After that he got the idea for galaxies. Satan suggested it would make the universe more visually interesting to group galaxies in even vaster structures. Yahweh agreed and made it so. He continued to tinker until he had a finished product that was, he modestly announced, good.

Yahweh laughed when another inspiration came to him. He announced merrily, "Watch this!" He spoke and the vast sphere of created objects obeyed. Its nature changed so that it ceased to occupy a volume of simple space. Then Yahweh commanded this four-dimensional continuum, which he now called space-time, to continuously expand, but not in a way that would enlarge gravitationally bound entities like solar systems, galaxies, and clusters of galaxies. Satan and Michael were very impressed.

"This will blow the humans' minds if they ever figure out how to detect the expansion," Yahweh chuckled. When he saw the archangels didn't get the joke, he explained, "You see, the universe will look eternally static to them, so that's what they'll believe it is until they can detect the expansion. They'll feel like a bunch of doofuses when they find out different."

Satan and Michael looked at each other. Another lame prank. Satan changed the subject by asking, "What happens when the ball of space-time expands enough to fill the volume it's contained in?"

"I'll decide that when it's about to run out of volume."

"You should let it crash into the containment wall, sir," Michael suggested. "I bet that'd be absolutely spectacular."

"Oh, it surely would," Yahweh agreed. "Maybe I will — and maybe I won't. We'll see what mood I'm in when it's about to happen."

Yahweh returned his attention to the earth, which was going to be the crown of his creation, which would eliminate boredom for him and everybody else in Heaven. First, he created the animals living in the water and all the animals gifted with flight. That was really interesting work. It took another thousand years of creating and eliminating species until Yahweh was satisfied. Next came the land animals, and once again another thousand years swiftly passed while Yahweh had fun creating and eliminating species until he looked upon all the living land animals and saw that it was good.

"Now here's the really good part," Yahweh announced eagerly. "Let's make humans in our own shape, like one of us. Let them rule over the fish of the sea and the birds of the air and the livestock and over all the land and over every reptile that creeps upon the land."

Satan immediately interrupted, "I've got a better idea."

"Don't you always," Yahweh growled with more than a little annoyance, yet he said, "Come on, I'm listening. I haven't got all eternity." Satan gave him an amiably teasing look that made Yahweh admit, "Well, yeah, I do." He then gave Satan a much less amiable look and went on, "But I don't want to spend all eternity jacking around with the creation of the universe! What have you got in mind?"

"OK, see if you don't like this. Don't make them like us. Make them an ape species similar to chimps and bonobos, but a lot smarter. Make them a lot less furry, so they can make themselves believe they aren't an ape species. Have them walk around on two legs all the time to free up their hands. You might want to consider a slight relocation of the thumbs so they can use their hands more efficiently than chimps and bonobos can. Make them have so many behavioral options that they'll believe they have free will. And remember to create them with the ability to disobey you. Just think of all the amusement animals like that will provide! Now, here's the best part. At some point get them to believe they're made in our image and are masters of the earth and all the critters on it! Imagine their ability to cause trouble multiplied by a bloated ego. What do you say, big guy? Is that going to be amusing or what?"

Yahweh laughed loudly as he gave Satan a godly hug. "Right this moment, I'm damn glad I created a smart ass like you!"

— Missing Text —

◆ ◆ ◆

NOAH SCROLL
(from Cave IV)

MY NEXT SELECTION concerns the period of the Noachian Flood. Certainly this event has to be the second greatest event in world history, yet in Genesis, chapters 6 and 7, the events leading up to the greatest of cataclysms to date are insufficiently detailed. Here my Terminally Ill Sea Scrolls demonstrate their superiority over the scraps of scribbles found at the Dead Sea, for in the "Noah Scroll" the drama of the pre-Flood days, when preparations were in progress, is magnificently detailed.

◆ ◆ ◆

NOAH MOVED SLOWLY, feeling every one of his 600 years. He was wondering if being Yahweh's favorite boy was really such a privilege. Once talking with Yahweh was a special thrill, but ever since Yahweh decided on the Flood and laid on him the burden of preserving breeding stock to repopulate the planet with humans and animals, Noah had been feeling that was too big a load for a 600-year-old man. If only he was two centuries younger — or even just one! — he would've had the energy. Noah wondered if Yahweh had picked him for lack of good sense rather than for possessing superior virtue. He had been wondering how much good sense he had ever since he had been crazy enough to get into fatherhood after 500 years of childlessness.

This latest from on high was not making his job any easier. He didn't even want to tell his sons and daughters-in-law. Why, he wondered, was the Lord so unreasonable and unrealistic? Such a sinful thought never would have occurred to him before that day when Yahweh told him about the Flood.

The day of the awful annunciation was cloudless and sunny. Noah was sitting in the sunshine and thinking about the big birthday party coming in a few months (he always celebrated starting a new century of life in a big way). In his hand was a jug of his best wine, which he swore was the secret of his impressive longevity as well as equally impressive virility through nearly six centuries. Just when he thought he had it made in the shade, the cork on the small table by his chair burst into flames, scaring the Sheol out of him. It didn't help matters when the flames started talking.

"The end of all living things is in sight," the deep, thunderous voice declared, "for the land is filled with violence because of them. Watch while I destroy them with the land."

Noah relaxed a little. It had to be Yahweh, though of course Noah didn't know Yahweh's name. Nor did anyone else at that time and in the times that followed, because Yahweh had not yet found exactly the right historical moment to reveal his name to humans.

Noah just called him "Lord," which was not terribly imaginative, but it was what his father had called Yahweh and his father before him, and so on for who knew how many generations; and Noah had a fondness for family traditions.

Noah settled down and considered what Yahweh had said. It seemed a somewhat extreme reaction to ordinary human behavior. So the old guy asked, "Isn't that overdoing it a bit, Lord?"

Yahweh replied, "I don't think so. The end has come for everybody and everything. I have decided this because the earth is covered with human violence, so I'm wiping out every living thing on the earth."

Noah admired his god's oratorical skills, yet he couldn't just let it slide (especially since he was one of the living things and did not yet know what Yahweh had in mind), so he said with sweet reason, "Couldn't some lesser punishment do, Lord?"

"What should I do, send them all to bed without their suppers? Come on, I'm the Supreme Being! No other god or goddess is more supreme than me! I have to do things *big*."

Noah shivered a bit at Yahweh's awesome annoyance, yet felt he had to try to talk Yahweh out of this drastic act. "OK, I'll grant that humans aren't perfect, but really, Lord, we ain't so bad."

"There's a lot of adultery going on."

"There's a lot of loving, faithful marriages."

"There's a lot of juvenile delinquents."

"There's a lot of kids who are good sons and daughters. And what about the infants and toddlers? How wicked can they be? Yet you want to drown them like unwanted kittens? Come on."

"Here's what I'm thinking: I'm just going to kill them all and sort them out later. Anybody doesn't deserve it, they get special liberty privileges and can wander around outside Limbo as long as they don't get to be a nuisance. If they don't like it, I can deal with that too!"

The belligerence in the voice coming out of the flames that did not consume the cork intimidated Noah, but still he found the courage to try to dissuade his angry god. "Surely, you don't want to act so inhuman, Lord."

"You're telling me humans don't murder every day, all day long, for the most ridiculous reasons? I've seen it all, and it isn't pretty."

"But most people don't murder," Noah pleaded.

"Most people also don't worship me!"

"But you don't make much effort to prove you are who you are. Don't condemn people for what they do or don't do in ignorance."

"Alright, smart ass, here's another justification: you humans invented politicians and bureaucrats!"

Noah looked aside in silent shame. The flames burned smugly.

Triumphant, Yahweh declared in his most awesome voice, "Yeah, got that right, didn't I? Humans have corrupted the earth. The planet is so corrupted by the ways of all flesh I don't even like the plants and other animals anymore. None of you obey the law!"

Just when hope seemed gone, a glimmer of it glowed in Noah's heart, and he said, "Look, Lord, maybe you could give us a uniform code of earthly justice. You can't accuse us of lawlessness. We've got plenty of laws! We got more laws, I think, than we got people to obey 'em! Every nation has different laws. Sheol, every dinky group of mud shacks that thinks it's a town has different laws! If laws were fleas, we'd have all scratched ourselves to death long before you finally got all peckish. What's legal here ain't legal there. I mean, who's being unlawful depends on location. What we need is one set of laws for everybody. Wouldn't that make more sense than destroyin' us for a confusion that's really failure of leadership from the top?" The instant the words were out of his mouth, Noah's face showed the horror that filled him. He croaked, "Er, uh, you know, meanin' no disrespect, Lord."

Yahweh, ever merciful to the Hebrews (or at least the ones he liked), pretended not to have heard the last part and said, "Hmmm, not a bad idea."

"Great!" Noah said much too enthusiastically. "Let's have 'em, then maybe we can get our act together."

"Maybe later, but not now, boy. That's not on my schedule. If I give humans universal laws, it'll be when I want to. The Flood script's written, and I'm not in a mood for rewrites."

Noah filled his voice with reason so sweet that it might have gagged a humanist and argued, "Lord, why punish us for not obeying laws you never revealed?"

The flaming cork burned brighter. "Damn it, I want to destroy the earth! I created it, so I can destroy it if I want! I've already announced it in Heaven. I just know Satan will have a field day ragging on me if I back down. And you damn Hebrews, if I ease up any on the heavy hand, you all turn into idolaters faster than you can say 'Baal.' So let me put it to you this way: I mean to bring a flood, and cover the entire earth, to destroy every living plant and creature under Heaven. There's going to be only dirt, rocks, and water left! It's going to happen whether you like it to or not. Now, I've been thinking I'd keep a small group of humans alive — I'm talking about you and your family, in case you can't figure it out — and breeding stock for all the other species to give you all a second chance, but you've just about argued me out of that. Now the question is, do you want to make me really peckish by continuing to argue with me about this plan, or do you want to get with the program?"

After 599 years, a guy becomes accustomed to living, so Noah said humbly, "when you put it like that, Lord, I say hard lumps to all them sinners!"

The flames burned warmly with satisfaction. "That's my boy! I knew I could count on you being all too human. Now, this is what I want you to do" ......

— Missing Text —

EVER SINCE THE DAY Yahweh had announced the flood to Noah, his life had been a tough trek that was uphill in every direction. First, his sons thought he had had too much wine (which, he had to admit, wasn't a bad guess). He persuaded them to cooperate after hours and hours of weeping and wailing and gnashing of teeth.

Would Yahweh help out? No way, even though the whole idea was his (and Noah couldn't help feeling resentful, but not enough to count as a sin, or so he hoped).

That was not the end of his troubles. The Ark was the joke of the town, but nevertheless it was seen by all to be a golden opportunity. The prices on resinous wood, reeds, and pitch went up 300% almost overnight. The unions soon knew they had him by the stones and struck for higher wages and creation of new, unnecessary jobs. Before he knew it he was paying unbelievable wages to a work force so large that it spent most of the time at the job site drinking wine and discussing the chariot races. Every other day a bureaucrat came around with some sort of new permit he had to buy or some new safety regulation he had to obey — unless he bribed his way out of it.

Noah was mortgaged up to his earlobes. He had taken out far too many loans at larcenous interest rates. Hebrews should have been ashamed to put it to another Hebrew like that while pretending they were doing him a favor! But Hebrews were just like every other breed of humans. Noah now had to bitterly admit he didn't understand why Yahweh seemed to like them better than other humans, though being Yahweh's favorite people wasn't all fertility festivals and free wine.

Noah figured he might just be able to make it through the next seven days, which he now knew by way of divine revelation was when the Flood was scheduled to begin. His dread was that Yahweh might yet go soft on him and decide a plague or earthquake was punishment enough. If no Flood happened, he would have to live another 600 years just to get out of debt!

One thing building the Ark had done for him: he now was firmly convinced the human species deserved to be wiped out.

Noah topped a hill and saw the Ark. What an ugly boat! No style at all. He hoped it wasn't sinful to wonder why Yahweh had designed such an unattractive tub. And the stench! He could smell it from the hilltop. As Yahweh had instructed, it was covered with pitch inside and out. Whew! Noah hoped the Flood wouldn't last long.

The unsightly boat looked done. There was just some interior work left to do. Noah glanced at the ominous, overcast sky and smiled vindictively. As the Ark got nearer and nearer to completion, the weather got worse and worse. It had been overcast for days. When he thought of all the rip-off maggots he would never have to repay, a warm satisfaction filled him.

He entered the construction site looking for Shem, the foreman. He found him confronting the union representative.

"We don't need the construction crews any longer," he was saying hotly. "The boat is built! There's only some interior decorating left to do. It's absurd I should pay all these men to sit around getting half smashed and talking about their adulteries and fornications!"

The union rep smugly replied, "We gotta contract! The old man here signed it. All our boys stay on at full wages 'til the job's done. You try to break the contract, we shut this site down! You try to do the interior work yourselves, we go to court!"

Shem whirled about to face his father. His young, handsome face looked much older than his 99 years, a sign of how heavy the stress of supervising the construction of the Ark had been from just about day one. He cried out, "How could you?"

"I had to get 'em back to work," Noah grumbled defensively. "The Lord was giving me Sheol about all the delays."

The union rep sniggered derisively. Like every person throughout the land, he thought Noah was bonkers. Shem's face flushed. Though he wondered about his father's sanity at times, he did have family pride. He turned on the union rep.

"That's enough, you! Everybody stays! Just get the job done with no more delays. I mean, it gets finished in six days with no more clamjamfry from you or anybody else!"

Noah pulled Shem away when the youth's face went purple, saying, "Come on home. We have to have a family meeting now that Japheth's back. I've been talking with the Lord again."

"Oh, *great!*" Shem groaned. "What now?"

"I'll tell everybody at once," Noah replied nervously.

Noah's son Ham greeted them at the door with a cocky, "Hi, Pops, how's it hangin'?"

Noah glared. "Your disrespect for your father will be your undoing, young man!" he cautioned the 82-year-old boy.

Ham grinned, feigning innocence. "Disrespect? Forget about it! Any guy that can still get it up at *your* age has *all* my respect."

Noah considered spanking the youth, but a look at the boy's muscular body put an end to that thought. Instead, he said gravely, "We must have a family meeting. I've been talking with the Lord."

"Yikes!" Ham groaned. "Break out the lube!" Nevertheless, he followed his father and his brother.

They found the wives in the kitchen gathered about Japheth with worried expressions on their lovely faces. No stranger would have guessed Mrs. Noah was just 20 years younger than her husband. She didn't look a day over 400. The 96-year-old boy was at the table eating voraciously. He looked as if he had been starved and physically abused for the past three or four decades. He had left right after the first revelation about the Flood to take a survey of all living creatures and select the lucky pairs to survive. He had been gone a long time — much longer than Noah had thought he would be — and had come back just yesterday. He had been a quiet, serious, humorless boy. Now he was disturbingly spooky.

"OK, people," Noah began as soon as he had their attention, "here's the latest from the Lord. Of the unclean animals, we still take a single breeding pair. The clean animals, now it's our wise and merciful Lord's will we take seven breeding pairs, and seven of all the birds, too."

Ham chuckled, "I guess the Lord wants to make sure we have plenty of guano to fertilize our fields with."

Noah opened his mouth to rebuke his uppity son, but Japheth stole the spotlight by jumping up. His gaunt, weather-battered face showed much agitation. "The Lord must be out of his friggin' skull!" he cried out. "Doesn't he know how many different species there are? Well, *I damn well know now!* There's millions of 'em! *Millions!* Even taking a single pair, no way we're gonna get 'em into a boat only three hundred cubits long, fifty cubits wide, and thirty cubits high! And we're supposed to feed 'em! Damn near every stinkin' critter out there has a specialized diet that it has to have to live. It'd take a thousand Arks just to stock all the varieties of food! And how're we gonna get 'em here? Huh? Huh? Do you have any idea how big this planet is? No, you don't! Ain't none of you been hardly a hundred thousand cubits away from this town in your lives. Well, *I damn sure know how friggin' big this planet is!* It's *huge!* If it was a human body, this stupid town and the whole region it governs would be about one friggin' hair! An' there's animals everywhere on it. Animals like nobody ain't never imagined ever existed! Millions and millions of species! *Everywhere!* All over! Near and far and farther than far! We couldn't get most of 'em here in six friggin' *years* an' the Lord's talkin' six *days!* There's millions an' millions an' millions an' —" Here he broke down into hysterical weeping.

It took the women a long time to calm down the upset lad. Meanwhile, Noah hoped Yahweh would make a flaming appearance and solve the problem. No such luck. He glumly accepted that he had to make a decision, so he made one. He said rationally, "Japheth has a point. So, look, we'll just round up all the local animals we can and see if the Lord will let us slide with that. All the rest of these animals Japheth's talking about, we never heard of 'em before, so who needs 'em, right?"

"Right on, Pops!" Ham exclaimed sarcastically. "If the Lord can drown every little baby for the crimes of the adults, I'm sure he won't be upset if a few million species of animals go extinct."

Noah glared at his smart ass son, but he stuck to business. He went on grimly, "The Lord also wants us to take along the microbes —"

"What the Sheol is a microbe?" Shem demanded impatiently. He just knew the lazy union pukes were goofing off while he was away from the construction site.

"Well, it seems all diseases are caused by little animals so small you can't even see 'em. If we don't take 'em along, well, then there'll be no diseases after the Flood. The Lord said he created disease microbes because there's nothing like a serious illness to make impious people remember our loving and forgiving Lord."

"That's definitely our Lord," Ham laughed. "The Lord is virtuous and benevolent; his compassion never fails. He keeps us from becoming humanists."

"Oh, bite me!" Shem snapped nastily.

"What does this all mean?" Mrs. Noah asked fearfully, for she could tell her husband was none too happy to be the bearer of this news. After 567 years of marriage, spouses get to know each other pretty well.

Noah sighed unhappily. What a burden it was sometimes being the holiest man on the earth! He reluctantly explained, "Well, it means we all have to become diseased. The Lord wants to ensure the repopulated earth also has ..." — he scrunched up his brow as he struggled to remember it right — "smallpox, polio, encephalitis, influenza, pneumonia, meningitis, tapeworms, trichinosis..." on and on he went with dreadful and awful names until even Ham was pale and trembling.

When Noah got into the sexually transmitted diseases, Mrs. Shem burst into wretched tears. "I don't want any STDs!" she wailed. "I've been a good girl all my life. I don't deserve any STDs!"

"Now, now," Noah said as soothingly as he could, "we must do the Lord's will."

"I'd rather drown with all the other millions of condemned species," Japheth cried. "We'll die anyway with all those diseases in us!"

"I second that emotion!" Ham exclaimed passionately.

The women didn't say anything—just wept and wailed and gnashed their pretty, white teeth.

"Now, now, it isn't all that bad!" Noah pleaded desperately. "A lot of the animals will carry a lot of the diseases, so it's not like we'll be carrying all of 'em. Remember, the Lord wants us to survive, so he'll make sure the diseases won't kill us." When that proved unmollifying, he tried religious exhortation: "Come and let us sing to the Lord. Let us shout joyfully to the rock of our liberation. Let us enter his presence with thanksgiving, and shout joyfully to him with music. The Lord is a powerful god, and a mighty king. He outranks all other gods. The depths of the land are in his hand. The mighty mountains belong to him. The sea belongs to him. He conjured them up. His hands molded all living things. Come and let us pay homage and kowtow to our Lord. He is our god. We are his sheep and our hearts fill with joy when he fleeces us."

"Happiness is trusting in the Lord," Ham replied bitterly, and for once the rest of the family agreed with him.

Noah was totally distraught. The holiest family on earth was on the point of rebellion, perhaps even on the verge of straying after other deities, and he couldn't think of a thing to do about it except cry out, "Lord, Lord, a little help here wouldn't be such a bad idea!"

"I'm glad Satan isn't here right now!" Yahweh said to Michael, who was by his side in Heaven watching the scene in Noah's kitchen. "He'd have a few things to say about this, wouldn't he?"

"Yes, sir. smart ass doesn't ever miss a chance to be in your face," Michael agreed.

They glanced over at the South Pacific island where Satan was enjoying some R&R in the flesh by pretending to be some kind of bizarre volcano god who required virgins to sacrifice their virtue in order to keep him from erupting — well, erupting, that is, in the way the islanders didn't want him to. Archangel Michael was envious. Really envious. He just had to get in one last R&R in the flesh before the Flood!

"These humans!" Yahweh said with much disgust. "I can't get any of them to obey me! I pick a group of them to be my favorite people, and it's as if I picked the one group with the most talent for disobeying me. Look, that's the holiest family on the whole stinking planet! Look! Ask the holiest family on the whole stinking planet to bear one little hardship and all I get is bitching and moaning!"

"Sir, meaning no disrespect now," Michael said cautiously, "but they're pretty much behaving just like you created them to behave. I mean, sir, if you dumped the Hebrews and picked some other people to be your favorite, would it be any different?"

Yahweh scowled fearsomely, and Michael would have soaked his pants if angels were biological and wore pants. After a very terrible silence, Yahweh said, "Yeah, yeah, I know, but you would think by now I could at least get eight of the maggots trained!"

Michael dared to say, "But, sir, wasn't your reason for creating them in the first place amusement? Don't tell smart ass this, but he was right. Those humans put on a show, and every day it's something different. Something amazing. And R&R in the flesh down there's the best thing you did for us angels since creating us. You've seen how high morale's been since you started the R&R program. I mean, sir, no angel wants nothing other than to worship you every moment for all eternity, but getting a little extra's sure nice. Them earth chicks! Every single one of the ding-a-lings falls for that 'I'm a god' line. Turn some water into wine or walk on it and they're all over you like you got the only serpent on the planet! You don't even need to pretend to be a goddess with guys. You just show up warm, willing, and female, and they're jumping outta their clothes like their brains're in their serpents. Sheol, lots of guys don't even require you being female, or even human! I ain't kissing buns, sir, when I say you get a hundred percent approval rating for creating the universe and the humans. Uh, not that you wouldn't get a hundred percent no matter what you created or didn't create, sir!"

"Yes, yes, I know," Yahweh admitted. "I just have this thing about obedience. I like being obeyed. I am who I am, aren't I?"

"Yes, sir!"

"Well, then, they ought to obey me even though I created them with the ability to disobey me! I mean, they could obey me if they really wanted to."

"Sir, I'm not being uppity, you know I can't do that; you didn't create any uppity in me or any other angel except smart ass. So it isn't uppity when I tell you it's not ever going to happen. You'd have to make them different to get the obedience you want, and, if you did that, then they'd just be another type of angel. How amusing would that be for you, sir? I mean, you were pretty bored before creating the universe and the humans. You haven't been bored much since. Seriously peckish a lot, yeah, but damn sure not bored."

"So maybe I should just let them do any damn thing they please no matter what I think about it?"

"Yes, sir. Why not? They don't live long enough to be good for anything except amusement."

"You mean I should stop interfering in their lives?"

"No, sir! You are who you are! Keep on trying to train them if that amuses you, and kicking their buns if they don't get in step. The way it messes up their heads cracks me up. I'm just saying, sir, lower your expectations so they don't get to you like this. I mean, sir, they're human, all too human! They aren't worth getting so worked up about."

"There's wisdom in what you say, Michael. I think I'll call off the Flood. Just so they won't think I'm turning humanist, I'll hit them with a plague and an earthquake. Maybe a swarm of locusts too. They really go bonkers when insects are all over them!"

"Yes, sir, that's always fun to watch, but will you permit one more suggestion?"

"I'm listening."

"Go through with the Flood, sir, just like you planned. Remember, the humans are for amusement, and wouldn't watching them deal with the Flood be about as amusing as they can get?"

Yahweh chuckled, "More wise words, Michael. I'm glad I created you. Well, I guess I better go down there and kick buns and take names."

Noah and his family were awed into silence when one of Mrs. Noah's dish towels burst into flames, but was not consumed. And those flames looked angry!

"All right, pukes," boomed Yahweh terrifyingly. "You will get with the program! You will do things *my way!* Knock off the bitching and the moaning right now! When you get to be God, you can destroy the world your way. While I'm God, I'll destroy the world *my* way! Got that? OK! Now enough with all this loose clamjamfry and get this Flood on the road. I'm tired of waiting, Take it away, Noah!"

The flames vanished, and Noah looked at the resigned, submissive faces of his family. "Any further comments?" he asked.

Not even Ham said anything.

"OK," said Noah, "let's go out and get diseased!"

HAM SCROLL
(from Cave VII)

MY NEXT SELECTION is the "Ham Scroll." Even though it is seriously fragmented, it sheds new light on the great Voyage made in the Ark and the events directly after the Disembarkment. Though these are treated with a bit more detail in Genesis (chapters 7, 8, and 9), nevertheless the whole amazing tale is glossed over all too briefly. The gloss remains, thanks to the ridiculous obsession with the Dead Sea Scraps, which are not fit to be in the same jug as my magnificent Terminally Ill Sea Scrolls. The whole world, especially my foolish peers, will be astounded by the revelations of the "Ham Scroll." It is the personal diary of Ham! It is a stupendous eyewitness account of the Voyage and Disembarkment.

◆ ◆ ◆

DAY 5 DF [During Flood–SP]: You wouldn't believe the rain! It's coming down like it's the end of the world! Ho! Ho! It *is* the end of the world! Pops says it's going to dump like this for 40 days and 40 nights. Well, I guess he's right, being as he's tight with the Lord. But Japheth says there's this mountain over something like 18,000 cubits high. If he's right (and he never was into joking before and damn sure ain't now), then it has to come down at nearly 19 cubits an hour to cover everything in 40 days. It doesn't seem to be raining nearly so heavy as that ......

— Missing Text —

GOT TO ADMIT I'm glad I'm on the winning team! You should've seen all the repentant people come begging to get on board after the rain started and the water was about buns high. Ain't one of them laughing now. Pops and Shem stood on the deck hurling insults down at them. Hey, I can dig they wanted a little payback for all the clamjamfry we took when we were building the Ark and loading the animals. It got so bad towards the end I couldn't get nooky in the town with shekels spilling out of my pockets. Not that I had money for nooky in my pockets too very damn often! This Ark sucked us all dry. We were flat broke when the rain started. We couldn't have afforded one more day. What I'm saying is that I had a grudge too, but I still wanted them to cool it, because the mob was really getting mean, and I thought they could still do damage to the Ark. As it turned out, they tried but couldn't ......

— Missing Text —

DAY 7 DF: Cripes, this voyage already is dragging my buns! You'd think if the Lord really loved us like Pops is always saying, he'd stop the biological functions of the animals aboard. Damn, there must be ten tons of dung to shovel overboard a day! And there's so damn many frigging birds on this tub ain't no way to shovel dung without getting covered with guano from on high! Then we have to shower in the rain, which is coming down so hard it's just about like being stoned to death! We all work the dung detail. Except Pops, who just lays back like some patriarch and drinks the wine we brought along. Man, the old guy just has to have his wine! We could've saved another dozen or two species in the cabin where he keeps it.

And Japheth didn't even need another excuse to get spookier, but Pops gave him one with that. You ask me, Japheth could use a good drunk, but Pops ain't into sharing. Like I said, the old guy loves wine as much as he loves nooky. The job ain't easy, considering we're all about dead anyway with the various diseases that could only be preserved in a human host. I don't know half the names of what I'm carrying and don't want to know! Man, I can't even sigh without liquid yuck squirting out of my buns! It's got to be one of the Lord's miracles that we're still alive and functioning just well enough to get the daily jobs done. I mean, I didn't even know what misery was before the Flood! Most of the time I think the ones that got drowned were the lucky ones. And the overcrowding! It's buns to bellies even in the family quarters. We each got about one square foot of living space between us. The animals are worse off, which makes shoveling dung even harder ......

— Missing Text —

DAY 15 DF: Japheth is really getting flaky over the animals we left behind. Pops sent him out to survey how many species of animals there were and where they were located and to pick a breeding pair. He came back really spooky, saying the earth's thousands of times bigger than anybody ever thought it was and there's millions of species. I think he spent too much time by himself. (Yipes! I hope his wife never lets on who kept her satisfied while he was gone! The guy looks unstable.) I can't buy the millions line. I doubt if I can name a hundred different animals. I doubt if I've seen even a thousand different animals in all my 82 years. Well, I mean before we loaded up the Ark. I couldn't believe how many different kinds of animals we found in the area we could cover in the last six days before the Flood. Maybe Japheth is right. Nah, can't be millions! I might buy a couple hundred thousand, though. Well, whatever, we loaded up the boat to the max with one breeding pair of unclean animals (which ain't done nothing but get more unclean on this tub!) and several pairs of the clean ones (which don't seem so damn clean anymore!), and left whatever we couldn't round up in six days to extinction. Hard lumps, I say, but it drove Japheth half-mad, and by the time he got back half-mad had become a short drive to full-mad. I ain't sure I want to be around when he completes the trip like he seems certain to do. We've got lots of sharp tools and weapons and there ain't no place on this tub to hide! Pops keeps telling him not to worry about it because the Lord hasn't complained, so he obviously never meant literally to save all animal species or he would have had us build a bigger boat and given us more time to round them all up. I think Japheth wants to reply with something blasphemous, but so far he ain't that far gone ......

— Missing Text —

DAY 41 DF: What the Sheol! The rain stopped right at sunrise just like Pops said it would. It's still cloudy out, but now we can look outside and see farther than five cubits. How long will the Flood last? Pops doesn't even know. Bummer. I hope it doesn't last too much longer. My wife's been seasick since the water first lifted the Ark, and she's carrying the chlamydial infections, which don't do a whole lot to improve her mood (not to mention her looks and smell, but we could do it in the dark, and nobody can smell anybody's BO because of all the dung anyway!). I haven't had any nooky since this tub first rocked. I wish now I'd gone the polygamy route since we got to save our wives, but who knew then what I know now? I mean, before the Flood I always thought "Who needs all the drama two or more wives create when we have a herd of young, sexy slave girls to ride all we want?" Well, now I'm the fool because we had to leave our slaves to drown with everybody else, and I never knew my wife gets just about terminally seasick until it was too late to get more wives, so it's been petting the serpent for the kid again! What a bummer.

I've been trying to get a little off Japheth's wife, but she's pretending she's all righteous now that she has Japheth around and won't give me any. It doesn't help me he ain't so spooky he don't like to get a little nooky just about every night! You ought to see what they're carrying! Man, I don't even want to know what those diseases are! They still do it to it real regular, though. Everybody else is getting plenty. Even Pops! 600 years old and still putting the serpent to Mom, who evidently can't get enough! I'm impressed to find this out, but I wish we had private compartments. That was the original plan until Japheth went totally bonkers about saving all the animals we could and Pops wussed out by letting him fill up all but one compartment of what was going to be our living quarters. It was the only way he could get Japheth to accept giving up so much space for the wine. Man, this sucks! We crammed into one compartment and there ain't hardly enough room to scratch our buns without poking somebody in the belly or buns! Let me tell you, a sheet partition may cut off sight, but sound comes through loud and clear!

— Missing Text —

DAY 103 DF: Today we found a family in a small boat. Totally unreal the amount of work they had to do to keep that pathetic thing bailed out while it was raining. I can't even believe they managed to do it with just a man and his wife and their three sons and two daughters. They looked about dead and were begging for food and water. I was at the bow and telling them we'd be glad to help when I realized Shem, who was at the helm, intended to run them over. I went about bonkers, but couldn't get to him in time to stop the murder. Pops and Japheth held me back or I would've thrown the maggot overboard! I demanded to know why he did it after cooling off some. He gave me this arrogant grin as he explained righteously how he was doing the will of the Lord, who said everybody but us were to be exterminated. I went bonkers again, screaming about how the Lord definitely didn't need any help murdering people. Guess which one of us got his buns kicked? Yeah, right, but it took all three of 'em! Shem always had a nasty streak in him, so I think this "will of the Lord" clamjamfry is just an excuse to kill without feeling guilty about it. Pops is no better, particularly when wasted on wine, and the only thing keeping Japheth reasonably sane is he now believes destroying the world and all the magnificent animals he got to see is part of some mysterious divine plan that has good intentions. He's en route to becoming one seriously pious puke. How could the Lord consider any of us more virtuous than all the other people in the world? I knew lots of people before the Flood and most of them were as good as any of us, except they weren't as into worshipping the Lord as we were. Well, the others were. I'm not saying I'm an unbeliever, but religious services have got to be the only thing more boring than celibacy! I wasn't much more into worshipping than all those people who're dead now, so why am I saved? For being Pops' son? What's just about that? Oh, man, I gotta stop thinking about it or I'll freak out like Japheth ……

— Missing Text —

DAY 137 DF: I guess the Lord forgot there were a lot of boats other than the Ark. We've met several. Most of them have been living on all the dead fish floating all over the surface of the water. (And how come that happened? Japheth's explanation about the fragility of most of the ocean's "ecological niches" sounds like he's pulling my leg, except he's never been the kind of guy who pulled legs, not even his own third leg, and is even less like that kind of guy now. Still sounds like nonsense to me. Nobody ever heard about any of these "ecological niches" before, not even the nerds who knew just about everything before the Flood.) If the Flood doesn't end soon, they don't stand a chance, because by the smell of things, most of the dead fish now ain't fit to eat. They'll have to start eating each other, and I don't mean the fun way! Shem and Pops have sunk all the smaller boats by ramming them. They've been keeping track of their kills on the wall nearest the helm using their initials. Pops is up by five and it's like nothing he ever did in 600 years ever made him prouder! Disgusting. They have been seriously peckish, I'm happy to record, because they have to let the bigger boats go. No way to ram those babies without damaging the Ark. I guess there'll be more than us repopulating the world unless the Lord keeps the Flood going long enough for all those other people to starve to death. Personally I hope they make it, but Pops is really bent out of shape. He was really turned on about being the last family on the earth and all future generations being our descendants. He can't stand the idea there might be others.

Damn, he's drunk again and outside singing to the Lord! "I am going to flatter the Lord's wholeheartedly in the assembly of my orthodox family on the Ark. The Lord's accomplishments are spectacular. All of those who derive pleasure from them float safely on the Ark. He has performed miracles to be remembered. The Lord is benevolent and permeated with favoritism. He has provided food and the Ark for those who reverence him. He is going to eternally be vigilant of the contract he made with me." How much longer is the frigging Flood going to last? I'm about ready to jump off this tub when we find the next big boat he and Shem have to let go. My wife is still too sick to put out! She's so sick she doesn't give a damn about my rights as her husband. I can't believe this is the same hot honey I married. Man, in the good old days she didn't know the word "No" and kept me so busy I hardly had any left for our slave girls or the harlots in the town, but I managed to save some for them, didn't I? Oh, man, those memories, they're like torture now! And I'll say it again: how pathetic is it I discovered about eighty days ago my own reason to be glad we brought the sheep along? ……

— Missing Text —

DAY 150 DF: Well, about damn time! The Lord finally remembered us! He sent a Sheol of a wind and the water is beginning to subside. Well, OK, I can't really tell that, but that's what Pops is saying and I got to admit he's tighter with the Lord than I'll ever be. How long before we can get off this stinking (and I do mean *stinking!!*) tub? Pops says 150 more days! Rats! Which, I've neglected to mention, we've got zillions of by now, but who's complaining? Mom has figured out more ways to make rat delicious than anybody ever dreamed possible before the Flood. Good thing. Food for us humans was getting pretty low before Mom decided to take care of the rat problem in her own unique way. After the first meal, which was pretty decent if you didn't think about what the meat used to be, Pops sang out, "Everyone who reverences The Lord and follows his rituals is going to get lucky. You are going to eat the toil of your hands. You are going to be contented and do well. Your woman is going to work hard and always be ready for a ride. Your sons will be like olive trees around your table and not lust for their inheritance. Your slave girls will always be young, pretty, and eager for a ride. You are accordingly going to see how The Lord blesses the orthodox." Needless to say, he was smashed half out of his mind, but that was just about the last time. The wine ran out not long afterwards. I wish it hadn't. I had forgotten what an unpleasant old coot he is when sober longer than a day or two. I guess I can stand it ……

— Missing Text —

DAY 1 AF [After Flood – SP]: Dry land! Well, drying land, but who's bitching? Wow! Whoopee! We went bonkers when we first got off that damn tub. I kissed the ground. Didn't even care how bad it smelled, how salty it tasted, how many bones and dead twigs and branches and other things I don't want to think about were in it. I rolled all about in the mud. I ran all around. Well, I guess I didn't actually run since the goop was knee-deep, but who's bitching? Room to move in! Space! Too much! Even Mom was acting like she was only about 200 years old. Even Pops, who's been sober now for longer than he's been sober in the past 500 years, was smiling and acting as goofy as the rest of us. Of course, everything looks like Sheol. After a year under water, and I mean really, really deep water, all the trees are dead, soaked skeletons. There's slime on the rocks that nobody has a name for. There's no grass or bushes or flowers or anything! And the remains of all the people and animals that died are everywhere. The ones that didn't get eaten, well, they didn't finish decomposing under the water. You wouldn't believe how nasty it all looks. They all went for higher ground, the animals and the people who didn't have boats. I don't even want to think about what their last days were like. So here we are on one of the mountains of Ararat, up to our knees in mud, and surrounded by what looks worse than any nightmare I ever had, yet we're happy like we're all kids and it's our birthday! Go figure. Things look grim, but we're off the Ark. We let the animals go right after celebrating, but they aren't in any hurry to scatter, not being able to move in the deep mud any better than we can (except the birds, but where are they going to go in a land that doesn't have any place that can be a new home for them?). I guess being a year jammed into that tub without even space to scratch and then set free in a lifeless land has kind of blown their minds. What they'll do for food when what little we have left is gone is a good question. It won't take the predators long to finish off the prey, which I'm afraid is going to include us. There's just about one day's worth of provisions left on the Ark. Pops says don't worry, be happy, and the Lord will take care of the petty details. I guess he's right ......

— Missing Text —

DAY 2 AF: Praise the Lord and I ain't even joking! We woke up to a world miraculously restored to what it was before the Flood, except for the people. I mean, the ground is dry, the plants are restored, and most of the animals are gone (we're assuming they've been miraculously returned to where they used to live). Judging by the numbers of birds and other critters that have always lived on the mountains of Ararat, the Lord decided not to wait for natural breeding to repopulate Earth. Not to sound any less grateful, but, really, it had to be that way, right? *Nothing* could have survived in the mess the earth was after the Flood, so the Lord had to make it like it had been if he wanted us to survive. I mean, how many centuries or even thousands of years will it take before the descendants of *eight people* can repopulate the earth, which, according to Japheth, is way bigger than any of us thought before he came back from exploring? The Lord will have to make sure nobody dies until they're old and everybody successfully produces kids, which women will have to pop out just about annually, *for centuries* just to repopulate the lands we knew about before Japheth came back to tell us about lands far, far away we and nobody we knew ever even heard of before the Flood.

Hey, what about the few animals and the *one* plant we saved? How long would it take *them* to spread over the earth starting from where we landed? If the earth was going to have plants all over it again, how could trees and flowers and bushes and all the food plants come back when all we saved was a few grapevines? There's also the fish! We didn't save any fish (never thought we had to!) and none of them survived because the Flood destroyed the water as a place where fish and all the other kinds of things that lived in the water could survive and thrive. I ain't ever telling anybody this, but I don't think the Flood was very well planned unless the miracles that happened overnight were part of the plan. In fact, if those miracles hadn't happened, I'd have to say the Lord had a bad case of the doofus when he planned the Flood.

So, Sheol yes! Praise the Lord! Seeing the wonderful restoration that saved everybody and everything on the Ark made me wonder if there're now people in all the places where people used to live before the Flood. I hope so, but Pops insists that repopulating the earth is our job. Well, I've always liked that work since I don't have to be the one who gets pregnant. So, once again, Praise The Lord for the miracles that made the earth life-friendly again.

Today, after Pops had a big barbecue on the altar we built for the Lord (good thing we did bring extra clean animals and the Lord left a few with us for the sacrifice), the Lord appeared as a chunk of burning wood, using one of the pieces we didn't need for the sacrifice. Very impressive the way the flames burned so brightly without burning the wood. He told us to be fertile and multiply and fill the earth. Well, I don't think any of us were planning on taking a vow of celibacy (especially not me!), so that seemed a bit redundant. I didn't say that, of course. After all, I was joyously grateful for the miraculous restoration of the earth, but it was an added incentive that those flames didn't look like there was any humor in them at all. The Lord also said we were supposed to "be the terror and dread of every animal of the land and every bird of the skies and everything that moves upon the land

and all the fishes of the sea." Evidently the idea is we eat them. What did he think we were doing with them before the Flood and with the rats during most of the Flood? I was wondering if he was going to order us to continue breathing, but kept that thought to myself. He mentioned plants too, so it was a good thing he recreated all the plants. We didn't save any plants, except some grapevines so Pops could get back into wine production ASAP. Oh, yeah, I forgot Mom and the girls saved seeds from the garden they had before the Flood.

The Lord also promised never to destroy the earth again, at least by flood. I would've been happier if he had specifically named fire and earthquake and volcanoes and drought. He seemed to leave these other options open, though Pops and the rest think he promised never to destroy the earth and people again by any means. Well, I'm not going to argue. They want to believe that, fine. All I know is, if people ever make him get all peckish again like he was before the Flood, I hope it's after I'm dead. One end of the world is all a guy ought to have to live through in a lifetime, even one as long as Pops'! The Lord then filled the sky with a pretty rainbow as a covenant, though I thought he could have given us a sign a little less ordinary than a rainbow. But what the Sheol ……

— Missing Text —

[DATE EVIDENTLY HOPELESSLY LOST – SP]: Whew! What a day! Pops has gone off the wagon. The vineyard he planted right after we got back to where our home used to be (and tell me why the frigging Ark couldn't have landed closer to here or why Pops couldn't have settled for any suitable chunk of land closer to the mountain where we landed?), well, the first batch of grapes fit for wine finally matured and he made wine out of all of them. The long ordeal of sobriety ended today for the old sot. Whew! He sure can guzzle that stuff down! Hey, I like wine and get off on a buzz every now and then, but Pops is way out of my league. Finally he ran off singing and dancing into the wilderness. Mom was worried and asked me to go find him, so I did. Shem and Japheth were busy with the crops and herds, so I didn't bother asking them to help.

Any break from the unending agricultural chores is good. Man, in the good old days we had slaves for all this grunt work and could buy all sorts of things made by artisans in the town. Now we have to do every frigging thing ourselves! And ain't none of us are very good artisans yet (and I'm never going to be; management is what I'm good at). The ladies ain't much help either. Decades of marriage and no kids for me and my brothers before the Flood, but now our wives get pregnant just about from our only *looking* at 'em! Even Mom — and being pregnant at her age doesn't improve her mood at all! Hey, while I'm bitching and moaning, let me add this: so far we haven't been too successful being the terror and the dread to the wild beasts that are predators. Maybe it's because we got squat for firepower and none of us can hit what we aim at except by luck. No wonder my family has been farmers for who knows how many generations.

Anyway, so I find the old sot. He was totally naked and running after a doe with amorous intentions. It was so funny I thought Shem and Japheth ought to see it. If that didn't restore what little sense of humor Japheth had before the Flood, the guy's hopeless. Those prudes went all righteous on me like seeing the old sot naked was some kind of sin. I mean, get real! We saw each other naked in the cramped quarters of the Ark just about every day, so what's the big deal now? They grabbed a robe and went looking for Pops. They found him passed out next to the doe, which looked real happy, and tried their damnedest to cover him up without looking at him.

Naturally the finks ratted me out as soon as Pops woke up. He was hung over so bad he looked like he had about an hour left to live, so naturally his mood wasn't too cheery. He got really mad and screamed, "Cursed be Canaan. He's to be the slave of his brothers' slaves. Blessed by the Lord is Shem. Canaan is to be his slave. The Lord is to expand Japheth. He's to live in Shem's tents, and Canaan is to be his slave." I couldn't help but laugh, which didn't improve his mood any. Who the Sheol was this Canaan guy he was ranting and raving about? Nobody in our family had that name and we hadn't seen another living person since the last boatload of starving folks we came across before the Flood ended. Shem and Japheth were as mystified as I was, though both were turned on by the idea of getting a slave again (what I mean is, management is a talent we all share). They like being farmers, but don't like doing the work themselves, not now, and not before the Flood. Shem asked who this fellow Canaan was. Pops said my descendants would be called Canaanites and would be slaves to my brothers' descendants. Shem and Japheth — being experts at being pukes! — really got off on thinking my kids were going to be their kids' slaves. That got me a little hot, but before I could say anything, Pops told the maggots it would be a whole bunch of centuries from now before my descendants would become known as Canaanites and eventually become their descendants' slaves.

Oh, man, I had to laugh again and I didn't care if they all got bent out of shape. Get real! Punishment suffered by somebody else who won't be alive until long after all of us are dead is not very effective. That's as stupid and irrational as calling it a sin to catch an old sot making a drunken fool of himself. Ho! Ho! That's some punishment! Shem and Japheth, but especially Shem, were real disappointed. I thought I'd probably get my buns kicked by the three of 'em, but I had to ask Pops in my most smart ass voice if it was righteous to punish people who had yet to be born for something they were totally innocent of. He must have been more hung over than he looked, because all he did was growl, "Get out of my face, boy!" So I went off to find my wife to see if she was recovered enough from giving birth to get back at doing our fair share of being fruitful and multiplying. I don't want there to be any shortage of slaves for the descendants of those two pukes! My hot honey was throwing her clothes off before I could finish suggesting a little afternoon delight. After all, we want to do the will of the Lord ......

— Missing Text —

ABRAM SCROLL
(from Cave XI)

MY FOURTH SELECTION is the "Abram Scroll," which covers one of my favorite Bible stories, that of Abram's excellent Egyptian adventure. This charming bit of history is really not well told at all in Genesis (chapter 12), but it is very well told in my amazing Terminally Ill Sea Scrolls. There is nothing like it to be read in the Dull Sea Scrolls. There are profound and revolutionary — yes, *revolutionary!* — theological insights to be gained from the fully detailed account of this remarkable and fascinating event in Hebraic history. This is, of course, not the place to reveal them, though I assure you I will reveal them at the appropriate time, when my foolish and arrogant peers have had time to study these selections after you have successfully gotten them published and all the world acknowledges the greatness of my discovery. Also, though I hope you do not take this as a personal insult and accept that the truth does indeed hurt at times, these insights would be very much above your level of education. Please do not feel rancor, my dear G. The glory to come to you as my colleague in one of the most tremendous publishing events since the invention of the printing press will compensate for such personal limitations. I am sure you will agree that it is best for you to learn to accept your limitations even as I will learn to accept mine if ever I should discover any.

♦ ♦ ♦

ABRAM STOOD on a hillock surveying all he owned. His tent was state of the art, the latest model, and very spacious. His slaves were tending his flocks. He could see his 55-year-old wife moving about the tent as she supervised the slave girls who were the envy of all Haran. Sarai was his sister as well as his wife. (They had the same father, but not the same mother.) An image of her full, voluptuous body seductively lying nude on the expensive pelts and down-stuffed pillows they slept on came to his mind. Drool dribbled into his gray beard.

"Oh, God," he prayed groaningly, "I just gotta be able to get it up tonight!"

He had come to the conclusion he had been an idiot to marry a woman 20 years younger than him, so perhaps his infrequent ability to perform during the past decade or so was divine punishment for being such a fool. What could he do, though? There was something about riding his own sister that had turned him on like he had never been turned on before. It still turned him on, but, alas, his waning potency could no longer match her passions, which still roared like the hungry lioness in the wilderness when the scent of prey is all around, yet none near her to satisfy her hunger. Yet whenever his serpent could rise up like the anaconda it had been in his youth and even in his middle-age, hosanna! Riding Leviathan couldn't be wilder, and certainly not as much fun!

Suddenly a nearby road apple burst into flames. The old man staggered and gasped as his startled heart thudded painfully in his chest as though about to explode. Abram leaned weakly on his staff after the first horrible moments passed. He clutched his sunken chest where his heart continued to beat erratically and gasped grotesquely, as if he had forgotten how to breathe. Thus it was not impiety that caused him to fail to notice the flames were not consuming the road apple.

Just when the old guy had regained his composure, he was rudely startled again by a booming voice issuing from the bright flames, saying, "If you'll leave your land and your kinsmen and your father's family and go to a land that I'll show you, then I'll make you the ancestor of a large tribe that will become a great nation. I'll bless you and make your name so famous that it will be used as a blessing. I'll bless those who bless you. I'll curse those who curse you. All the clans of the land will bless themselves by you."

"Oh, it's you, God," Abram said with much relief. He did not know Yahweh's name, which Yahweh had not yet revealed to his favorite people, so he just called him God, which wasn't imaginative, but the big guy had never complained, so Abram lacked motivation to come up with an appellation less ordinary. "What's up today?"

"We both know what won't be up today, don't we, old boy?" Yahweh teased.

"This I don't need, even from God," Abram muttered unhappily, then more loudly asked, hoping to change the subject, "What can I do for you?"

"I've already told you. You're going to pack up and move out. I've picked out a nifty new place for you to live."

Abram was appalled to hear this and protested, "Come on, God, cut me some slack. I finally got it made here. I'm set for life. What do I want to leave for? I mean, I'm seventy-five years old. I'm retired. I didn't even want to leave Ur, except my old man, who was, just between you and me, completely bonkers the last decade or so of his life, dragged us off and we ended up here. The fool lost all his wealth, that should've been *my* wealth, t in bad real estate deals. 'Stick to money lending,' I said, but would he listen? If I would've known he was going to live only two hundred and five years, then die leaving me nothing but bad debts, I never would've left Ur with him. God, trust me, I've done all the moving I ever want to do. Besides, I'm already the patriarch of a large tribe. Even though Sarai and I don't got kids, I got about a platoon of daughters from my previous wives, may they rest in peace, and more grandkids than I can remember their names. Does a guy need a son to be a tribe's patriarch? I don't think so. Don't get me wrong, God, I would've appreciated a son, but you didn't bless me with one, so I'm stuck with having my nephew Lot live in my tent to get the kind of help old men are supposed to get from their sons. I'm fine with that. If you want to do me a favor, just make me a stud like I was fifty years ago."

"That could happen if you cooperate, old boy," Yahweh said seductively.

Abram's face filled with joy nearly as bright as the divine flames. "Yes, anything, anything. I'm outta here. Won't be nothin' but dust in the air, I'm leaving so fast. No lie, God. You know you can trust me. So, how about doing it right now?"

"Abram, Abram, you think it was last week I created you humans? I don't arrange anything until I actually see you obeying my will."

"How long before I'm a stud again, then?"

"After you settle in Canaan."

"Canaan! That's where my old man wanted to take us until he thought he could make a killing in Haran's real estate market. What's so special about Canaan?"

"I want obedience, not questions, Abram. What do you really want? Answers to questions or a studly serpent like you had fifty years ago?"

Abram burst out in pious poetry, "Judge me, God, for I have adhered to my sincerity. My trust in you is not going to waver. Evaluate me, God, and test me. With or without a studly serpent, your benevolence is in front of my eyes. I have followed your orthodoxy."

The flames vanished, and Abram went down to his tent to do the will of Yahweh. Right away Sarai, who had not experienced the divine revelation, accused her husband of being as crazy as his father had been. She had been against following her father-in-law to Haran and had not forgotten the hardships of the first years after the move. Now that they were rich and living easy, at the top of Haran's social ladder, she wasn't willing to risk it all by moving to someplace she never heard of.

"No way!" she declared loudly and with many insults about his mind being as limp as his serpent usually was.

Abram tried to impress her with more details about his encounter with Yahweh, but she laughed before he finished; flaming road apples were to her only proof of how senile he was getting. Abram was distraught, and knew not how to get her to agree to the move without doing a patriarchal number on her, which he was reluctant to do because he didn't want to be like his father.

He left the tent in a rolling and tumbling dudgeon because Yahweh could've shown up to help persuade Sarai — just a minute or two would've done it, probably less, and it was his plan, right? — but no, he didn't, just left Abram to take the clamjamfry. How the Sheol was he going to sell Yahweh's plan to Sarai without using the old patriarchal heavy hand? The only good thing was he had only one wife now! He shuddered as he imagined how it would've been if Yahweh had dumped this load of road apples on him back when he had four wives.

He didn't miss polygamy at all! One wife was enough and sometimes — like now! — too much. If a man needed more nooky than one wife could provide or simply enjoyed variety, slave girls were the smart solution. And that thought reminded him that obeying Yahweh would bring back the glory days of being studly enough to satisfy Sarai and still have plenty for his slave girls, who rarely got rides with him nowadays.

"There has to be a way to persuade Sarai instead of forcing her," Abram muttered as he walked. "Maybe Lot will have an idea." He wasn't optimistic, hence it was a good thing he could not see how much Yahweh, the archangels, and tens of millions of angels were enjoying his unpleasant predicament.

Lot was at that age when adventures are fun even if they are loaded with ordeals; therefore he was cheerfully willing to make the adventurous move to wherever Yahweh wanted his uncle to go. Lot's enthusiasm made Abram feel better before he explained the problem with Sarai. Lot could understand Sarai's attitude, yet was youthfully confident he could persuade her to cooperate. Abram gratefully accepted the offer. After two hours alone with young, manly, handsome Lot in the tent, Sarai approached her husband with joy all over her face and announced she was willing to move to Canaan if that was what he wanted. Abram scowled, especially after noticing how unsteadily Lot was walking, and did not experience the happiness he had been expecting.

And then Abram began to wonder just how sincere her submission to his will was when she started having headaches those few times he had a studly serpent. Every time only a few hours alone with Lot could cure them! Supposedly he had a special talent for scalp massages! Abram scowled more and more often, perhaps because his serpent usually was snoozing by the time she was feeling no pain again. Or perhaps because Lot seemed to be so tired yet so happy after giving her one of his massages! Alas, what was he to do? He wanted to regain a studly serpent and that meant getting his old buns to Canaan as fast as possible, so he decided to ignore his suspicions and concentrate on getting the move moving.

That was not the end of his problems. None of his slaves wanted to go, though, being slaves, none dared actually bitch and moan about it when he or Lot was

around. However, they showed how little their enthusiasm
was by how badly they dragged their buns in packing up
all of Abram's possessions for the journey. Even if they
had been happy about the move, packing up would have
been one long, tremendous chore. The stuff he and Sarai
had accumulated! He thought most of her stuff was just
so much sentimental junk, and she had more clothes
than any ten women needed, but he did not dare try to
get her to toss out any of it after the ranting and raving
that resulted from just one little, mild suggestion that
she ought to think about it. It all ended in a headache
requiring more than four hours alone with Lot before it
passed and she felt well enough to begin packing again.
More scowling for Abram!

If all that was not ordeal enough, his daughters and
sons-in-law worked their mightiest to prevent him from
leaving. Miserably he realized all they were seeing was
all his wealth being taken so far from them that most
likely they would never be able to get their fair shares
when he died. The more he stubbornly resisted them, the
more viciously insistent they became. They thought, he
realized much to his disgust, that his wealth was actually
their wealth and that he had no right to do anything that
might threaten their possession of it after he died. He got
much pleasure from proving how wrong they all were!

Finally they were ready to go. They said goodbye to all
their family and friends in Haran, and then the enormous
procession moved out. The weeping and wailing and
gnashing of teeth rising from his angry daughters and
sons-in-laws were to Abram like hosannas and alleluias
sung at an altar. He was tempted to moon them, but
decided a show of silent dignity was more fitting at his
age.

Before the first day ended, Abram acknowledged how
fortunate he was to have Lot coming with them. His vast
flocks and herds would have been scattered all over Sheol

if Lot hadn't been around to vigorously supervise the unhappy slaves who tended them.

Abram was impatient, but also 75 years old. No way he was moving anywhere very fast. Not that it made any difference. Even at his age he could have walked to Canaan faster than he was riding to it in the ponderous procession of pack animals and herds and flocks. Each morning his tired old bones and aching muscles protested every single cubit they had traveled the previous day. Sometimes he would have a studly serpent in the morning, but, alas, Sarai always woke with a terrible headache and would send him out whether he was stiff or limp to tell Lot to come make the headache go away. And it always did, but by then Abram had exhausted his studly serpent with a slave girl and there was no riding Sarai, who was more fun to ride than all his slave girls put together. All he could do was scowl as he reminded himself of the glory that would return to him once they were settled in Canaan.

The tiny horde went on and on until they reached Shechem in the land of Canaan. There they paused. Everybody was about as miserably tired as could be. Sarai was too exhausted to get one of her headaches. Even if she still had had that much energy left, Lot could not have done her any good. He felt as old as his uncle!

"I'm gonna die!" the old man muttered as he accepted a goatskin of water from one of his slaves. He drank long, even though the water was not even close to being as good as the pure, sweet water he had enjoyed on his lands in Haran. As soon as he set the skin down, blazing flames ignited all over it, yet did not consume it.

"I'm going to give this land to your descendants," Yahweh boomed in his typically dramatic way.

Abram was too tired to be startled. "I hope you mean this is where we're gonna settle," he grumbled. "I'm about done for. I'm too old for this clamjamfry!"

"Not here for you," Yahweh said, "but one day your

descendants will settle here and everywhere throughout the land of Canaan. They will be a great nation."

"They may not be so overjoyed, you know."

"What makes you say that, old boy?"

"Well, for one, unless the rest of Canaan's a lot different, what I've seen so far is not prime real estate. It'll be sweat and heartbreak to raise herds and crops on this land."

"The soil is cursed because of Adam. Wresting food from it is going to exhaust you, every day of your life," Yahweh reminded him.

Abram was too physically worn out to be appropriately pious. Grumpy was the best he could do, so he griped, "Yeah, yeah, you've said that before. But we both know some places — like Haran, for instance, if you get my drift — require less exhaustion than others. Besides, this land already is full of people. So far they've treated us pretty decent, but these Canaanites don't look like they'll turn over their homeland peacefully just because my descendants have been given the deed to it by you. I mean, they don't even believe in you!"

"So who promised you a rose garden? If I made it easy, do you think they'd appreciate it? Look, with me on their side, how can your descendants lose? Sure, they'll have to exterminate the Canaanites and, yeah, their own body count is going to be high, but they'll win, and winning isn't everything—*it's the only thing!*"

Abram was appalled. "But, God, that's genocide you're talking about! There has to be a kinder, gentler way."

"What, you've become a humanist in your old age? Sure, there are different ways it could be done, but I want it done *my* way. What's a little genocide compared to not doing my will?"

Abram was not yet ready to give up the argument. "Look, God, I appreciate what you want to do for my descendants, but is here really the place to do it? I saw some maps in the last town we stopped at. Sure, the coast is ideally situated for sea-going trade and Canaan's a natural land trade route between Egypt and the northern kingdoms. But that means every king with visions of glory and empire will want to conquer this land. If it's great for getting goods from one place to another, it's great for getting armies from one place to another. Let's face it, Canaan's one of those places that's going to be conquered about as often as empires are going to be built and destroyed and built and destroyed and built again. Are you going to save my descendants' buns every time they get invaded? Even you might get tired of that."

"As long as they worship me and submit to the laws I want them to obey, I will ensure they're always victorious."

Abram groaned, "Oh, God, what's the chance of that? We're only human! Come on, you can do better by my descendants than that. If you want them to rip off somebody's land and exterminate them, why can't it be the Nile Valley and the Egyptians? Now, there's some prime real estate! Fertile like you wouldn't believe and a lot harder for enemies to attack. They'd appreciate that land a Sheol of a lot better than this land, so they'd be more motivated to worship and obey you like you want them to. Come on, how about it? Do it for old Abram, God. Look how I've suffered doing your will already. Doesn't that put any points on the scoreboard?"

"Your words have moved me. But you must show how much you love your descendants and want the very best for them. If I have you settle in Egypt instead of Canaan, and thus make the Nile Valley the land where they shall be a great nation, then no studly serpent for you, not even infrequently."

Abram thought about never again riding his voluptuous, lusty sister and replied, "So maybe I'm wrong about Canaan. Who says a little work won't make this place another Nile Valley?"

Yahweh chuckled, "You humans, you're so reliably all too human!"

"So, I get my studly serpent back now?"

"When the journey's over, Abram, and not before then."

"Oh, God, when is it going to be over?"

"That's for me to know and you to find out—when I tell you," Yahweh replied, and then the flames vanished. A second later they reappeared just long enough for Yahweh to add, "Say, do me up a nice altar here. I'm in the mood for some formal worshipping."

Abram groaned as he got to his feet to do what Yahweh wanted. He had no enthusiasm for the project, but Lot came through again. He kicked buns and took names until the slaves were hustling to gather the materials for the altar. Abram hardly had the strength to build the altar and might not have been able to do it without more help from Lot. After the long, formal services giving thanks to Yahweh, the horde prepared to move out. Lot and Sarai stayed behind so he could cure her latest headache. They caught up with the slowly advancing horde four hours later. Abram was so grateful for the young man's recent help that his scowling wasn't nearly as ugly as it usually was. From there Abram and his tired, grumpy, unhappy horde moved on to the mountainous district east of Bethel. Here they found a valley so perfect for herds and flocks that Abram allowed himself to believe this little, uninhabited paradise surely had to be where Yahweh wanted him to settle. The joyous hosannas that greeted his announcement cheered his old heart. His splendid tent was put up and then Lot's smaller, less gorgeous tent, followed by all the tents of the numerous slaves. Sarai supervised the sweating, glaring slaves until everything in the tent she shared with Abram was just perfect. "And this better be the last time I have to do this!" she announced to her husband when she showed him the finished results. The herds and flocks spread over the meadows and verdant hillsides.

Finally, after glorious sleep, Abram built an altar to

offer thanks to Yahweh and gathered all his household for the services. Before he could finish the long, happy prayer prior to starting the fire on the altar to offer up fragrant sacrifice, the whole altar burst into flames and from them boomed the awesome, frightening voice of the unhappy supreme being. Yahweh said, "Did I tell you to settle here? Move it out. You're way behind schedule." Then the flames disappeared.

Abram, almost shattered by bitter disappointment, nearly told Yahweh to kiss his wrinkled buns, but he was a pious and righteous man, so he stiffened his upper lip and ordered his household to pack up and move out ASAP. He anticipated much grumbling and discontent, loud weeping and wailing, theatrical gnashing of teeth and throwing of dust. He was surprised to see everybody obeying. They weren't happy, but they were packing up.

Lot summed it up with a proverb: "It's hard to argue with God when you hear him yourself."

"What, they think I would do this if God hadn't told me to?" Abram protested indignantly.

Lot replied with a weary shrug and went off to supervise the preparations to move on down the long, seemingly endless road. On and on they went. They made their way stage by weary stage to the Negev, a desert region south of Bethel. In one semi-arid part that was not as bad as the other parts, the bleached bones of a lizard burst into divine flames and Yahweh's voice boomed out cheerfully, "You're home, Abram. Remember to thank me for the golden shower of unending benevolence and everlasting love I've given you."

"Alleluia," Abram said with as much enthusiasm as he could muster, which was not much since every bone and muscle in his body felt twice as old as it was.

The flames vanished, and Abram went to his household to tell them the good news. They were so glad the journey was over that they didn't bitch and moan about the less-than-prime real estate that was to be their new home. That came after they had rested, but eventually they all changed their minds. Things were fabulous for five years. Abram had arrived rich and continued to get richer, and he showed his appreciation to the slaves who had made the long, hard journey with him by making them the best fed and best dressed slaves in all the Negev.

Abram got the reward for obedience. The power of an unfailingly studly serpent returned to him. Sarai was so impressed that she forgot about being mad about having to leave Haran and later the valley near Bethel. Her headaches miraculously ended, and Abram was riding tall in the saddle again. Even better, his restored virility allowed him to also resume riding his slave girls without depriving his lusty sister. Life didn't get much better than that!

Lot continued to live with his uncle. Sarai had more than enough energy to keep on enjoying the handsome young man's companionship. She told her husband she enjoyed his charming conversation and would not be happy to lose it. Considering how often they got together for private chats, Abram suspected Lot was providing her with more than pretty words, but he didn't try too hard to catch them. He was definitely getting his fair share of rides, and Lot did a lot of work around the place.

Abram's household prospered and morale rose and rose. It was like living in a paradise — or as close to it as was realistically possible. Then everything went to Sheol when famine came to the land. Abram became poor so fast that his old brain just about exploded. With brutal suddenness he was reduced to poverty. Only Sarai and Lot remained after selling all the slaves and everything else to avoid abject poverty. It didn't work, so they soon had the clothes on their bodies and nothing else.

Abram was about as demoralized as one of Yahweh's favorite boys could be. Such a grievous blow, having to start over again at the age of 81! Abram wailed piteous pleas and prayers to Yahweh, but he never got so much as a firefly in response. Sarai, who had never known destitution, really came down hard on him. Such bitching and moaning the world rarely sees! "Do something, you old coot!" she demanded repeatedly.

Half-mad with despair, Abram finally did something. He announced, "Look, we're hopelessly out of luck here, so let's go to Egypt. Who knows, something may turn up."

"Egypt! Are you bonkers?" Sarai demanded. "Let's go back to Haran where we have friends and family who'll help us out. Who do we know in Egypt?"

"What, you want I should return humiliated by failure and have to hide my face all the rest of my life?" Abram demanded back indignantly.

"Oh, like that's going to be a long time!"

"Oh, wife, you're my sister, remember? That gives me double rights and power over you. No more Mister Nice Guy, is that what you want?"

"Don't start any of that patriarchal clamjamfry with me, you old coot! You're just another gerahless maggot without God backing you up. When we need him the most, there ain't been any flaming anything since the famine started."

"Virtue is rewarded with good fortune," Abram insisted piously, "and I'm going to find good fortune in Egypt, so there!"

"Well, maybe *I* won't be there helping you look, so there back!" She turned to Lot and smiled her sexiest smile, which was awful powerful sexy for a 61-year-old woman. "Come on, Lot, let's return to Haran."

Lot smiled charmingly, but nevertheless said, "Would my father welcome me if I deserted his brother and my uncle when he most needed me? Besides, I've always wanted to visit Egypt. Now seems a good time for it."

Impious resistance melted from Sarai's heart and

obediently she followed her husband. Abram scowled, but what could he do? She was going with him, wasn't she? If her motives were not exactly what he wished they were, at least the headaches didn't come back. In fact, once they got going, she seemed to suddenly realize she actually was going to see fabulous Egypt and excitement filled her. If they hadn't been so desperately poor, the journey to Egypt wouldn't have sucked at all.

As they neared Egypt's border, Abram became increasingly worried. People they had met on the long and winding road were full of gossip, and the hottest item was the pharaoh's legendary promiscuity. He liked "fresh meat" daily, they all tittered, and had scores of "meat finders" engaged solely in providing "new dishes" for his "menu." No woman was safe, especially foreign "dishes," who provided the "exotic flavors" he truly "savored." If it was female and it would hold still long enough, Pharaoh would "feast" on it. If the woman belonged to a man — husband, father, brother, uncle: it made no difference to pharaoh — that man best cooperate. Horns, they tittered merrily, were better than a tombstone.

Abram saw a new danger facing him. So one night after a pleasant ride and before Sarai went to have some private conversation with Lot, the old man said, "Listen. Since you're an attractive woman, it's certain that when the Egyptians see you they'll figure that you're my woman and kill me to acquire you for a 'meal' for pharaoh. Or perhaps kill me after he has tasted your delights and decides he wants you for himself. So I implore you, pretend that you're only my sister, which is no lie, after all, so they'll spare my life for your sake and maybe even treat me well."

Sarai sneered contemptuously. "Well, well, the man of God's scared God won't save his wrinkled, old buns! Where's your faith? How can the Egyptians kill you when you haven't sired a son yet? Didn't God promise your descendants will have that cesspit we just left? And everybody but you believes descendants from daughters don't count, right? It seems to me, a mere woman, that your life's guaranteed until you sire a son. Besides, what's the worry? I ain't exactly dead, but I ain't exactly hot enough to drive men to murder. I'm sixty-one, you know."

Abram replied, "Ah, Sarai, don't you know what a voluptuous beauty you still are? Don't you know what a wild ride you are? Youth and beauty, what's the big deal? When I ride you, my serpent sings hosannas and alleluias. Pharaoh's probably never had a real woman like you. Anyway, you don't look a day over forty-five!"

Sarai smiled lovingly. "Maybe I don't want to chat with Lot yet," she said in a sexy voice that thrilled Abram all over his old body, but most especially that most important part of his body that had been restored to vigorous youth. As she pulled him down for another ride, she said, "Nevertheless, darling, I think you worry too much."

Abram replied with this proverb: "Trust in God, but take precautions."

The three vagrant Hebrews reached the bustling capital of Egypt without incident. They were ragged, hungry, and didn't have a single gerah in their pockets. The border guards would not have let them into Egypt, but, luck being with them, they were all asleep. Abram shrugged when he noticed that everybody else freely crossing the border in both directions acted as though this dereliction of duty was SOP.

They were so broke that they would have asphyxiated if air had cost even a gerah a day. They were hungry. They had no place to sleep. Yet they weren't alone. The hordes of the destitute were all around, most of them doing humiliating things to arouse enough amusement or empathy in the citizens who had shekels to get them to part with some small share of their affluence. It was, the miserable trio quickly perceived, a hard, degrading way to make hardly enough gerahs to keep starvation from precluding the next day's performances.

Abram was in a black depression. He was old, and poverty sucked. He felt ready to gladly die. Where was Yahweh when he needed him? It wasn't that long ago he could hardly scratch his buns without something bursting into nonconsuming flames. Now he felt as though Yahweh did not exist at all. Even worse than that was being totally devoid of ideas about what to do next.

Sarai felt more confident. She hadn't lived to be 61 without learning she always had a gold mine with her that would keep her from starving if it came down to that. So she was excited by the urban environment. Nothing was like anything she had seen in her life. Haran was a slum compared to the splendors of Egyptian civilization. Lot shared her enthusiasm. He was young and handsome in a huge city filled with rich women who knew how to appreciate young and handsome men. Even their horrible poverty could not put a bummer on his optimism. If nothing else, he would be able to bore his family for the rest of his life with tales of his sojourn in Egypt.

"What are we going to do?" Abram moaned and groaned. He raised his wrinkled, gray-bearded face to the sky and sobbed, "Have pity and help me, God. I'm in deep road apples now. Poverty fills my eyes with tears, thirst torments my throat, hunger gnaws my guts." He glanced around to see if any divine flames were burning. His disappointment almost killed him.

Sarai laughed gaily, "I don't think we're getting any help from God today and probably not tomorrow. Remember what the proverb says: 'Praying is a virtue, but you can't rely on it to help, so it's best to do it yourself if you can.' We'll be better off if we take matters into our own hands."

"What can we do?" Abram whined.

"Well, I'm thinking of turning a few tricks. Haven't you been paying attention? There's action in just about every doorway and alley in this city. Young, not so young, old. These Egyptians sure are a horny bunch!"

That about killed the old man when he realized his wife wasn't joking at all and not even slightly repulsed at the idea. He gasped, "No! No! God would turn his face from us if I allowed you to do this abomination."

"You mean he hasn't turned his face from us yet?" Sarai asked sarcastically.

Lot, who worried to see his uncle in such distress, suggested, "Let's go find where the Hebrews live. Our own tribe'll help us out. If not, then we should consider more drastic options."

"My plan's more fun!" Sarai teased the men.

At that moment one of the pharaoh's meat-finding crews spotted the three destitute Hebrews. The four men smiled with joy to see the voluptuous beauty of Sarai. The pharaoh was currently on a diet of older women. What a hassle it was finding women over 50 who still looked good enough to be a feast fit for a pharaoh! One look at Sarai's amazing voluptuousness and they knew they had a lock on the bonus money the pharaoh awarded to the most successful meat-finders.

They approached their target with grinning confidence. It was too good to be true! The meat and the two guys with her were obviously foreigners and vagrants, which made procuring the meat simple. They surrounded the pitiful trio of starving Hebrews and put them under arrest. Abram and Lot ended up in a jail that was pretty close to being as vile as a jail could be, but at least they were inside and would be fed. They were so bad off that getting arrested seemed like good luck.

The meat-finders took Sarai to the gorgeous palace and handed her over to female slaves to clean up. They fed her gourmet delights as it was obvious she needed nourishment if she was going to be a good feast for the pharaoh. Meanwhile the happy meat-finders went to the pharaoh and sang her praises to him. Lust filled him gloriously. He ordered her brought to him as soon as she was made ready.

Sarai pleased him from the moment he first saw her. He pleased her. He was a gorgeous hunk of middle-aged man! They spent the next several hours in the most satisfying feasting of the pharaoh's horny life. Sarai was still hot to be devoured when the pharaoh had passed any hope of getting a studly serpent again without some hours of rest and recuperation. So he sent for a gang of aristocrats who shared his craving for fresh meat and watched the incredible Sarai wear them all out. She was magnificent! She was the woman he had dreamed of every day since puberty.

The next day the pharaoh declared to his astonished court, "I have found a woman worthy of being my wife!" He had Abram and Lot released from jail and brought to the palace to have possession of Sarai formally transferred from her brother to him.

Abram, being human, all too human, saw in this remarkable turn of events a chance to make some profit. So he said to the pharaoh, "Sire, it's not right you take my sister to be your wife without giving me suitable payment for her."

The pharaoh's face darkened and he replied, "You uppity old maggot! Three days ago you were starving in the streets! You're not even Egyptian! You got some big stones to demand payment, I'll give you that, but you ain't gonna have 'em much longer!"

"Suggesting," Abram hastily said, "I was just suggesting."

"*I'll* suggest something, you uppity puke! I'm the *pharaoh!* I don't *pay,* I *take!* And I take all I want, especially from grubby foreigners! I was going to give you a room in one of the lesser palaces and a decent income out of my regard for Sarai, but I think I'll *suggest* something else!"

He turned to an official and ordered, "Take this Hebrew road apple out and castrate him! Then stuff his stones in his mouth and cut his head off! Stick his head on a post in the Hebrew ghetto as a warning to all of them. Feed the rest of him to the crocodiles!"

Abram turned pale. He trembled so hard that he seemed about to break into pieces. He was getting to his knees to beg forgiveness when one of the pharaoh's ministers asked, "Sire, do you intend to be faithful to Sarai?"

The pharaoh laughed, "You gotta be kidding!"

"Well, then, give the old maggot a good payoff. Hey, make him rich and let it be known to all Egypt you rewarded him because Sarai is really fine feasting. Believe me, just about every father or brother or uncle who possesses fresh meat will go blind with greed and fall all over themselves trying to get you to taste their daughters or sisters or nieces in hopes of being similarly rewarded. Up to now they hide their meat from you, and you pay enormous sums to keep an army of meat-finders looking for fresh meat. If you take my advice, sire, and make this road apple rich, endless fresh meat will be yours. The beauty of it is, you'll never have to make another payment! The greedy pukes will always blame the girl for failing to be a good enough feast!"

The pharaoh immediately perceived the devious brilliance of the plan and he rescinded his execution orders. Abram's dazzled joy then did not come close to the happiness that filled him the next day when he received flocks, oxen, donkeys, men and women slaves, she-donkeys, and camels in abundance. He was the talk of Egypt from one end of the Nile to the other. He was wealthy beyond his wildest avaricious dream. He sold enough of everything to buy a modest palace and still had plenty left over to live the kind of extravagant life that had been his secret fantasy from the first day he understood the power of shekels.

As predicted, just about every family with a good looking female member wanted to score big like Abram. Schools sprang up all over Egypt to teach girls and women of all ages the erotic arts. Each one claimed to possess the secret knowledge of the pharaoh's "diet." Cosmetics and perfumes, always a lucrative trade, boomed big time. The pharaoh had so much fresh meat delivered to him daily that he began to believe it truly was possible to have too much of a good thing.

Abram shared all his sudden and vast wealth generously with Lot. Now that they moved among the highest levels of Egyptian society, the handsome young man had a chance to meet numerous rich widows eager to have a young hunk for their second or third or fourth or so-on husband. Lot selected one nearly as old as Abram because he figured she would die while he was still young enough to enjoy the wealth he would inherit. It was a splendid wedding. And an even more splendid wedding night: the old woman died of a heart attack brought on by the seventh wild and satisfying ride during almost three hours of uninterrupted sexual indulgence. Just like that Lot was nearly as wealthy as Abram!

The slaves who had witnessed Lot's display of awesome virility, and how many times his wife had experienced sublime glory before dying, quickly spread the tale of the instantly legendary performance. Now Lot had hordes of wealthy women of all ages willing to risk the same kind of death with him. Lot and Abram piously believed Yahweh had to be responsible for their new wealth and happiness; only a supernatural explanation made sense, at least to them.

All proceeded to live happily ever after. Sarai got off on being the queen of Egypt, but she got off more on being married to a man who loved her for being as promiscuous as he was. How he loved watching her feast! Or being just one dish of one of her feasts! Or even just hearing from her details of her feasting before sharing details of his latest feasting. Sarai hardly remembered Abram at all.

Which did not bother Abram, who was too busy riding his lovely, young slave girls and engaging in all the other amusements of the very rich. He would have forgotten about Sarai if her astonishing feasting was not the hottest gossip item from one end of the Nile to the other. Lot partied frequently with his uncle and enjoyed being one of the most desired men in Egypt. Did either care about the pathetic plight of the Hebrew slaves then in Egypt? Forget about it!

Up in Heaven, Satan observed all of this with glee. Humans never failed to be all too human. Finally, after letting Abram, Lot, and Sarai live happily ever after for three years, he went to find Yahweh to bring him up to speed. He found him out in the sticks touring planets at the end of creation.

"Hey, big boss, what's happening?"

"Evolution, smart ass. Most fascinating. It's very entertaining how the natural processes change all the planets continuously without me doing anything. Life is already happening all by itself on many of them. Evolution is much more amusing than instantaneous creation like I did on the earth."

"Well, evolution's pretty much inevitable given the fundamental interactions between matter and energy you established when you created the universe. So what's so surprising?"

"I didn't say it was surprising, smart ass. I said it was fascinating."

"What are you going to do if some species evolve so they're intelligent and have lots of behavioral options, like the humans?"

Yahweh smiled. "Wouldn't that be fascinating? I guess we'll have to wait and see. It shouldn't take too long. Maybe three or four billion years."

"Wow, that quick? Really?"

"Oh, yeah. Natural selection works fast."

Satan chuckled. "You know, boss, it would be a great practical joke if you created on the earth all the evidence a human would need to believe the universe and space-time and galaxies and humans were created by evolutionary processes. Imagine the confusion and conflict and cultural hate and discontent that would happen when humans finally got advanced enough to scientifically analyze that evidence. I mean, think about it! There would come a time when some humans would start believing deities, including you, don't exist because their science can't prove you or any of the others exist, and, this is really good too, religious humans, even the ones who believe in you, won't be able to prove them wrong. It'll drive the religious humans bonkers if that happens. Of course, before they become that scientific, you'd have to stop doing miracles down there, or only ones that no rational human would believe are miracles. Oh, boss, can't you see what it would eventually be like on the earth? Imagine the ridiculous theories they'll invent when they try to find atheistic explanations for how the universe and life and everything else got started and why everything works the way it does. If you do it, we would die laughing if we weren't immortal."

Yahweh grinned. "You know, you get the most devilish ideas! I'm going to do it. Imagine the looks on the atheists' faces after they die and find themselves in Limbo."

"Yeah, an eternity of embarrassment! Messing with their heads is so easy, but such fun!"

Satan fell silent. God cocked his head, squinted and asked, "Is that all you want?"

Satan grinned. "Have you been keeping an eye on the earth lately?"

Yahweh's good mood vanished as he groaned, "What are the humans up to now?"

"Your favorite human at the moment has been engaging in some interesting behaviors."

"Oh, wonderful! Why can't they just obey orders? I'd like to get *just one of them* trained right — just one frigging human who would actually choose to do my will all the time!"

Satan laughed, "Instead, they act just like you designed them to act!"

"Oh, shut up, smart ass. No, tell me what Abram's done and then shut up."

Satan told Yahweh about all that happened since he'd started his planetary inspection tour. It did not please the supreme being.

"Who told that loose puke to go to Egypt? Now I have to hustle his wrinkled, old buns back to Canaan!"

"Will you leave Sarai with the pharaoh?"

"No way! I decided long ago she's going to be Isaac's momma and, by Me, she's going be his momma! Except now I'll wait until she's around eighty before she conceives. Yeah, we'll see how she likes giving birth at that age!"

"That means Abram'll be around a hundred years old," Satan reminded Yahweh.

"He'll be *one frigging thousand* if that's how I want it!"

Satan chuckled, "You're the boss, Big Boss."

"Damn, ease up on the heavy hand for one second and even the Hebrews start acting like I don't exist! Here I am about to announce to Abram I'm changing his name to Abraham because I'm going to promote the Hebrews from my favorite people to my *chosen* people. Even better than that, I'm going to make it so that in not too many generations all the Hebrews will be Abram's descendants. He'll be the father of a multitude of nations and I'll formally give ownership of Canaan to him and all the Hebrews descended from him. All these goodies I'm planning to give to an old coot who can't keep obeying me when it's raining road apples on his head! All this for a guy who can't tell a test of faith when I give him one?"

"I suppose he would plead ignorance if you confronted him about it. You know, the good old 'You didn't tell me, so how could I know?' excuse."

"What, I have to explain every frigging thing like they're never any smarter than a three-year-old?"

"I think it's more like they're too full of doofus to be as clever as you sometimes want them to be. Remember, doofus is one of the big reasons they're so entertaining."

"Yeah, well, sometimes I just want to be obeyed instead of frigging entertained. I am, after all, who I am!"

"So, boss, you want me to clean up this mess? Always glad to be of service, that's me."

"Not this time, smart ass. I'll do it myself."

"What are you going to do?"

Yahweh grinned. "I'll punish the pharaoh with a new disease."

It was a target so tempting that Satan couldn't resist taking a shot. Doing his best humanist number, he asked, "Why punish the pharaoh? If Abram had told the truth about Sarai, the pharaoh never would have taken her to be his wife. He made a law against polyandry and, for some strange reason, actually obeys it himself. If Abram had told the truth, the pharaoh would have rode her for a while and then given her back to Abram. That's just malicious rumor he would kill some poor guy to snatch his woman. His supply's greater than his demand, so he isn't likely to get too radical about any one particular woman. You know that."

"How about letting me run the universe? I created it."

Satan asked mockingly, "What, you don't want to run it fair?"

"What's 'fair'? I created that too. I'll tell you and anybody else what 'fair' is: 'fair' is whatever I say it is.! Right now I'm thinking 'fair' would be to cook your uppity buns in a lake of fire and brimstone until they aren't so damn uppity anymore."

Satan just chuckled, "I serve the purpose you created me for, boss."

"Maybe that just shows omniscience isn't the same thing as smarts!"

And so it came to pass that the pharaoh and all the Egyptian men who had feasted on Sarai suddenly found the most precious part of their male bodies covered with chancre sores and dripping the most ghastly, stinking goo imaginable. When they drained the serpent, the burning sensation was as though they were whizzing boiling oil. The screams and shrieks filling the palace of the pharaoh and all the lesser palaces where lived the similarly accursed aristocrats terrified all the land of Egypt. The wisest doctors could do nothing, which cost them their heads, but even that unjust exercise of totalitarian power did not make the pharaoh feel any better. It was said from one end of the Nile to the other that everybody else was next to suffer the affliction. Suddenly the temples were full of pious worshippers expressing their religious fervor with a flood of gold and silver coins. The angels who spent their R&R in the flesh pretending to be the gods and goddesses the Egyptians worshipped kicked back and watched the love offerings pile up.

After three days of torture the like of which no man before then ever had suffered, Yahweh spoke to the pharaoh. The miserable monarch was staggering from the royal bed to the royal chamber pot, his eyes flowing tears of dread of the agony he was about to suffer, when suddenly the royal chamber pot burst into flames that did not consume it. The terrified pharaoh lost control of his bladder and the resulting agony felled him like an arrow through the guts. He wriggled and flopped around on the floor, screaming out his agony. The slaves in the royal bedroom did not respond; they were like statues, seeing and hearing nothing. The slaves outside the bedroom heard nothing and went on about their business.

"Enough with the screaming, already!" Yahweh boomed awesomely.

"Whatever god or goddess you are, just kill me now!" the wretched pharaoh begged desperately.

"Oh, show some guts, man! You humans are such wusses! Now, listen up, road apple! You married Sarai, which makes me just plain mean peckish. She's Abram's wife, and I've got work for her to do. Divorce her pronto and send her and Abram back to Canaan. When you've done that, this plague will end."

"I didn't know she was his wife!" the pharaoh wailed piteously.

"Sure, I know that. That's why I've gone easy on you."

The flames vanished and there was not the slightest bit of scorching to prove that the pharaoh had not hallucinated the whole thing in his extreme agony. The slaves in his bedroom remained stock still and remembered nothing. The pharaoh, however, knew it was real. He ordered Abram brought before him ASAP.

"What have you done to me, you old puke?" the pharaoh demanded when the frightened old man was trembling before him in the audience chamber. "Why didn't you tell me she was your woman? Why did you say, 'She's my sister,' causing me to make her my woman?" When Abram proved too terrified to speak, the pharaoh turned to the nearest miserably suffering minister and barked, "Go smack that Hebrew road apple upside the head and see if that doesn't jar an answer out of his lying mouth!"

Abram's voice revived instantly, and he replied, "Well, I guess, ah, because I guess, er, well, you see, uh, er, well . . ."

The pharaoh turned to the same minister and growled, "He still needs that smack upside the head."

"No, sire, no! No, I don't need no smack upside my head or anywhere else! OK, it's this way: I thought if I told the truth, you'd kill me to get her for yourself! And it wasn't such a lie, sire; she really is my sister."

"You frigging maggot! What gave you the crazy idea I'd kill anybody to score some meat? Do I look like the kind of moron who thinks meat's important enough to kill for?"

"I guess not, sire."

"Damn straight, road apple! Sarai's something else, but she's just meat! If you'd've told the truth, I'd've feasted for a while then tossed her back." Sarai, who was by his side in her place as queen of Egypt, glared at her husband, who ignored her as he went on, "You made me break my law against polyandry and that's why we've been cursed with this plague!"

"Uh, well, I thought —"

"You old puke, you're too senile to think! Now, here's your wife!" He shoved Sarai towards Abram so hard that she collided with him and knocked him on his buns. "Take her and go!"

"I'm queen of Egypt!" Sarai shouted indignantly. "You can't treat me like this!"

"Don't you wish! Now get out of my face and then get out of Egypt!"

Abram, always more all-too-human than it was smart to be, said from the floor, "What about all the stuff you gave me? Can I take it with me?"

"Are you for real, road apple? No! You return to Canaan as poor as you left it!"

Suddenly an awesome voice boomed, terrifying everyone except Abram, who knew it was Yahweh. The old man's morale soared. He knew Yahweh was virtuous and compassionate and benevolent and would save him no matter how enraged the monarch was. The thunderous voice delighted Abram as it asked, "Pharaoh, how would you like this plague to last for the rest of your life?"

The pharaoh saw the light. He let Abram and Sarai go with all the vast wealth he had given Abram. To ensure they went as fast as possible, he assigned a large military unit to escort them to the border. Lot, with all he possessed, was deported as well for the crime of being Lot—Abram's nephew. He and Sarai were not happy for a long, long time. They spent much time alone consoling each other during the journey, but eventually got over it. They were returning to Canaan, a cesspit compared to Egypt, but now they were richer than they had been before the famine. When you're rich, it's hard to believe life sucks for any serious length of time.

Abram returned in triumph to the land of Canaan, which had recovered from the famine and was enjoying unusual prosperity. The old man pitched his tent in the valley near Bethel where he had first stopped in Canaan. He hoped this time Yahweh would let him stay in the lovely place. Here at the altar he had built earlier he offered formal worship to Yahweh, who appeared like he had before and told the old man to get his wrinkled buns over to Hebron, where he would make a new home at Oak of Mamre.

Abram was too happy to be upset. He said merrily, "Well, God, all's well that ends with me being rich, eh?"

"No more trips to Egypt or anywhere else without checking with me first," Yahweh warned.

Abram gloated piously, "God, I'm so wealthy now you ain't created the famine that could wipe me out! You name the place, there I'll be as long as you want me there. I'll sing hosannas and alleluias every day if that's what you want."

"A nice altar and weekly formal worship will suffice."

"You got it, God."

And so it came to pass that what came to pass passed.

TAMAR SCROLL
(from Cave II)

BY NOW, dear G., I'm sure you're astounded by your good fortune to be associated with a project as stupendous as publishing the Terminally Ill Sea Scrolls, and, if I may suspend my usual modesty for a moment, to be associated with a scholar of such superior achievements. When I am justly famous and doing all the talk shows, I promise you'll be fairly mentioned, though, of course, you surely understand that not a lot of the glory will be yours. After all, who did all the truly important work? Was it not me? Your part, though important, is not to be compared to my long years of study and translation. The brilliance of my achievement, once it is shining all over the planet, will be what astonishes and amazes all people. Your achievement of assisting in getting my magnificent Terminally Ill Sea Scrolls published will surely bring you justly deserved honors, but it would not be rational of you to expect them to bring you glory such as I am fully confident will be mine.

My next selection is the "Tamar Scroll," which shall prove how justly deserved that glory shall be! Onan, so wrongly castigated as a perverted masturbator, is here fully exonerated and shown to be deserving of pity rather than condemned for the vice of self-pollution (though, to be honest with you, the perversion is understandable, especially when a man has a wife who neglects, whether by intention or by ignorance, her duties!). The real reason Tamar behaved in the scandalous way she behaved is finally brought to the light of human knowledge. And, most amazing of all and surely to be a fact having profound theological ramifications, the name of Judah's wife is finally brought out of the darkness in which both the Old Testament and the Droich Sea Scrolls have inexcusably consigned it (only the insufficiency of my peers perpetuates the inept translation of "daughter of Shua" [that is, "Bathshuah"] as this vitally important woman's name). Also revealed, which shall also cause much rethinking among the so-called experts who mock me now and shall surely suffer the humiliation of apologizing in the future, are the true names of the father and mother of Tamar. Thus, my dear G., even a man of your low level of education can appreciate the colossal importance of this scroll.

◆ ◆ ◆

ZADOK, a prosperous moneylender in Chezib, married Zebudah, the fifth-born daughter of one of his biggest debtors. Because she was the hottest, most beautiful babe in town, he offered a two-thirds reduction in her father's debt for the mohar payment, which the desperate man agreed to joyously. Zadok and his voluptuous new wife commenced to be fruitful and multiply. Fifteen children in 25 years he sired, an accomplishment he bragged about to all those seeking to borrow from him, because they had no choice but to listen. Amazingly, only three kids had died so far. Truly he was a man blessed by Yahweh.

When Zebudah gave birth to her fifteenth child, another son, she failed to recover promptly. In fact, she never regained her full strength, and Zadok sadly realized he better start checking out the daughters of those most hopelessly in debt to him. He did not want to replace his wife, but he was wise enough to understand the wisdom of being prepared. If that meant he would enjoy again the delights of tight nooky, well, that proved the proverb: "God Most High consoles his chosen people when tragedy afflicts them." When asked why he didn't have several wives, which a man of his wealth could have afforded, he always replied with this proverb: "Sometimes even one wife is too many." When asked why he didn't ride his young slave girls like every slave-owning man did, he had another proverb: "Ride a slave girl like a wife and pretty soon you have a slave girl acting like a wife." The proverbs were part of the weird doctrine of monogamy that Zadok and a few other hardcore orthodox Hebrews tirelessly tried to sell to the Hebrew community as the more moral, hence more Yahweh-pleasing, way to live.

At this time, Tamar, Zadok's seventh child and third-born daughter, was twelve years old and had just recently burst into all the glories of womanhood. The men of Chezib lusted for her mightily, but only those who were prosperous knew they stood a chance of possessing the stunning, voluptuous beauty. Zadok enjoyed the pursuit of his daughter. She was twice the prize his other two daughters had been and he had been able to score excellent marriages for both of them — marriages that had brought in heavy mohar and also had been very, very good for his business. He expected to make an even more rewarding marriage for Tamar, so was in no hurry to give her up. Besides, with his wife so sickly and Tamar the oldest daughter living in his house, he needed her to fulfill all the duties his wife formerly had performed so excellently. In fact, there was one duty Zadok was particularly tempted to have her perform after Zebudah died, but he was too piously committed to his peculiar hardcore orthodoxy to betray it by celebrating the Rites of Lot with her. People, especially his debtors, called Zadok a lot of insulting names, but hypocrite was never one of them.

Zebudah suspected she had not long to live. This troubled her mightily. She had been a baby factory for her husband as she had been taught to be, and this was her reward! Bitterness filled her heart against Yahweh and she grew determined to save her daughter from a similar fate. Let being fruitful and multiplying be her choice, not her destiny! It was too late to save her two oldest daughters. Both were popping out babies as though they alone shouldered the responsibility of ensuring the continued existence of humans on the earth. In other words, they were perfect fools like she had been at their age!

Tamar could still be saved, and her mother intended to save her. Not only that, she now knew of a way to save her. If only she had known in her youth what she had recently learned too late to save herself now!

When Zebudah recovered enough of her strength to be able to get out of bed, she called for Tamar to come before her and said, "This clamjamfry sucks, but it'll be different for you."

Tamar stared at her mother with amazement. In her arms she held her infant brother at one of her lovely, soft, and firm breasts. The baby had a liplock on her plump nipple and suckled contentedly. Since he wasn't hungry, it mattered not to him there was no milk. Tamar wondered if the pleasure of her brother's happy suckling was a sin, especially when she felt so little love for the obnoxious brat, but she was too embarrassed to ask about it. Her father had hired a Hebrew wet nurse for his newest son when it became obvious his wife was too sick to nurse the baby herself, but Tamar gladly and guiltily offered her young breasts to the infant's eager mouth between feedings. It was the best way to keep the little demon from screaming and screaming and screaming. The only time he was reasonably bearable to be around was when suckling on a breast.

She told herself it was good practice since she would

surely be married soon. How humiliating it would be to celebrate her 13th birthday and not be a wife! There were a few girls in town who were her age and already had been married for two or three years. So, she told herself, she would be married soon and probably would give birth to her first child before her first anniversary. That meant practicing breastfeeding with her infant brother was really being smart and not being a pervert.

Tamar said, "I'm like not understanding, I'm sure, Mom."

"Let me put it this way: you're a woman now and will be married soon, so do you want one of those about every year for rest of your life?"

"Like no way, I'm sure! But like I'm sure I'm not into celibacy."

"What if I tell you I'm certain I know how you can avoid babies and still have the fun of being ridden by men?"

"Like tell me right now, Mom!"

"Put down the brat and I'll take you to the place that's going to save you from brats."

Because the wet nurse was visiting her sister for a few hours, Tamar found the next oldest sister, a charming girl just eight years old, and commanded her to take care of their infant brother for the duration. The baby began screaming hideously the instant Tamar's succulent nipple was pulled from its mouth. Tamar's sister pouted unhappily as she received the obnoxious demon, who promptly filled his swaddling clothes with the foulest dung ever to come out of an infant.

"Oh, I'm like so grateful, you know," Tamar's sister griped sullenly while trying not to puke up lunch.

"Like bite me, hussy," Tamar replied tartly before returning to her mother's side.

Slowly and painfully Zebudah dressed to go outside the house for the first time since giving birth. She took them by a long route that enabled them to arrive at their destination without being seen by any of the people who knew them. This strange behavior intrigued Tamar, but her mother hushed her when she asked about where they were going. Tamar was shocked when she found them arriving at the small rear gate of the temple of Anath.

This place was scorned among the most orthodox Hebrews, such as her father, as a place of perversions and idolatry. Here Yahweh was not worshipped as the supreme being. The hardcore orthodox Hebrews hated the fact that many Hebrew men and women worshipped the Goddess as well as Yahweh or, much worse, worshipped the Goddess as though Yahweh did not exist. Tamar's aunt, her mother's sister, was quite brazen about worshipping both, answering Zadok's scolding with a sassy proverb: "Two wagers offer double the chance of winning. And even if that was not true, worshipping Anath's more fun than worshipping God Most High." Once when Tamar asked her why she thought the Canaanite religion was more fun, the woman replied cryptically, "Ask me that again when you've had a few riding lessons!" then laughed rather naughtily.

Tamar knew her father strongly disapproved of his sister-in-law's behavior and lamented that the Hebrews who worshipped only Yahweh were not numerous enough in the land of Canaan to do anything about the worshippers of Anath, especially those who were Hebrews. He said to his children often enough to bore them with it, "The day will come when God Most High will cease to tolerate the religious bigamy or outright apostasy of the Hebrews, then it will be all over for Anath and her worshippers!" Tamar didn't like it when her father and other Hebrews who thought like him got intolerant like that.

When she reached the age where she could expect to be married and start her adult life as some man's wife, Tamar began wondering why it was so important which deity got worshipped, since she hadn't seen any evidence of Yahweh or Anath or any of the others caring much about it. She thought the best thing people could do was just be nice to each other, help each other out when they could, and let everybody be happy in whatever way made them happy as long as they weren't hurting anybody else. She liked that proverb she had heard some wandering preacher say on a street corner one day a couple of years ago: "The good man does not do to others what he would not like them doing to him." She wondered what deity that guy had worshipped. It couldn't have been Yahweh, since her father and the other intolerant Hebrews had been really upset about the guy preaching on the street corners as if Yahweh wanted people to have freedom of speech and religion. Tamar thought her father and the other Hebrews who thought like him ought to make that proverb part of their religion.

A young, beautiful priestess answered the knock at the gate of the temple, and Zebudah announced, "Tell the Adath that Zebudah, wife of Zadok, and her daughter Tamar, wish to see her."

"She won't want to see you," the young priestess replied bluntly.

Zebudah produced a purse full of shekels of silver and said, "Perhaps she'll make an exception this time."

The priestess snatched the purse eagerly, saying, "It could happen! Wait in the garden!"

Zebudah and Tamar took a seat on a wooden bench in the lovely garden. The very young priestesses, some not yet women, tending to the garden gave them strange, hostile looks, but did not say anything to them. Tamar didn't have to be very clever to guess it was because they knew her father was one of the intolerant Hebrews who condemned their religion and called the priestesses harlots. It made her sad, but what could she do?

When the Adath arrived, she sent all the priestesses away, then stood before Zebudah and asked, "Why have the wife and daughter of Zadok come to this holy place? He must not know, since I'm sure he wouldn't approve."

Zebudah replied, "What a husband doesn't know makes a marriage happier. My daughter has recently become a woman and I want her to know the secret of how to enjoy being ridden by men without becoming pregnant. Endless childbearing has been my lot and the last one has no doubt killed me or come close to it. I want my daughter to have a choice about it."

"What makes you think we who serve the Goddess know such a secret?"

"My sister thinks you do and what she thinks she ends up telling me."

"Hmmm, why am I not surprised? Well then, what makes you think we who serve the Goddess would share any of our secrets with the daughter of a man who hates us and our deity so much? I doubt if you brought her here to convert...."

"I care about none of that. I worship God Most High because my husband does, but I can see with my own eyes it doesn't make much difference which deity people worship; joy and sorrow, wealth and poverty, sickness and health, these blessings and curses come to each person as though none of the deities exist. All I want is for you to teach Tamar the secret of avoiding pregnancy. If you can get her to convert as well, so what? If she ends up like my sister and worships Anath and God Most High, so what? You and my husband may not like that attitude, but I've lived long enough to know only a fool really believes a deity is going to help when he or she needs it."

The Adath smiled. "Here we say this proverb: 'The prayer quickest answered is the one you answer yourself.'" Then her face became solemn as she said firmly, "I would like to teach your daughter, but that's not possible. If your husband found out, it would cause a lot of trouble we don't need."

"Perhaps it is possible," Zebudah said calmly as she produced another purse full of shekels of silver.

The Adath smiled warmly as she took the fat purse, saying, "It could happen. Anath works in mysterious ways. This could be one of them."

Zebudah turned to Tamar and gave her a proverb: "Prayers are received with joy in Heaven; shekels are received with joy in temples."

The Adath, showing no offense as she tucked the purse away in her robes, said, "We prefer this proverb: 'Virtues are gold and silver in Heaven; gold and silver are gold and silver on the earth.' When do you want the lessons to begin? Any ideas about keeping this a secret from your husband?"

"Now is better than later because later may be too late," Zebudah declared. "As for my husband, he's easier for me to fool than he thinks he is."

Tamar could not help feeling fear when her mother left her alone with the Adath. She wasn't a very religious girl, but she did believe in the deity her father worshipped and she knew she was offending Yahweh. It was true she couldn't see much evidence of him being offended by all the ways her father so often said the Hebrews offended him, yet there was no way of knowing when a sin would be one too many sins for him. And Tamar didn't want to be singled out by Yahweh as an example. However, she also believed she could trust her mother's judgment. She decided to do as her mother wished. After all, it was entirely possible Anath would protect her from the wrath of Yahweh, assuming what she was doing would actually make him angry enough to want to punish her.

The Adath sat by the beautiful, voluptuous girl and said reassuringly, "There's no reason to be fearful, dear."

"I'm like trying not to be," Tamar said bravely.

"That's a good girl. I must say, you're the most adorably sexy girl I've ever seen. It's amazing you're not already married."

"Oh, I'm like so wanting to be married! I'll be like thirteen in seven months, you know, and I'll like just die of humiliation if I'm not like married before that."

"Well, I'm sure your father doesn't want that to happen, but, knowing his reputation, he's going to want some serious mohar for you. I'm sure some man will pay it. When it comes to their serpents, men will do foolish things with their money to keep them happy. However the important question right now is do you want to know the secret your mother wants you to learn? It's not a decision your mother should make for you, though I understand and approve of her motivation."

"Oh, for sure! Brats like suck, but like so does celibacy, I'm sure."

"Indeed it does, dear. This, then, is the secret: the serpent of the man longs to worship the Goddess in the temple of the woman. When the serpent worships in the Temple of Life, the result is almost always pregnancy, though sooner for some than for others, and occasionally never if it's the will of the Goddess. Our secret is knowing women have two other temples for the serpent to worship in. We call them the Eunuch's Temples, which is how Anath enables her priests to be ridden as though they are women by the men who come here to worship — or just to have some fun. A lot of Hebrew men who worship only your God Most High come here to trade gerahs for rides, which is why the orthodox Hebrews call Anath's priestesses and priests harlots. They don't understand that Anath isn't against riding just for fun and that it's also considered to be worship if done in the temple, even if one of the people involved believes it's just for fun."

Tamar knew what a eunuch was, since castrated male slaves were common (her father had several). She also knew the priests of Anath had castrated themselves to qualify for their jobs (this peculiar self-sacrifice was one of the rituals of Anath and other goddesses that the Hebrews who worshipped only Yahweh despised the most). None of that knowledge told her what either Eunuch's Temple was, how it was possible for a girl to have Eunuch's Temples, and where they might be on her body. She had been raised to be a good Hebrew girl and had been shielded from as much naughty knowledge as possible. "I'm like totally not understanding," she confessed.

The Adath smiled as she asked, "Do you understand what the serpent of the man is?"

Tamar was glad to be able to show she wasn't entirely ignorant, so she replied enthusiastically, "Oh, for sure. I have like lots of brothers. Pet the Serpent is like my most favorite game to play with my older brothers. When Mom like found out, she went like all bonkers. She like went, 'You only play Pet the Serpent with your husband!' I'm like, 'Why?' Then she's like not sparing the rod on my buns until I'm like promising I won't play Pet the Serpent with my brothers anymore, but I'm like still doing it, you know, only like more carefully, cuz it makes my brothers treat me nice. If you like pet the serpent long enough, it like pukes up this gunk. It's totally yucky, you know, but it makes my brothers like totally happy. Lots of times Daddy gives me this look like he wants me to pet his serpent, but he's like not doing anything about it."

The Adath chuckled, "I do believe Anath brought you here because you're a natural-born priestess, dear. Do you also know what the Temple of Life is?"

"Is it like where babies and pee come out?"

"Yes, dear."

Shock suddenly appeared all over Tamar's gorgeous face. "No way a serpent like fits in there, I'm sure!"

"Now, dear, don't you think, if something as large as a baby can get out of there, something much smaller than that can fit in there?"

"Is that like what happens when men are like riding women?"

"Yes, except we call it worshipping in the Temple of Life."

"So like what're these Eunuch's Temples where the serpent like also worships?"

"One is located right next to the Temple of Life. You may have heard some of your people calling it the Muddy Road."

Tamar was even more shocked, and looked it. She cried out, "Like totally gnarly! No way no serpent's goin' in there!"

"Yes, way. That's the secret your mother brought you to learn. When the serpent worships in the Eunuch's Temples, pregnancy never happens."

"I'm like gagging here, I'm sure!" Tamar protested. "And where, like, is this other Eunuch's Temple."

"You're speaking with it, dear."

Tamar turned green and said, "Gross! No way!"

The Adath laughed. "Dear, dear, ignorant child. It is one of the most ancient and exquisite methods of birth control. It's much more effective than exterior ejaculation, which is, if what your aunt, the one who worships here with her husband, says is true, the much more common method used by your people — well, at least in this region. I imagine, like all other peoples, Hebrews behave to some degree differently in different regions. When priestesses everywhere don't want to get pregnant, they use the Eunuch's Temples. It is the most common birth-control method among Canaanites, and you would be shocked by the number of Hebrews who practice it. The next time you see a woman your mother's age, either Canaanite or Hebrew, and she's only had three or four children, don't believe it was Anath or your God Most High who limited the size of her family. I'm sure your mother and her sister know this. I suspect your mother's belief in Anath's priestesses knowing some other mysterious birth-control method is nonsense from her sister, who is really quite a silly woman."

That was a load for Tamar to think about. She did know women who had small families and the only explanation she had ever heard was that Yahweh had decided not to bless them with large numbers of children. Now she was being told it was people, not Yahweh, controlling how many kids they had. What an astonishing thing to discover, yet she decided immediately she preferred it that way. If Yahweh was a trustworthy family planner, would her mother's health have been ruined by too many births? What about all the poor people with huge families they couldn't support? But none of that meant she wanted a serpent in her Eunuch's Temples, and she emphatically said so.

The high priestess's eyes sparkled with wise amusement as she replied, "Oh, you dear, dear girl, I promise that not only will you learn not to gag, but you'll learn to enjoy it just as much as any woman has ever enjoyed the serpent worshipping in her Temple of Life. In fact, you're coming here now must be Anath's will, because we are blessed with the divine presence of Tammuz, Anath's son and lover. Who better to teach you how to enjoy the Eunuch's Temples?"

Tamar's protests were blown away by the force of her astonishment at being told she was going to meet a supernatural being. She did not doubt for an instant the existence of Tammuz, the divine stud who rode his mother like a man rides his wife. Not even the most orthodox priests of Yahweh denied the existence of the competition. To accept the fact of their existence was not a sin. The sin was to worship them. Tamar became very excited. She didn't know anybody who had met an actual supernatural being. Her girlfriends were all going to die of envy!

Tamar gasped when Tammuz came into the garden as though he had been waiting inside to hear his name as the cue for him to come out. He was the most beautiful young man Tamar had ever seen or could even imagine. He had gloriously flowing locks framing a dazzling fifteen-year-old face. His sensuous lips filled her with longing to drink endless kisses from them. His blue eyes sparkled with joyous lust. His body was mostly concealed in white robes that left his powerful arms bare, but Tamar had no doubts about it being too exquisite to be mortal. The Adath enjoyed how stunned with sexual arousal the young Hebrew girl was as she beheld the god approaching her.

"I hear I'm needed," Tammuz said when he stopped just three feet from Tamar and locked eyes with the totally enthralled girl.

"My sweet Lord, she has come to learn the arts of the Eunuch's Temples," the Adath said needlessly, her voice full of adoration.

"Mmmm, my favorite places to worship," Tammuz murmured seductively. He was actually Uriel, who was enjoying some R&R in the flesh. Tammuz was the archangel's favorite character to be on the earth, because the priestesses and priests of Anath always put out like crazy for the son of their supreme being.

Tamar could not speak. She felt as though her insides had melted. She no longer knew anything except that she would do anything Tammuz wanted her to do. It was as if she had not been alive until her eyes saw him.

Tammuz opened his robes and showed off his long and thick serpent, which was standing proudly, to the virgin's startled eyes. He said amorously, "No reason not to start now."

"It's like too big, I'm sure!" Tamar protested, ashamed of her fear yet unable to ignore it.

Tammuz and the Adath laughed, then the god said soothingly, "You'll soon learn how wrong you are, darling."

Tamar did learn that and a lot more. Every afternoon she eagerly went to the Temple of Anath for more lessons. Uriel enjoyed teaching her so much that he begged for an extension to his R&R. By then the other archangels and just about every angel in the lower ranks were hot to replace him as Tammuz, so Yahweh denied the extension and had Gabriel organize the horny horde into an orderly daily rotation after a lottery to determine which ones got to participate. To prevent Zadok from interfering or ever punishing Tamar, Yahweh, who was highly amused by the angelic lust for the voluptuous girl, cast a spell of ignorance over all the Hebrews and Canaanites in Chezib-Timnah region except Zebudah and the priests and priestesses of Anath.

For two years Tamar took lessons in the arts of the Eunuch's Temples from Tammuz, never knowing that every day Tammuz was actually a different angel. When Yahweh's amusement began to wane, he declared it was time to let Tamar get on with her life. The angel currently being Tammuz told her and the Adath that Tamar had no more to learn about the arts of the Eunuch's Temples and thus must come no more to the Temple of Anath unless she became a believer in Anath. Bets were made all over Heaven about her decision. Satan and Yahweh had a wager, the archangel betting on her not converting and Yahweh, because he could see how tempted the girl was, betting she would change her religion. Tamar was severely tempted, but she dearly loved her father and hence could not break his heart by becoming one of Anath's worshippers. Yahweh became very peckish; he hated losing bets. Tamar never knew how close she came to being supernaturally punished.

When Zebudah, who never regained her health, died the day after Tamar finished her unusual education, Yahweh declared Tamar off limits as an R&R site. All those angels who did not get a turn being Tammuz with Tamar moaned and groaned about unfairness, which enraged Michael because it gave Satan an excuse to tease him unmercifully. Raphael and Uriel were flying furiously all over Heaven to restore discipline. There were so many angels on their faces giving them twenty or thirty or more that daily routine in Heaven was thrown way off schedule.

As soon as Tamar was no longer daily enchanted by Tammuz's company, she began suffering intense humiliation; she was now *14* and unmarried! All her girlfriends were married and all but one already had given birth to her first child. She was teased unmercifully, even by her own siblings. Nevertheless she did not give her father a hard time and even pretended to cheerfully accept her duty to become the female head of the household until her father married the sweet young thing he had selected for his next wife. The wedding was to take place as soon as possible after Zadok had observed all the mourning rites.

Zadok's future wife was two years younger than Tamar and almost as beautiful. When Tamar got to know the girl (she looked ready for it, but in fact had not yet had her first flow of blood that would make her officially a woman), she found her full of conflicting feelings. She was tremendously happy to be marrying one of the richest men in the land; however she was not enthused about her future husband being older than her father and even less enthused about becoming the stepmother of eight children. Because she liked the girl's charming personality, Tamar felt a little sorry for her, but, as she told her, there was nothing unusual about a girl her age, or even younger, marrying a man her father's age. She advised her to think only about how wealthy her future husband was and also about her father, who was hopelessly in debt to Zadok, being liberated from that burden because the mohar for her had been the cancellation of his debt. Tamar did not tell her how eager she was for her father to marry again; it would liberate her to get married, which would end the humiliation of being unmarried at her advanced age.

At this time Judah was looking for a wife for Er, his first-born son, who was 27 years old and whining constantly about wanting a wife so he could stop riding slave girls like a teenager. Judah told him, "You want a wife, go find a wife like I did. And, anyway, every man rides his slave girls no matter how old he is or how many wives he has."

His son insisted, "Dad, fathers are supposed to arrange marriages! That's the way it's done in all the best families. No top-shekel girl wants any of that romance stuff today. That's for peasants. If you get me a pretty enough girl, I won't want to ride slave girls."

Judah replied, "You don't know anything about marriage if you believe that, unless you've converted to that weirdo monogamy theology some of the hardcore orthodox have become infatuated with. Have you?"

Er replied in turn, "No way! But why can't I just ride my wife if that's what I like best?"

Judah sighed with frustration, "Are all kids your age as ding-a-ling as you are, or is that just you?"

"Dad, I'm modern. What was good enough in the old days when you were young, well, that's not the way it is today, so just deal with it and arrange my marriage, OK?"

Judah eventually gave in. The winds of change were blowing, so what else could he do? In his youth, while visiting Hirah, his Adullamite friend, Judah had fallen in love with Zeruah, the daughter of Shua. She was so voluptuously beautiful that he didn't care that she was a Canaanite or that she wasn't dealing with a full deck. Judah was prosperous enough to provide mohar for himself and obviously was also a sure bet to become wealthier, so Shua told his daughter to forget Anath and convert to the religion of the Hebrews, which Judah had said she must do if she wanted to marry him. He told her what he thought was the world's wisest proverb: "Go for the shekels and worry about your soul later; the righteous are starving all around us, but the rich aren't." Zeruah, who had very little ability for that kind of thinking and even less interest in theology, did not care whom she worshipped as long as she had handsome and studly Judah for her husband, so taking her father's advice was no problem.

Judah wed Zeruah and they were happy. Zeruah always enjoyed Judah's serpent worshipping in her Temple of Life, and Judah discovered riding her was so much fun that he greatly reduced the amount of time he had been spending riding his slave girls or riding harlots when he was traveling on business. Er was born eleven months after the wedding. Next came two daughters, then the second son, Onan, born four years after Er. Three more daughters arrived before Zeruah gave birth to the third son six years after Onan. The third son was named Shelah. Following him came four more daughters. The last child nearly killed Zeruah and she never regained good health — or her desire for her husband's serpent to worship in her Temple of Life!

Judah was sad that his riding days with his wife were over, but he had plenty of young, sexy slave girls and every town had harlots who were skilled at making serpents happy. He thought about marrying another wife, but decided to make Zeruah happy by waiting until after she died. Alas, he wasn't being truly altruistic. Lots of wealthy and almost-wealthy men he knew had two or more wives, so he knew how often polygamous marriages were filled with drama. That didn't make him one of those loony monogamists. Those crazy orthodox guys believed not only in having just *one* wife, but also that the wife should be the *only* woman a guy rode! Judah preferred a monogamous marriage for himself, but there was no way he wanted the sexual boredom of a monogamous lifestyle.

Zeruah was terrified of becoming pregnant again, so she loved her husband even more when he did not insist on his right to ride her. She was deeply moved when he let her know he wouldn't marry another wife as long as she lived. She knew he was riding his slave girls and harlots when he traveled for business, but that didn't bother her because it was entirely normal male behavior. She knew that some of the most orthodox Hebrew men had only one wife and would not ride harlots or their slave girls if they were slaveholders, and that they were trying to persuade all Hebrews to practice this weirdness called monogamy, but she was glad her husband was not pious in such a peculiar way. She believed in the wisdom of a currently popular proverb: "Religion is a good thing, but it's silly to be so religious that people think you're weird." Yet it saddened her that she was no longer making his serpent happy.

When she told her husband about this regret, Judah told his wife about a popular service harlots provided that did not involve a serpent worshipping in a woman's two other temples (Judah had learned the first time he had suggested it that Zeruah was not ever going to allow his serpent to worship in her nether Eunuch's Temple). Zeruah, like most women who were determined to be the good girls they had been raised to be, always had been good at ignoring things she didn't want to know, thus she gagged just hearing about it. It took a few days of thinking about it for her to accept the fact that her vocal Eunuch's Temple was the solution to her dilemma. She did grow to like keeping her husband's serpent happy that way, but never grew fond of swallowing. It wasn't exactly living happily ever after, but it was close enough.

They had established their household in a valley near Chezib by the time Shelah was born because it put them closer to Timnah, where Judah's Adullamite friend lived. Both owned vast herds and flocks. They discovered all sorts of ways they could work together to cut their costs and dominate the market. Indeed, by the time Judah was looking for a wife for his oldest son, they had driven the competition out of business in the region all around Timnah and Chezib. In Chezib, only Zadok the moneylender was wealthier than Judah the herder, which was why Judah went first to Zadok to see if his daughter Tamar, whose voluptuous beauty was legendary throughout the land, would be a fitting wife for his son Er.

Zadok received Judah joyously. The son of a man as wealthy as Judah could not be a more perfect match for his gorgeous daughter. Sure, Er was known to have certain disadvantages, but Zadok expected a daughter of his loins to see that his advantage, meaning his father's vast wealth, which he would inherit some day, overwhelmed any disadvantages. He knew so many ways two men as rich as they were could make loads of shekels together! What glories of profit-making could come from the union of the two wealthiest families in Chezib, especially if Hirah, Judah's equally rich Adullamite friend, became a third partner! After they were settled comfortably and had enjoyed some wine and polite conversation, Zadok called for Tamar to come before them.

Tamar's voluptuous beauty blew Judah away. His serpent rose to honor the gorgeous 14-year-old girl. All the legends about her beauty had poorly prepared him for the stunning reality of the utterly delicious girl. As her father had wished, she wore clothes that were almost scandalous. No doubts were left in Judah's mind about how exquisite her firm, young body was. However, there was one thing more and that one thing was what gave truly awesome power to her physical presentation. It was the horniness that glowed all over the frustrated teenager!

Only her fingers (or the fingers and tongues of her favorite slave girls) had been in her temples for worshipping since Tammuz had sadly told her that her training was through and that she must not return to the temple except as a true believer in Anath. Alas, she could not give up Yahweh because that would have broken her father's heart.

Fingers and tongues were fun, but she was the kind of girl who would always believe serpents were way better. Her father stubbornly refused to celebrate the Rites of Lot with her despite all her seductive ploys. When his morality arguments failed to persuade her, he gave her a proverb: "Don't bite the fruit you have for sale." After speaking the proverb, he went all patriarchal on her and would not permit the matter to be discussed again, which precluded her from telling him she knew how he could bite her all he wanted and no shopper would ever be able to tell he had (which, she had to admit, also meant she never had to confront the challenge of overcoming his religious prejudices against birth control in general and the Eunuch's Temples in particular). He could be so peculiar when it came to anything that had some relationship to shekels or religion! She had brothers who could have played Abram and Sarai with her, but they would not risk the economic punishment their angry, orthodox father would have inflicted on them if he caught them.

By the time Judah came to formally propose marriage between Tamar and Er, she was wondering how to get the worshipping she craved behind her father's back. So, when she approached her father and his distinguished guest, her desperate horniness shone all over her, making her beauty flash like Yahweh's lightning.

"Judah has come to propose marriage between you and Er, his first-born son," her father announced happily.

Tamar knew that, of course, but it was polite to pretend she didn't and was surprised to be so honored. However, pretending the latter was a struggle, and she managed it only to make her father happy. The sad fact about Er was that he would have been the biggest joke in Chezib but for Onan.

They said of the three sons of Judah, "If brains were gerahs, they wouldn't be worth a shekel." They said of

Er, "When God Most High was passing out brains, the angels were beating Er with the ugly stick!" And this too was said of him: "He couldn't keep a flock together if the sheep didn't feel sorry for him." Also this: "It's a good thing Judah's shekels are uncountable, because Er can't count!" The unkindest thing, though, was this: "That boy couldn't get laid in a brothel with bags of shekels in his hands!" (That last was untrue, of course, since harlots gave men rides for gerahs and not for love or pleasure. Er, however, never did anything to prove the insult wrong; his father owned too many young, sexy slave girls, and thus it seemed silly to him go all the way into town just for some nooky, which proved he wasn't as stupid as the jokes said he was. However, he was as ugly as the jokes said he was, which wasn't a problem for him with slave girls.)

In other words, Er was not exactly the husband she had been dreaming about, but she knew she had no choice. Although her father did love her and would hate to use his right to force her to marry Er, there was no way he would allow her to refuse a match that by his standards was made in Heaven to benefit him on earth. Before she could start to resent how unfair life could be, she remembered one of her father's proverbs that applied to her situation: "A wealthy man cannot ride a camel through the eye of a needle, but being poor sucks worse than that." Suddenly she was thinking realistically. While living at home, she enjoyed the lifestyle her father's wealth provided. But that wealth would one day be inherited by her brothers. If she wanted to live all her life in the style she had become accustomed to, she needed a wealthy husband. Er, thanks to his father, would certainly be a wealthy husband no matter how many other wonderful things he would never be.

Here, one of her mother's proverbs gave her the wisdom she needed at the moment: "The husband who can be trained is better than one who can't." It was the proverb she had taught and retaught her daughters whenever Zadok's stubbornness could not be sabotaged by any of her overt or covert tactics. If Er was only half as stupid as he was said to be, Tamar had no doubts about being able to train him.

"Oh, father!" Tamar exclaimed with joy that seemed authentic. "I'm like so happy, I'm sure! I never like dreamed, you know, of being married to a man like Er. God Most High is being like very good to me."

And so it came to pass that when Judah rose to return to his palatial tent, he had good news for Er.

The people in Chezib, Timnah, and throughout the entire region were stunned when they learned an ugly doofus like Er was going to score the sexiest, most beautiful young woman they had seen or heard about in ages. Even when the huge, spectacular wedding took place, many watched as though they couldn't believe what they were seeing. When the poor guy fumbled his lines, Tamar was the one they felt sorry for. All the young girls looked at tall, scrawny Er and shuddered to see his gaunt, pockmarked face, which was dominated by big, slimy-looking lips and a nose so large that they all thought he would need a week to finish if he ever started blowing it. And he did look as stupid as the jokes said he was. It was too yucky for any of them to even imagine Er's serpent worshipping in Tamar's Temple of Life — but not too yucky to joke about!

When the ceremony was over and she was at last alone in the luxurious tent that was now her home, Tamar was too horny to give a damn what Er looked like. He was a man and he had a serpent! Anything else, *forget about it*! Er was also very excited. He was going to ride his own wife — and she was the stunningly beautiful girl every guy throughout the land had wanted to marry! Who was laughing now? He was sweating like a virgin when he laid his bride out on the pile of soft furs and expensive pillows that would be their marriage bed. Tamar's slave girls had removed all her and Er's clothes immediately after they were in the bedroom. She restrained herself from jumping her husband. At last she found something to admire about him: a serpent damn near as big and beautiful as Tammuz's!

Er wondered what the small jar of olive oil was doing by the bed and wondered twice as hard when Tamar began smearing his serpent with it. Then all his wondering vanished when the pleasure of her slippery hand filled him with delight vastly exceeding any the slave girls ever had given him. Skillfully Tamar guided her husband's serpent to her nether Eunuch's Temple.

Er's serpent had never worshipped there before. He knew about the practice. All the pious Hebrews, even the moderate ones, insisted it was supposed to be offensive to Yahweh because it was associated with what the eunuch priests (and also priestesses who wanted to avoid pregnancy) did with those who participated in the sexual worship of Anath (hence the derogatory Hebrew expression "Muddy Road"). That was why all of them said publicly they would never, ever do it — and also why the hardcore orthodox loudly wished Yahweh would reveal to the community a law forbidding the Muddy Road to all Hebrews. Therefore Er believed good Hebrews didn't let their serpents worship in either of the Eunuch's Temples. The guy was stupid enough to believe what people preached about sexual behavior was what they practiced when their lust was roiling and boiling. That was why he was both shocked and reluctant, but how could he refuse his wife?

Tamar saw his reaction, guessed the cause of it, and said sensuously, "Oh, darling, the daughter of a Hebrew as like orthodox as my father wouldn't do something offensive to like God Most High, you know?"

"Well, uh, yeah, I guess," he agreed uncomfortably.

"You'll be like lots happier if you do things like my way, I'm sure."

How could he look down at her adorably sexy face and refuse to submit, especially when he foolishly assumed she was only talking about which Temple she wanted his serpent to worship in. And so began the training of Er, who wasn't as stupid as the jokes said he was, but was sufficiently stupid to enable Tamar to become the boss in the family. But what did he care? By the end of his honeymoon, he was the happiest man on the earth and certainly the most envied by men in Chezib and Timnah. Tamar was just as happy. Her husband was ugly and he wasn't close to being as smart as she was, but when it came to riding, she quickly discovered he was able to learn to do it as well as Tammuz ever did!

Er lived happily ever after for three years. And so did Tamar. He had a natural inclination for monogamy that she found rather charming, but she insisted he ride one of their slave girls at least once a week. She didn't want him giving people another reason to laugh at him. Er had learned well that happiness was doing things Tamar's way, so he rode slave girls with his eyes shut so he could fantasize they were his wife.

It wasn't long before one of their slaves let it be known that Er and Tamar were practicing birth control, revealing also the method used. Like most slaveholders, they quite often behaved as though slaves were furniture and thus did things when slaves could observe them that they never would have done in the presence of any free person. It was one of the facts of life that went with having the luxury of slaves.

Zadok strongly disapproved; he believed birth control was immoral and having kids was one of the most important religious duties for Hebrews. However, he wasn't Tamar's or Er's patriarch and they weren't breaking any laws, thus he was limited to scowling and reprimanding, which were not effective at all.

Judah and Zeruah were disappointed, yet also understanding of Tamar's explanation that she and Er wanted to enjoy being just a couple for a while before complicating their marriage with kids.

The Hebrew community was officially disapproving, yet everybody knew that many Hebrews practiced birth control and a significant minority of them used Er and Tamar's method, so they weren't pointing fingers too hard at the couple to prevent other fingers from pointing all over the place. After all, the poor, who were almost always members of extended families living in small digs barely big enough for one nuclear family, had even less privacy than the slave-holding rich. The art of pretending not to know almost everything about everybody was greatly valued in a highly communal community — which was bizarre since gossip was the most popular form of entertainment. There was a proverb that explained it: "Up is down and down is sideways if everybody behaves that way."

Er might have been bothered about all of that, but Tamar told him to ignore everybody and just be happy with her. His happiness was so vast that he couldn't ignore that advice. He did want children, especially sons, but he also now knew he didn't need kids to be happy with Tamar. It did bother him that his father and mother were disappointed at not being grandparents yet (nobody believed grandchildren produced by daughters were as valuable as those produced by sons), but it didn't bother him enough to spoil his happiness. He was confident that when Tamar was ready to start having kids Yahweh would reward their efforts to be fruitful and multiply.

Judah did his best to conceal what *really* made him miserable. Er's tent was near his tent and the bedrooms were positioned just right so that every night of the week he heard Tamar's uninhibited enjoyment when Er was riding her almost as clearly as he would have if he had been on their bed watching. His serpent became aroused every time and that meant Zeruah or one of their slave girls (who slept in the bedroom to provide prompt service when required) had work to do.

Zeruah was amused by how her son and daughter-in-law's astonishingly frequent and enthusiastic riding made her husband so horny. She envied Tamar, though, remembering how passionate — and almost as frequent! — she and Judah had been when they were young, and sometimes was tempted to risk her life just to enjoy being ridden by Judah again. It pleased her that her husband's first choice at night was to let her make his serpent happy in the way she was still able to safely do it instead of calling to one of the slave girls for a ride, but she knew he liked riding the best. She often thought of this comforting proverb: "When life's not as good as it used to be, that doesn't mean life is as bad as it could be."

Three days after celebrating their third anniversary in the way they liked the most, Er staggered happily out of his tent to go see if his slaves were tending his flocks and herds properly. He could have stayed in bed. As long as Judah's sharp eye and rigid discipline prevented his son's incompetence from being abused by his slaves, Er's flocks and herds would be tended with the same excellence with which his father's flocks and herds were tended. However Er thought he was being a successful herder, so he acted as though he was.

Above the white cotton balls of the clouds, Michael and Satan hovered, their vast wings flapping majestically. They watched Er walking to the pasture where one of his herds grazed. Michael said, "Look at that road apple diddly-bobbing along like he thinks he's going to live happily ever after."

"He looks like death warmed over," replied Satan.

"Yeah, but look at that doofus grin! There ain't a priestess in the world who can make a serpent happier than Tamar can, and I know that for a fact!" It wasn't often he got one up on Satan, so he really enjoyed it when he did.

Annoyed, Satan said, "I'm tempted to take some R&R in the flesh even if I have to look as ugly as that loose puke. I'm tired of all the ways everybody reminds me I missed out on being Tammuz with Tamar."

"Now you know we can't mess with Tamar no more, smart ass."

Satan chuckled, "When will you realize I was created to be the exception that tests the rule?"

"Well, maybe, but if I was you I wouldn't be making the Commander in Chief peckish like you do sometimes." Michael grinned rather nastily as he added, "I got to admit, though, I wouldn't mind seeing what he'd do to you if he ever decides he's had enough uppity from you."

"Let me worry about that, Mikey. Hey, wouldn't it be a blast to wipe that doofus grin off that road apple's face?"

Michael laughed. "Yeah, his head and buns are so disconnected he doesn't know what a loose puke he is." The archangel formed lightning in his hand. "Bet you my next R&R in the flesh I can make him squirt and dump at the same time."

"I'll bet you two R&Rs in the flesh you can't do it without killing him."

"You're on, smart ass. Watch this." Michael hurled the lightning down at Er and struck him square on top of the head. The human didn't die instantly, but he wasn't going to live much longer as he jerked and flopped on the ground while squirting and dumping copiously. The furious archangel thundered, "*Damn!*"

Satan laughed, "You didn't correct for windage! You *never* correct for windage!"

"Oh, bite me! Damn, now what do we do? Do you think the Commander in Chief had any big plans for him?"

"He's never mentioned any to me."

"Damn, damn, *damn!* I wish the big boss had given us the power to resurrect humans. I'd zap the poor maggot back to life if I could."

"Oh, don't sweat it, Mike. They die young all the time; they're used to it, or should be by now."

"So, what? We just hope nobody in Heaven saw it and go on like he just up and died like humans do all the time."

"Why don't we just admit what happened? Really, I don't think the boss will care. He hasn't before, right? When it comes to killing humans, we're not in the same league with him."

"Well, what do you think the humans will say happened?"

"If they don't put the blame on Er, I'll give back the R&Rs I won," Satan replied. "Haven't you figured out humans yet? They won't blame anybody in Heaven. They never do. They'll say Er sinned in some way and was justly punished by Yahweh for it."

"Sin? What sin? The guy was more moral than most humans and he worshipped the Commander in Chief more sincerely than most Hebrews do."

"Doesn't make any difference. That's how humans think. They're free to be rational, but they hardly ever are."

Michael shrugged. "Yeah, you got a point. Besides, you know, he wouldn't've lived much longer than three or four more decades anyway."

"There it is. They're born to die quick and they know it, yet most of them do everything they can to make themselves and other people miserable during the time they're alive. That's one of the big reasons why they're so amusing. Now come on, we have some R&R schedules to rearrange."

"See if I ever bet with you again, smart ass," Michael grumbled as they started the flight back to Heaven.

Satan laughed, "I might believe that if we'd been created last week!"

So it came to pass that Er's death was ascribed to some sin so horrible that it required Yahweh to execute him in such a dramatic fashion. The annoying thing was not knowing what the sin was. Though he was the second biggest joke in Chezib, everyone always had acknowledged Er lived as blamelessly as any human could. "Unless ugly's now a sin, the boy, may he rest in peace, wasn't clever enough for serious sinning" was the common eulogy for the poor guy. Eventually other interesting stuff happened, and Er's hideous sin, whatever it was, ceased to intrigue people.

Tamar, Judah, and Zeruah were the only ones made miserable by Er's sudden death. Judah and Zeruah had lost a son who had been, alas for them, the best of the three. Tamar had lost a husband she had come to appreciate as a lover and as a spouse not nearly clever enough to be a patriarch in their tent or cruel enough to want to be one. He kept her satisfied in bed and happily accepted her benign domination. She had stopped seeing him as ugly before their first anniversary. Indeed, her love for him had moved her to start bringing his serpent to her Temple of Life in the past month because she knew how much he was looking forward to having a son. How sad she had not conceived before he died.

Judah was sad, but an idea came to him that pretty much pushed his grief out of his mind. His lust had inspired him to think about the Rites of Lot and to ask why they should not include daughters-in-law and fathers-in-law as well. Wasn't Tamar now a member of his family, like a daughter to him even as he was like a father to her? That no person knew of a daughter-in-law celebrating the Rites of Lot with her father-in-law did not mean it could not happen. His thought processes, boiling in the oil of his lust, made him believe it was his duty as a religious leader to pioneer this unexplored theological territory.

When he had convinced himself that he and Tamar were qualified to celebrate the Rites of Lot together, action followed soon after she had finished the required period of mourning. Never once doubting she would consent (he knew a woman as horny as Tamar wouldn't willingly continue the celibacy of the mourning period if she had a chance do some riding after it was over), Judah dressed in expensive robes and groomed his beard, singing, "Hosanna, hey sanna, sanna, sanna, ho! Hosanna, hey sanna!" His joyous voice attracted his wife to their bedroom. Zeruah was surprised to see him dressing as though he wanted to impress somebody.

"So what's with all this happiness and the fine clothes even though our first-born son isn't dust yet?" she asked, her voice filled with disapproval.

"I'm going to Tamar to comfort her with the Rites of Lot," Judah announced. He was pleased with the perfect tone of righteousness in his voice.

Zeruah glared at her husband. "You should be ashamed of yourself! Her period of mourning has only just ended! And whoever heard of daughters-in-law and fathers-in-law celebrating the Rites of Lot?"

Judah smiled as persuasively as only a man who knew every trick in the book could. "Now, now, dear, who should know these things best, me or you?"

"I know that I've never heard of *that* before!" But his confident, relaxed tone leeched at her certainty, and it showed.

He wheedled on, "Well, dear, think about this proverb: 'What hasn't been done before is not necessarily what can't be done.' Trust me, I've looked into my heart and know the righteousness of what I know to be true."

Zeruah, who was only slightly more intellectually gifted than her deceased son, scowled trying to figure out how to refute those persuasive words. All she could come up with was a different argument. "Aren't I supposed to be dead first?" she demanded.

Judah gave her another one of those wonderfully persuasive smiles. "Dear, dear, don't trouble yourself about things involving theology. Trust me to know the will of God Most High. It is true that, if Tamar was my daughter, flesh of my flesh, then, yes, you would need to be dead before we could celebrate the Rites of Lot. But she is not the daughter of my loins. She's a daughter-in-law who has lost her husband. I've searched my heart and all I know about theology, so now I understand what my duty as a father-in-law is. You can trust me when I say the Rites of Lot include fathers-in-law comforting widowed daughters-in-law with both physical comfort and spiritual comfort."

There had to be an answer to that, but Zeruah couldn't think of it. Even if she had been more intelligent, she was a Canaanite who had converted to the Hebrew religion without any real religious feeling for it and even less interest in its theology. Against Judah in a battle involving Hebrew theology, she was like an unarmed woman fighting a fully armed soldier. Their friends included three Lotite couples, and from them she had acquired what little she knew about the Hebrew custom. Believing she would have to be dead before Judah could celebrate the Rites of Lot, she never saw any reason to try to learn anything more about them. Now she realized how wrong she had been, and blamed herself for having no arguments to keep her husband from going to Tamar.

"Very well, if you say it's right, it's right," Zeruah conceded unhappily. "It just doesn't feel right to me."

Judah embraced her and gave her a comforting kiss before providing her with a comforting proverb: "Theology succeeds where reason fails."

Judah stepped back from his wife, eager to get to Tamar, and at that instant Zeruah fell into a deep sleep and collapsed onto the bed she shared with Judah. Before panicked Judah could get to her, she and the bed burst into flames that did not consume. Judah, however, did not notice that at first. He shrieked in terror as he scrambled back from the conflagration. He looked wildly about for some means to put out the fire. He didn't figure out what was happening until a booming voice came from the flames, saying, "You shall not ride Tamar until you don't know you're riding Tamar."

Judah knew it had to be Yahweh, though he called him God Most High because Yahweh had yet to reveal his name to the Hebrews. He trembled as his fear drained away. Now he could see the flames were not burning up his wife and the bed.

"Give a guy some warning, will you? And what on earth is not riding her until I don't know I'm riding her supposed to mean, anyway?" Judah complained, trying to conceal his irritation.

Yahweh ignored the question and chuckled, "Maybe next time I'll warn you, maybe I won't."

Judah decided not to comment on that, so he said respectfully, "Why have you honored me with your presence, God Most High?"

"The Rites of Lot are off, though I admire your creative interpretation of them."

Judah cried out, "Ah, Sheol, come on! Three years of torture listening to her get off every night, now you tell me I can't ride her?" He realized immediately he would have to do better than that, so he rose to passionate eloquence, "Listen to my petition, God Most High, and allow my invocation to reach you. Don't hide your face from me when I am so horny. Bend your ear to me. I'm calling this day, so answer me promptly. My days vanish like smoke. My serpent burns like a fireplace. My heart has be struck, and shriveled like grass. All this because my lust for Tamar has gone bonkers. When I sigh for her, my serpent sticks out without shame. I resemble a pelican in a desert wanting her. I resemble an owl in the arid land needing her. Hearing her get off night after night after night all these years, I stay awake and resemble a sparrow isolated on a rooftop. My wife swallows my lust, but I am a vast marsh of lust that can never be drained. I ride my slave girls, but they cannot carry me across this desert of lust. Not riding Tamar would be like enemies taunting me all day long. If people find out I didn't ride her when I had the opportunity, those who praise and respect me now will say I'm a fool. Wouldn't you rather this be the history for the next generation, so that even the humanists are going to reverence your name? God Most High has gazed down from the heights of his sanctuary, looks down at the land from the skies, to hear the moaning of the father-in-law, and to free him to pursue happiness with his daughter-in-law even as Lot was allowed to pursue happiness with his daughters?"

"I'm impressed. Nobody can say you don't know how to use your tongue," Yahweh replied cheerfully. "Now shut up so you can listen up. Here's a new law to add to the Code of Conduct of the Hebrew community in the Chezib-Timnah region so that one day all Hebrews will understand the law that shall be the duty of all Hebrews to obey. Since Er died childless, Tamar must not marry a stranger outside the family. His brother must go to her and make her his wife. In other words, she's married and therefore not a widow. A formal wedding ceremony isn't necessary, but it's OK if the riding is delayed until after one is held. The first son she bears shall become Er's, so that his family will not be blotted out among the Hebrews. There's also a provision for when the brother is too young to marry. In that case the wife is to return to her father and be celibate while waiting for the brother to become a man. You know, it'll be like a wife waiting for a husband who's on a long journey. That doesn't apply with Tamar, but I thought you should know about it. So what all that means for you is, forget about riding Tamar."

Judah groaned, "Why me, God Most High? What did I do to deserve this? Come on, cut me some slack here. You know how I've suffered. I'm not saying this new law isn't a good idea, but it can wait, can't it? A generation? A year? A week? Come on, a week, just a week. You can give me a week with Tamar, can't you?"

"Sure I could, but I won't. Of course, you have all your behavioral options, so you can disobey me all you want."

Judah tried to conceal the temptation raging in him as he said, "Yeah, that's right, but, uh, uh, I mean, like, well, you know, would that make you as peckish as whatever Er did?"

"Let me put it to you this way: obey me and you will continue to be wealthy all the rest of the days of your life; disobey me and you shall ride Tamar in poverty all the rest of the days of your life."

The flames vanished. Judah moaned and groaned in misery for a few days then admitted not even Tamar was worth poverty. Zeruah, who was still certain her husband's theological interpretation of the Rites of Lot was somehow wrong, even if she couldn't figure out how, danced with joy when Judah explained why he would not be celebrating the Rites with Tamar. She sang merrily, "Come and let us sing to God Most High. Let us shout joyfully to the rock of our liberation. Let us enter his presence with thanksgiving, and shout joyfully to him with music."

"Enough already with the celebrating," Judah griped unhappily as he left his wife to tell Tamar about the new commandment God Most High had decided she would be the first Hebrew widow to obey.

Judah entered the tent that Tamar had shared with Er. From the bedroom came sad sighing. Judah parted the flaps covering the opening to the bedroom. His eyes were blinded by the sight of his daughter-in-law sprawled supinely on the pile of furs and pillows. She wore a single, light robe that was open to reveal most of her glories. His knees weakened and it was as though his serpent leaped towards her. His breathing turned to a difficult gasping, drawing Tamar's attention. She sat up and looked up at her father-in-law in a way that told him she would not have argued about his interpretation of the Rites of Lot. It took several seconds before she "remembered" her robe was open. Languidly she closed it over her fabulous body.

The slave girls who served his daughter-in-law as her personal attendants watched with eager fascination. The five lovely, young darlings believed Judah was there to do what he had so obviously been wanting to do since Tamar became part of his family. As soon as Judah entered, they began anticipating watching and then gossiping about it wherever they could. Judah could see their thoughts all over their pretty faces, and it felt like salt rubbed in a wound. He sternly ordered them to get out of the bedroom and they promptly obeyed the family patriarch, even though they were Tamar's possessions. They didn't go far though; they clustered close to the flap covering the entrance to the bedroom so they could hear every sound.

"Like what's up, Dad?" Tamar asked seductively, her eyes locked with his, communicating horny invitation.

Tamar didn't waste time thinking about how her behavior so soon after Er's death would be reported by the dismissed slave girls, who would be gossiping about what they would hear instead of see; she wanted what she knew Judah wanted to give her. Her sadness about Er was being withered in the heat of her lust. She was now not only willing but eager to give Judah what he wanted. Him or some other guy. Any other guy! Her mother had had a proverb for this situation as well: "The dead leave the table, but the living still have to eat." Her father-in-law, still a dashing hunk, looked utterly delicious to her. Though not theologically sophisticated, she had been thinking about the Rites of Lot and had decided on her own there was no reason why they couldn't include fathers-in-law and daughters-in-law even if the mothers-in-law were still alive.

Judah came so close to disobeying Yahweh that it scared him. His face became somber with righteous duty as he replied quickly, "God Most High has chosen you to be the first to live by a new law for the Hebrews of Chezib and Timnah."

Tamar pouted when she saw that Judah was not going to surrender to his lust for her. "It's like gonna suck, you know," she moaned through parted lips that seemed to be begging for a kiss.

Judah held in his mind the image of himself trying to live in poverty and that kept his resolution firm. He relied on the wisdom of a proverb to reprimand her: "The road of righteousness is paved with the pleasures we refuse to enjoy."

"Like I said, it's gonna like suck."

Judah moved closer to her, but his fear of the strength of the temptation battering at his determination to obey Yahweh kept him from sitting by her on the soft bed and giving her even softer body a comforting hug. He said almost sadly, "Here's the way it has to be. You're going take another husband to provide a son who'll be called Er's son, so Er won't be so dead he's forgotten. Or something like that."

Tamar brightened. "Cool! That like doesn't suck at all, I'm sure. Let's like obey God Most High right away. I'd be like a great number-two wife for you, I'm sure."

"There's more. The husband has to be Er's brother."

Tamar laughed. "Oh, for sure, I can see me like marrying Shelah. He isn't a whole lot older than me, which is kind of like weird, but he's cute," she said enthusiastically. She didn't add that she was certain he would submit to her dominance as easily and as happily as Er had. She knew Shelah only liked being ridden by men as if he was a woman, but she was young and silly enough to believe she was the kind of irresistible woman who could cure that problem. Unfortunately she suddenly thought of a problem that seemed much more serious. "Hey, he's like a worshipper of Anath. God Most High can't like that, I'm sure. Doesn't that mean the law like doesn't include him?"

Judah was a respected religious leader among the Hebrews (even the hardcore orthodox like Zadok acknowledged his theological acumen, which often compelled them to reluctantly surrender to his opinions) and thus didn't like thinking about his youngest son's apostasy. "Well, he still worships God Most High. Lots of Hebrews are religious bigamists. I don't like it, but I still have hope he'll see the light when he's more mature."

Judah didn't really believe that. Shelah, like Er, had been born with a light load of intelligence, but the real problem was he didn't have the slightest desire to ride women and had not tried it even once; he liked being ridden by men, which was perfectly moral for Anath's worshippers and a common way men (too often, in his opinion, Hebrew men) worshipped the goddess, though usually the guy being ridden was a eunuch priest. He also knew men (again too often, in his opinion, Hebrew men) rode men or boys simply for fun, though usually they didn't exclusively ride men or boys. Judah, who had no desire at all to ride men or boys, didn't really understand it.

"But what if like he doesn't?"

"Well, I don't know. God Most High didn't say anything about how apostasy affects the law. Anyway, Shelah's not a problem here. God Most High didn't specify it, but I'm assuming the duty to obey the law falls to the oldest living brother. That's how I would do it if I had made the law."

Tamar showed her revulsion. "Like no way! I'm so totally sure! I'll convert to like Anath if I have to."

"You're forgetting you're a woman. I'm the patriarch

of this family and you're my daughter-in-law, and that means I decide these things for you now that Er is dead. You're not converting to Anath and *you will accept* the fact that you're now married to *Onan*," Judah said grimly. He didn't like doing the patriarch number, but could do it as well as any if he had to.

"Oh, yuck! Like no way for sure!"

"God Most High commands and we obey."

"Then I'm like out of here like first chance I get for sure!"

Judah knew Tamar well enough by now to know the young woman was fully capable of carrying out that threat. The patriarch tactic wasn't going to work unless he made her a prisoner, which he could not do. He would have to try cunning, charm, and persuasion, which were talents he possessed in abundance. "Try it, you might like it," Judah urged, as though he knew something wonderful about Onan that Tamar did not.

"Like no way for sure. He's like this total freak." Her voice, though, revealed she was intrigued.

"Try it," Judah suggested like a salesman working on commission. "Just try it. If it really does suck, well, can't you run away then? I know the boy's not exactly anybody's dream for a son or a husband, but he's not cruel, and, who knows, maybe all he needs is a good woman to get his head and buns wired together."

Tamar wasn't quite as stubborn when she stated the real problem, which wasn't that Onan made Er and Shelah look like geniuses. "How's that gonna like work when Onan's idea of a good woman is one covered with wool and walking on four legs? There's like no way he'll want me, I'm sure."

"Well, there's that, but, trust me, Tamar, Onan's never had an opportunity to ride a woman like you!" Judah said and was happy to see Tamar suddenly seeing Onan as an opportunity to prove just how supremely powerful her sexual powers were. Then he joyously remembered something that would surely convince Tamar to obey the new law. Judah smiled triumphantly as he said to Tamar, "By the way, in case you don't know, his serpent's bigger than Er's was."

Tamar's eyes became wide and bright, and her scowl became a smile. "Like it couldn't hurt to try, I'm sure," she said enthusiastically.

Judah discovered that the joy of his victory didn't last long. It just wasn't right that the glory of Tamar would be his second-born son's to enjoy. The freak didn't deserve it! He would never appreciate the incredibly sexy and sensual young woman like Judah could. It seemed to Judah that Yahweh hadn't thought thoroughly enough about this new law before revealing it. He struggled not to think impious, rebellious thoughts as he went up into the hills where Onan lived with his small herd of sheep.

There were 30 of them and all of them were female. They were the only things the guy loved. Wealth meant nothing to Onan. Judah wasn't sure Onan actually knew his father was one of the wealthiest men in the land. What really annoyed Judah was the fact that Onan was the only truly happy man he knew!

Judah hated seeing his disappointing, disturbingly strange son with his sheep, so usually he sent a slave to fetch the young man when he needed to participate in some family event or have him fulfill his obligation to engage in formal worship. Onan couldn't be relied on to show up voluntarily because he was oblivious to the passage of time. What season it was didn't mean anything to him other than the weather. The phases of the moon, so mystifying and religiously important, were just something up in the sky that was interesting to look at. Onan always came obediently and never caused any trouble when among people, but it was clear what little mind he had was back in the hills with his beloved flock. Today, because of the unique duty his 26-year-old son now had to perform, Judah thought it best to fetch him personally.

He heard Onan before seeing him: a high, squeaky voice sort of panting, "Eee-hee, eee-hee, eee-hee!" Jonah stopped with a groan. The boy was riding one of his "wives." Judah sighed as he waited for the mating to conclude. He wished he had become a merchant or moneylender instead of a herder. If he had chosen one of those urban careers, perhaps Onan never would have developed a preference for riding sheep. What would he do if Yahweh came down to reveal a law that prohibited human-animal sex? He could only hope that, if Yahweh was considering such a law, it would be revealed after his funeral!

He thought about the day he had discovered Onan's preference for sexual companionship. He remembered all the futile effort of trying to get the boy to give up sheep for slave girls. None of his young, sexy slave girls had succeeded in seducing Onan. He remembered finally surrendering to reality and giving his son a small herd of ewes to live with in the hills. The boy had been living happily ever after since that day — and Judah had to endure the humiliation of being the father of such a son. Fortunately, being so fabulously rich and also a respected religious leader meant being powerful enough so that people said what they said about him and Onan only when he wasn't around to hear.

"Why me?" Judah moaned, as he did every time the fact of Onan's existence was put in his face. And it was in his face often enough. The most orthodox (thus the most intolerant) Hebrews urged making a law for Hebrews that would criminalize what Onan did with his sheep. Judah fought them by arguing that Yahweh would have revealed that law if human-animal sex offended him. So far, Judah's charisma, talent for theology, and dominant social status had kept his son from being turned into a criminal. Such trouble he endured — almost as much as the humiliation he suffered! He often wished Onan and his ewes would just wander off to ever more distant pastures until they were far enough away to cease being an embarrassment.

His thoughts turned to imagining the freak riding supremely voluptuous Tamar, and he just about couldn't stand it. He raised his arms imploringly to Heaven and cried out, "God Most High, is this some kind of joke? Onan and Tamar?! Come on, say it doesn't have to happen! What kind of child would come of it? If Er was alive, he'd be smart enough to tell you he wouldn't want his house restored by anything coming from the loins of Onan." Judah looked around. Not even a glowing ember gave him hope of a reprieve from above. What could he do? With Onan there was a chance he'd obey the new law. There was no chance of that happening with Shelah.

Suddenly the "eee-hees" were replaced by a louder squealing like that of some grotesque animal being skinned alive. Judah shuddered. It was a sound of lust more hideous than any Er ever made, and Er's triumphant squealing had been repugnant enough. How had Tamar endured it?

Judah went over the top of the hill, and there was Onan cuddling with one of his big, fat, woolly "wives." He was sighing softly affectionate nonsense syllables to her. She looked very contended — perhaps even happy. The other "wives" were scattered about eating the succulent green grass.

The boy was naked. He looked a lot like Er, only uglier. And unquestionably hairier! His body was covered with black hair just about thick enough to qualify as fur. His beard was long, wild and tangled. So was the hair on his head. He only bathed when brought home for important family events and formal worship services, so he stank powerfully.

Onan saw his father and greeted him with a goofy grin. "Da-eee," he squealed delightedly.

Judah sucked it up and did his duty like a true man of Yahweh. "Onan," he said seriously, so the boy would know to listen up as best he could, "God Most High has made a new law for the Hebrew community of Chezib and Timnah. When a married man dies without leaving a son and he has a brother, that brother automatically becomes married to his sister-in-law without a formal wedding, though they can have a formal wedding if they want to. The brother must sire a son with his new wife and this son will be recognized as his dead brother's son so the dead brother's family will continue to exist among our people. Do you understand?"

"Heeee, heeee, heeee," Onan replied happily.

Judah groaned, then tried it again. "Onan, pay attention, you freak! You are married to Tamar now and have to ride *her*. Do you understand that?"

"Heee, heee, Tam-eee, pree-eee," Onan said as he nodded vigorously.

"Yeah, right. You are married to her. She is your wife."

Onan's simple, uncomprehending grin made Judah move closer than he wanted to and pat the "wife" his son was cuddling on the head. "Wife. Tamar your wife. Like this 'wife.' Tamar now like this 'wife' and you must ride her so Er will have a son to carry on his name."

"Heee, Tam-eee, wife-eeee meee-eee?" Onan asked, his eyes showing some degree of excited comprehension that surprised Judah.

When it came to sexy, Judah hadn't met the woman who could compete with Tamar. Could it be possible that she was sexy enough to get Onan to change his lust from ewes to her? With sudden hope, he replied eagerly, "Yes, Onan. Your wife. You are married to Tamar. You get to ride her and give her a son for Er. After that you can keep on riding her so you can have sons and daughters like me. Wouldn't that be wonderful? Your current 'wives' can't do that for you."

Tamar had been the first woman to arouse normal lust in Onan. He never spoke of it in a way normal people could have understood because he was incapable of communicating such complex things. Since he was totally unaggressive, he never revealed it with an inappropriate action that normal people would have understood as an expression of sexual lust. He couldn't understand a lot of things, but he understood that Tamar was going to become one of his "wives" and join his flock. Onan trembled visibly as he giggled and grabbed his big serpent, shaking it as he squealed with glee, "Hum-eee, hum-eee, hum-eee."

Judah groaned miserably. What a batch of wretched, disappointing sons he had! The only thing they had inherited from him was the impressive size of their serpents! What had he done to deserve three lame-brain sons? How could two of them grow up to be perverts? All his daughters were perfectly normal girls who had average or close to average intelligence, had delightful personalities, and none of them were perverts. If this was how Yahweh was testing his faith, Judah thought he was doing it way too harshly.

Judah brought Onan home. The boy's "wives" followed him faithfully. What an embarrassment! At least only his family and slaves were present to see the freak show. He had slaves clean Onan up. Judah wasn't sure it would work out with Tamar and Onan. He wasn't even sure Onan really understood he was supposed to ride Tamar like she was one of his ewes, so there was the possibility the young man might refuse to do that even though he obviously had some kind of feelings for Tamar. How weird those were, who knew? Judah decided the intelligent thing to do was to see if a test ride was successful before spending any shekels on a formal wedding. He knew Onan wouldn't care about and most likely would not understand a formal wedding, but he was sure Tamar would want one (she certainly had enjoyed her first one), and the Hebrew community would lose respect for him if he didn't spend a lot of shekels on a wedding festival they could enjoy. He was sure Tamar would agree to a test ride since the young woman was obviously horny for serpent.

Judah personally delivered the boy, now clean, smelling nice, trimmed, and dressed in decent robes, to Tamar. He explained his thinking about the test ride and, as he had expected, Tamar had no problems with that. He didn't stay a second longer than necessary. The unhappy patriarch trudged off to tell the priests and all the Hebrew community about the new law Yahweh had revealed to him.

Onan gazed at Tamar with excited eyes, which bulged rather spookily, and just went "heee-eee, heee-eee, heee-eee" over and over. Tamar noticed only one thing about him. That was the awesome tent his serpent was making in his robe. The horny young woman was hot for some long, thick serpent. When Onan made no move to approach her, she ordered one of the slave girls to undress him. Tamar looked at her naked husband and, though she noticed his repulsively hairy body, her hormones overwhelmed her aesthetic judgment — especially when revealed in all its mighty glory was the serpent of her dreams!

"Makes your Tammuz look like a girly-man," Michael teased Uriel, as Yahweh, all the archangels, and a few million angels observed from Heaven.

The insulted archangel replied, "Wait until my next R&R in the flesh! I'll show them a serpent that'll make a high priestess get so horny she'll start sweating!"

"I've heard them say size doesn't matter," Gabriel observed.

"That's what guys with little serpents tell each other," Uriel scoffed.

"That may be true," Satan chuckled, "but I have noticed some women do appreciate men who can provide intelligent conversation. Onan doesn't have much talent for that."

"Tamar isn't that kind of girl!" Michael laughed. "One ride on that thing and she'll love him like she loved Er. Ask any angel who was Tammuz with her," he said, enjoying the annoyed look Satan gave him.

"I'm like totally impressed, I'm sure," Tamar told Onan in a voice thick with lust.

She touched it with her adoring hand, and instantly Onan started shaking all over and squealing sort of like Er used to do at the moment of glory, only it sounded much more ghastly. A second later his serpent puked up copiously. Tamar gasped from the shock of his astonishingly quick response and jumped back. When it was over, Onan stood there staring at her with spooky eyes, grinning like the happiest doofus on the earth, and going "heee-eee, heee-eee, heee-eee."

"Well, that was like not what I thought would like happen for sure," Tamar sighed. "Next time should go like better, I'm sure."

But it did not. Onan was ready for seconds in an impressively short time, but one touch by her after his serpent had fully stiffened brought on the same startlingly abrupt results, just somewhat less copious. The slave girls struggled to suppress their laughter as Tamar gave him a frustrated glare, but her horniness made her optimistic that erupting twice ought to give him some kind of control the third time. After all, she knew by now he performed admirably with his "wives." Er had taken her to watch from a distance one time when she had expressed curiosity about his brother's bizarre lifestyle. She knew it wasn't uncommon for people to occasionally have animal lovers, but to make such relationships a permanent lifestyle? What could be weirder than that?

The third time was exactly the same. Onan obviously was enjoying himself, going "heee-eee, heee-eee, heee-eee" over and over and over until Tamar began to get a little annoyed. She, however, wanted and needed what Onan had to offer. After some serious thinking, she guessed that the problem was his not being used to women. If she could make herself look more like one of his "wives," then he should be able to perform more like he did with them. Tamar told two slave girls to take one of the furs that made her bed and put it over her body as she assumed the classic four-legged position Onan was more familiar with. His rapidly stiffening serpent proved he got the idea quicker than he usually got ideas. He promptly mounted her, but he was squealing and shaking all over when he attempted intromission and the touch of his serpent against her warm, firm, gorgeous flesh made it instantly erupt again. Tamar sobbed with frustrated desperation.

"That's one seriously defective road apple," Michael chuckled.

Satan laughed and said to Yahweh, "Now that's entertainment, boss! I didn't think that new law would be this much fun."

"Yeah, but the entertainment I wanted was Onan and Tamar successfully married and Judah suffering tormented lust every day. This isn't making me happy," Yahweh said ominously. "That doofus is too doofus to live." And Yahweh reached down from Heaven and gave Onan a finger-thump upside the head, killing him instantly. "What a waste of a serpent!"

Down below, Tamar almost plotzed when Onan dropped dead. She was filled with dismay as she remembered Er's equally sudden death, and wailed, "I'm like not believing it happened *again*!"

While millions of angels laughed, Satan teasingly asked Yahweh, "What about his 'wives'? The ladies are going to be mighty lonely now."

Yahweh grinned. "Well now, why don't you take some

extended R&R in the flesh and keep them all happy until the very last one dies of old age."

The other archangels laughed as Satan protested, "What?! Me be *Onan* for that long?"

"Yeah. Do you have anything better to do?"

"I've got a feeling that doesn't mean Tamar's included," Satan grumbled.

"Hey, you may be a smart ass, but you aren't a dumb smart ass," Yahweh chuckled.

And so Satan went down to Earth and shape-shifted into a biological replica of Onan. He magically relocated the flock of "wives" to a remote verdant valley where humans couldn't bother them. There they lived happily ever after until the last one died of old age. They never knew the "husband" who rode them and cared for them wasn't the real Onan. Satan was joyous when his long years in the flesh were over and he was liberated from the obnoxious rôle to return to being Heaven's only uppity archangel.

After Tamar reported Onan's sudden death, it and the equally mysterious disappearance of Onan's "wives" were the hot topics for weeks in the region dominated by Chezib and Timnah. The most frustrating thing was trying to explain was the disappearance of Onan's "wives."

Onan's death was easier to deal with. As it had been with Er, so it was with Onan: everyone knew the freak had been struck down by Yahweh for some terrible sin. And once again it was frustrating not to know what it was. The hardcore orthodox Hebrews immediately seized the opportunity and insisted the sin was Onan's having sex with his ewes, but they couldn't sell it. Onan's behavior with his "wives" had been going on for too many years without him being punished for that to be convincing. And other Hebrews (especially shepherds) occasionally enjoyed four-legged lovers and had never suffered anything that could be called supernatural punishment.

When the hardcore orthodox insisted Onan's death proved the community needed to make human-animal sex illegal for Hebrews, only a minority agreed with them.

That wasn't the end of attempts to exploit Onan's death to get a sexually repressive law passed. Because slaves had witnessed Onan's frustrating (for Tamar) sexual encounter with Tamar, the details of it quickly became known, which let the hardcore orthodox claim that Onan's sin was spilling his seed on the ground. That would be grounds for outlawing male masturbation and exterior ejaculation, a popular though unreliable birth-control method. Petting the serpent being a popular Hebrew pastime, they couldn't make that one stick either, and were reduced to passionate prayers begging Yahweh to reveal these laws. Those prayers were as effective as prayers usually are.

Eventually, more interesting stuff happened, and it pushed the mysteries and controversies into oblivion.

The hardcore orthodox Hebrews were not entirely unsuccessful, though—they did have enough influence to get every Hebrew in the community thinking about their theological hypotheses. No laws forbidding human-animal sex, exterior ejaculation, or male masturbation passed, but gradually human-animal relationships lost respectability and were practiced less often and more furtively. Male masturbation and exterior ejaculation remained as popular and respectable as ever, but those practicing them were careful not to spill their seed on the ground.

Judah and Zeruah were not exactly torn up by Onan's mysterious death, but they put on a decent show because they were leaders of the Hebrew community and thus role models for young people. After the funeral, when he was alone with Zeruah, Judah groaned, "What do we do now? By the new law God Most High revealed, Shelah is now Tamar's husband. Oh, why is this happening? I'm glad we didn't have a formal wedding for Onan and Tamar before this disaster happened. What a waste of shekels that would have been! What the Sheol did the boy do to make God Most High so peckish? He was a freak, but he was a harmless freak."

"Is Shelah much better?" Zeruah asked, her voice surprisingly hostile. "Tamar might be the most beautiful, sexy, and horny girl there ever was, but Shelah won't ever respond. She could be twice everything she is, and his serpent will never become studly for her."

Judah sighed heavily, "Oh, this is so awful. I wish God Most High would reveal a law that requires children to honor their fathers and mothers!"

Zeruah, who hated what Shelah did with men more than she had ever let her husband know, said viciously, "I wish God Most High would reveal a law that would let us stone to death stubborn and rebellious sons like Shelah! Oh, and also wastrels and drunkards like my sister's worthless boy!"

Judah was shocked at the toxic hatred that his wife had revealed for their third-born son. Judah, like any good Hebrew, didn't like apostate Hebrews, but he wasn't one of those intolerant orthodox Hebrews who wished Yahweh would reveal laws commanding that they punish apostates with stoning or some other hideous death. He certainly hoped Yahweh never revealed such a law while he was alive. To find such hardness in the heart of his wife, who was not very interested in religion of any kind, was difficult to fathom. But then he did not have to go among women as the mother of three sons who were like punishments inflicted by Yahweh. Her social status as Judah's wife meant that other women's malicious enjoyment of her humiliation wasn't flung in her face, but it could not protect her from all the insidious ways women had for letting her indirectly know their enjoyment of her misery.

"Well, I'm not upset that much with the boy, but I understand how you feel," Judah said soothingly. "Anyway, there's no way to find out if Shelah will refuse to obey the law until he returns. Until then, well, Tamar won't like what I have to tell her."

The day after Er's funeral Shelah had left with a large party of Anath's worshippers to go on a pilgrimage to Babylon, where the largest and most glorious Temple of Anath was located, for a big religious festival that the Goddess's worshippers were supposed to celebrate at least once in their lives. He wasn't due back for another month. Judah strongly suspected his son would not be returning. During the past three years Shelah's interest in becoming a herder had evaporated, and during the last six months before Er's funeral he had spent almost all his time at the Temple of Anath. He had not said anything about it to his father, but Judah could read all the signs his third-born son was showing. Judah strongly suspected Shelah would become a priest of Anath in Babylon, which meant he would castrate himself in the initiation ceremony. If his son did that, Judah hoped he would never come back.

Judah went to Tamar and told her the new law meant she was now married to Shelah. Tamar was less than thrilled. Because Shelah was on a journey, she was condemned to celibacy! That wasn't the worst of it. Although actually still a member of Judah's family, she would have to give up the luxurious tent that had been her home since her marriage to Er and return to her father's house. There she would have to live like an unwed daughter even though she was a wife and Judah was her patriarch! Her father would be her temporary patriarch until Shelah returned, but he couldn't order her to do anything Judah disapproved of. It was confusing to her: she was now unquestionably married to Shelah, but somehow she would not be a full member of Judah's family again until her husband returned from Babylon, yet she was supposed to be celibate because she was a wife even though she was living like an unwed daughter in her father's house again! Shelah would have to die before she would become a widow and be free to marry again.

"This like sucks, you know!" Tamar protested petulantly

and Judah had never known until that moment how sexy petulance could be! "Could a law be like, you know, anymore stupid?"

Judah sighed as he struggled with his temptation and then, winning another unhappy victory over it, said, "Well, what can I say? God Most High revealed the law to me, so I know it wasn't some religious loony's hallucination. We're Hebrews and God Most High is our God, so there it is."

"It still like sucks! I should've like converted to Anath."

"What, and break your father's heart? You're too good a girl to do that, Tamar."

"Oh, for sure," Tamar admitted, pouting in a way that was so sexy that Judah's serpent began getting studly. He left quickly before he was conquered by his temptation.

Zadok welcomed his daughter home. He was very glad she had not conceived during her marriages. He was certain Er would have sired a child no man would have wanted for a grandchild. He was overjoyed that Onan had died before he had put seed in his daughter. Who knew what kind of monstrosity a freak like Onan would have sired?

Unfortunately the good news about Er and Onan was spoiled by the bad news about Shelah. Everybody knew about that particular apostate and how his lust was exclusively for men riding him as though he was a woman. What Hebrew father would want his daughter married to a man who lusted only for other men? Then add to that Shelah's apostasy and it was enough to make even Zadok wonder if Yahweh had really considered all the possible consequences of the new law he had revealed to Judah. One thing for sure was that Er would never have a son to carry on his family if it depended on Shelah getting Tamar pregnant. Zadok might have been more upset about it if he had not had his own miseries. Tamar, who had been expecting emotional support from her father, was miffed to find him less concerned about her troubles than she felt he ought to be. When she came home, her father was in the process of selecting his third wife. He had married the second one a month before Tamar and Er's wedding. During the little over three years of their marriage, she had been pregnant three times. She had died four days after Er's death while trying to deliver the third child, who also had died. Now once again he was looking over young, sexy girls freshly arrived at marrying age and belonging to fathers hopelessly in debt to him. The current crop was decidedly substandard, yet he had to have a wife! He was horny and would not break his commitment to monogamy by riding his slave girls. Since he was no longer married, Tamar thought that was carrying his bizarre monogamy theology too far, but her father insisted that monogamy meant a man could ride only a woman who was his wife.

That, however, was not the problem that was tormenting him the most. During the past three years his genius for business had deserted him. Several investments turned into disasters. He had lost a large amount of his wealth. When Tamar finally got him to admit how much, she was almost indignant, but she was more mature now and so reminded him as kindly as possible, "Oh, Daddy, you're like still richer than just about everybody in the land!"

"Hah!" he exclaimed in a voice that was twisted with a mixture of rage, grief, and humiliation. "One-third my wealth I've lost! *One-third!* My shekels, oh, my shekels!" he lamented. "Why didn't I emerge from the belly dead, or stop living after I came out from the innards? Why did the knees catch me? Why did I suck the tits? I should have lain there quietly and remained silent. I should have gone to sleep, for then I would have been at rest. Sing hosannas and alleluias for Sheol, refuge of the unjustly punished. There the heretics cease harassing, and there the exhausted are at rest. Prisoners relax together, and don't hear the voices of triumphant business competitors.

The potentate and the peasant are in Sheol, and the slave is free of his owner. Sighing comes to me more readily than food, and my howls are exuded like water. What I feared most has happened to me, and what I was afraid of has overtaken me. I have no peace, I have no rest, only agonies have occurred. A man thinks he's successful, thinks he's God Most High's favorite son, then doesn't he find out his life on earth is nothing more than unending corvée, his time turned into profitless drudgery? Like a slave moaning for the shade, I moan for Sheol. The businessman seeks profit, only to suffer exposed delusions such as have been assigned to me. I've received nothing for investing my precious shekels but losses like knives in my back."

Tamar patiently waited for her father to gush out all his self-pity. She thought he was being about as silly as he could be; even after his losses, only Judah and perhaps two other men were richer than he was. When he quieted down, Tamar decided to encourage him with a saying that her father believed should be the Hebrew motto: "Oh, Daddy, you always like say, 'In God Most High We Trust', so shouldn't you like do that now?"

That only fired him up again. "God Most High?" he yelled, forgetting the hardcore orthodoxy he was known for. "Who do you think has done this to me? I, who have worshipped him more truly than most Hebrews do, including Judah, I'm the one and not Judah who loses his wealth? God Most High allows this calamity to befall me? Well, girl, my complaint is bitter to this day. I am groaning under his heavy hand. If only I knew where to find him, I would go to his throne. I would plead my case in his presence, and spout arguments from my mouth. I would understand the meaning of his response, and comprehend what he wanted to tell me. Is he going to indict me with his enormous authority? No. He would encourage me. He would know he is confronted by an honest man, and I should permanently be reprieved by my judge and have my lost wealth restored. My shekels, oh, my shekels! God Most High, how could you permit this to happen to me?"

Yahweh, Michael, Satan, and a few tens of millions of angels up in Heaven were enjoying the show. Satan asked provocatively, "Are you going to let him get away with being that uppity, boss?"

"Nope," answered Yahweh cheerfully. "I'm going to snark some more of his investments so he'll lose about half of what he has now."

"I don't know, sir," Michael said, clearly not happy with the disrespect Zadok had shown his Commander in Chief. "You ought to lay some serious heavy hand on him. Sheol, you ought to kick buns and take names just to show them who's God. A bunch of loose, whining pukes, that's what they are! Do they think being the chosen people is all fertility festivals and free wine? I don't know why you like them so much."

"Don't worry, Mike," Yahweh assured him. "I've got some plans for the Hebrews that'll make them wish they were suffering only as badly as Zadok. You think they're whining now? Just wait!"

It occurred to Tamar that her father's horniness was making his problems seem worse than they were. Horniness certainly didn't improve her attitude! She knew exactly what would make both of them feel better about the road apples life had dumped on them recently. Tamar said seductively, "I'm like not even a virgin now. We could like celebrate the Rites of Lot, I'm sure."

Zadok sighed miserably. "Ah, dear girl, you probably know I've long been tempted, but how can I? Have I not preached hardcore orthodoxy all these decades? I've argued for making laws for our community that require girls to be celibate so they're virgins when they're married and widows to be celibate until they remarry.

Even if I was now willing to change my mind, you're not a widow. This strange new law God Most High revealed to Judah means you're still a wife even though your first two husbands have died and you're living with me like an unmarried daughter. The Rites cannot be celebrated with married daughters; they belong to their husbands, not to their fathers. Even if your husband was here and gave permission, we couldn't; I would be a hypocrite if I didn't practice now what I've always preached. Often I've said riding another man's wife is adultery if she becomes pregnant even though a husband agrees to it. I've also often said riding another man's wife even with her husband's consent should be condemned just like adultery is. Our community has not agreed to make it a crime, but most of our community does not respect sharing wives with other men like slave girls are shared.

"Even if you were a widow and somehow I was again your patriarch instead of Judah, how could I celebrate the Rites with you when I've argued that the law about the Rites be changed so that they are illegal? And then there's my commitment to monogamy, which would be violated by the Rites. If I changed my mind now to satisfy my lust, I would be a double hypocrite and then how could I face our community? Even the Canaanites would mock me. We wouldn't be committing a crime, but people would lose their respect for me. My shame would be hard to endure. I've been righteously judgmental for decades, so people would be justified to condemn me as a hypocrite and I wouldn't like that.

"But you're not a widow and your husband isn't here to give his consent. That means we'd have to celebrate the Rites in secret. If we could keep it a secret and you got pregnant before Shelah returns, then you obviously would be guilty of committing adultery! What a scandal you'd be in then! Nothing could save you. If you named the father, I would be buried in the same pile of road apples you would be in, though I wouldn't be punished as harshly as you."

Tamar considered herself a religious person, but had never been interested in being educated beyond a very general understanding of her religion. There was a lot she didn't know about the Hebrew religion, but she wasn't totally ignorant. She knew enough to ask this: "Why should people like care? God Most High hasn't revealed like a commandment that forbids adultery, you know."

Zadok sighed, "I wish God Most High would reveal such a law! And a law against attempted adultery. I also pray for a law against the Rites, as well as one making the Vows of Abram and Sarai illegal. But we can't just wait for God Most High to give us laws. Remember what the proverb says: 'The righteous don't need a revelation to know sin from virtue.' Hebrews are God Most High's chosen people and that means we're supposed to be more moral than other peoples. I know Judah disagrees and most of our community think like him, but about adultery without the husband's consent almost all of us agree, so there's no problem with the lack of divine revelation. Most Hebrews *like* the law that makes adultery without the husband's consent illegal. Who needs God Most High to tell them it's wrong for a wife to get pregnant by another man behind her husband's back and thus burden her husband with the costs and troubles of raising a mixed-seed child or possibly one that was started by none of his seed?"

Tamar couldn't think of an answer to that one, but she knew something her father didn't. So she smiled in a way that severely increased her father's temptation. "So, what if I like know how to not get like pregnant?"

"Oh, sweet girl, when have I preached that birth control is righteous? How could I do differently now? Besides, even if we avoid the crime, there's still the public scorn and shame of not practicing my preaching. You've heard often enough my proverb: 'If you preach orthodoxy, you must practice orthodoxy.' I can't become a hypocrite. Would the joy of our rides really be worth that?"

Tamar was horny enough that she suggested, "If we were like careful, nobody would like know, I'm sure."

Zadok sighed, "Oh, darling daughter, look around the house. We're surrounded by slaves. How could we keep them from knowing? Maybe once, maybe twice, maybe even thrice, but not if we did it regularly, and we would never be able to stop after one or two or three times. What slaves know, eventually everybody knows! They're the worst gossips on earth! We'd have to give up having slaves and do all their work ourselves! Would you want that?"

Tamar hadn't thought of that. Like most people who lived surrounded by slaves and depended on them to do just about everything, it was simply natural to be oblivious to their constant presence. And, when she thought about it, like most people who lived surrounded by slaves she was totally unwilling to live without them. So Tamar conceded that her father was right and reluctantly abandoned thought of celebrating the Rites of Lot together.

Still concerned about her father's disturbed mental state, she told him to celebrate the Rites of Lot with one or more of his other daughters who were old enough for marriage but still unwed and living at home. Zadok wouldn't do it; he believed the Rites of Lot were immoral and that was all the reason he needed not to do it. Besides, even if he would have been willing to endure being exposed as a hypocrite, he was not willing to give up the shekels. His unwed daughters' virginity would ensure he got the highest possible mohar for them, and at that moment his hottest lust was for every shekel he could get.

Zadok still had numerous children at home who needed mothering, and the house slaves needed a mistress who would manage their labor. It was a lot of work and responsibility, which was why Tamar was not happy to be once again the female head of her father's household. She couldn't refuse to do her duty. She could only hope Zadok found a new wife soon. She didn't want to be rescued by Shelah's return from Babylon. No woman who liked men riding her as much as Tamar did could want to be married to a man like Shelah, yet she was because of this bizarre new law. Being married to Shelah was tolerable only as long as she did not have to live with the sexual rejection he would inflict on her every day. He was a really nice guy even though not very bright, but he was who he was, and the more she thought about it the more she realized she had been very silly to believe she was beautiful enough and sexy enough to change him—at least in that way.

Judah's third-born son didn't return when expected. Zadok did not select a new wife; more business losses greatly reduced his wealth and he became unwilling to cancel any man's debt as a mohar payment for his daughter. Nor did he want to part with precious shekels to pay mohar. Tamar's ordeal continued. It was the celibacy that she hated the most. Fingers were no substitute for serpents. Like any normal rich girl or woman, she frequently enjoyed her favorite slave girls, who were skilled at making celibacy less stressful for their mistress, though they couldn't satisfy her like serpents could. Nevertheless, Tamar decided that, if Yahweh revealed a law, or Hebrew men made one, that forbid the fun women could have with each other when men were not available to them, she would convert to Anath no matter how much it broke her father's heart.

Tamar saw Judah frequently. So far the business deals involving Judah and his friend Hirah the Adullamite were the only ones that her father could rely on to be successful. In fact, her father, father-in-law, and Hirah were part of a fabulously successful business partnership that essentially ruled the region dominated by Chezib and Timnah. The other two men proved how sincere their friendship with

Zadok was by not exploiting their partner's economic crises to crush him and turn the ruling trio into a ruling duo. That made Tamar adore Judah in a way she had not when she had been married to Er and treated by Judah and Zeruah more like a daughter than a daughter-in-law.

Tamar was concerned about Judah's unhappiness and more and more wanted to restore the joy in his life. She understood why he was in such misery. Shelah had not returned from Babylon when expected and each passing week without his return made it less possible to believe he would return. She was certain she knew why Judah was very reluctant to attempt to discover what the explanation was: he didn't want to know for a fact that his third-born son had castrated himself and was now serving as a priest in Babylon's famous Temple of Anath.

Zadok sympathized and also appreciated beyond what words could express how Judah had not exploited his financial vulnerability. He wanted Tamar's legal status moved out of the strange category it was in, but was reluctant to pressure his unhappy friend. Letting more time pass was his decision, which was made easier because Tamar really was excellent at being the female head of the house and he didn't want to spend shekels on another wife until he had regained his former wealth, or at least close to it.

Then, three days before the anniversary of Onan's death, Zeruah died of a fever. Judah's unhappiness deepened into depression. His joy in life was gone. Only his profound sense of duty kept him going day to day and continuing to be a role model for all of the young people in the Hebrew community. Tamar wished she could comfort her father-in-law, but he seemed to have lost every passion in his life, including the one he'd once had for her.

Tamar wasn't happy, and her father-in-law was more miserable than she was. She wanted to help herself and him, but what could she do? She could marry Judah!

Oh, how she liked that idea! She knew he was a man who knew how to ride a woman, until she was exploding with glories! But there were the problems of Shelah and that stupid law that made her married to him as long as he was alive. What to do? Tamar didn't know until one day a few months after Zeruah's death she was in the marketplace and a friend said to her, "Like listen, your father-in-law's going up to like Timnah for the shearing of his sheep, I'm sure."

Tamar gave her a look and replied, "Well, duh! He's been doing that this time of year like forever, you know?"

However, her friend's silly comment did start the voluptuous young woman thinking. The result was a plan to seduce her father-in-law. Since there was no way any respectable woman could travel to another town unescorted, she told her father she was going to travel with an old friend and her escort to visit a mutual friend, who had recently moved to Timnah, and stay there a few days. She knew a spot near the rear gate of the Temple of Anath where she could conceal a change into a male disguise, which allowed her to leave Chezib without an escort the day before she knew Judah would depart for Timnah. She went to the tiny village located at the fork where the road to Enaim branched off the road to Timnah. The village existed to serve the small farmers in the area and the travelers wanting refreshment for themselves and their animals. It was a grungy, one-harlot dump, but it was better than barren dirt.

When Tamar arrived, the owner of the small inn was depressed because recently the fever had passed through the little village and reduced it to a no-harlot dump. He had yet to find a replacement for his daughter, who had been the local harlot. No decent harlot was willing to relocate to such a dismal gehenna, and he did not have enough money to buy a slave attractive enough to be as successful in the profession as his daughter had been. Tamar could not have asked for a more perfect opportunity.

When she revealed that she was a woman and suggested she might be willing to take the position, the owner's serpent just about spewed with joy that such a voluptuously gorgeous young woman would be working for him. Naturally he insisted on a free ride to evaluate her job skills. Tamar had not thought of that contingency, but realized a professional harlot would not hesitate to comply. She only wished he had higher standards of personal hygiene! An hour later the exhausted, thoroughly satisfied innkeeper hired her. He gave Tamar his daughter's room. Tamar told him she was not ready to start working that night, but would be the next day. He did not argue. Already visions of shekels of silver flowing like the Nile were dazzling him.

When Judah arrived at the Fork (no person called the dump by its real name, not even its scroungy citizens), Tamar was on the road in front of the inn waiting for him. She had already serviced three customers and was convinced she could become one of those superstar harlots who became rich. It was tempting, but she decided she would be happier if she became Judah's wife.

Tamar was wearing gorgeous, sexy Egyptian veils that swathed her heavily while leaving no doubts about how utterly fabulous her body was. Judah stared at the astonishing sight. A harlot that beautifully adorned was about the last thing he expected to see in the Fork. He felt a stirring of lust for the first time in a very long time. He recalled the good old days when business trips were lots of fun because of all the harlots he rode. Could he recapture some of that carefree vivaciousness after the tragedies that had afflicted him?

Tamar said to him, "You like want to party?"

Judah's serpent leaped eagerly beneath his garments. The harlot's voice was almost exactly like Tamar's! He laughed and asked the bodyguards who were with him, "What do you think, boys? Should I party hearty or get on about my business?"

These were hired men, not slaves (it being well known that slaves rarely were motivated to defend their owner's life with their own), and all had been working for Judah for many years. The commander of the bodyguard chuckled, "There ain't no guy I know what needs a good party as much as you, boss."

"There's wisdom in your words," Judah admitted merrily. He felt as though he was emerging suddenly from a long, dark tunnel. He looked down at Tamar from his camel and said with teasing formality, "Please take a walk with me and let me get into you."

"Let's use my room. It's nicer than this place looks. How much will you pay me to let you get into me."

Still teasing, he said, "I'll send a kid from the flock."

"Oh, like I'm that stupid! Like will you leave a marker until you send it?"

Judah laughed, "Do you have any idea what a kid from my flock is worth? It's about ten times what any guy with any brains would pay for a trick in the Fork."

"So do like ten tricks with me," Tamar said in her sexiest voice, which was very sexy indeed.

Judah stopped joking because his body was now reminding him painfully how horny it had become during his long period of celibate depression. "Maybe I might," he replied with a voice full of lust. "But I've got plenty of shekels, you know. Your boss will want money instead of a kid."

"Oh, I'm thinking he'll take like whatever an important customer like you wants to pay, you know, so the deal's like for a kid. No kid, no ride, I'm sure. Like just give me a marker."

"What kind of marker should I give you?"

"Mmmm, how about like your signet and bracelets, and like the staff in your hand?"

Judah started to object. The expensive bracelets were a 25th anniversary gift from Zeruah, the staff, which Hirah had given him years ago, cost almost as much as the bracelets, and his signet was too valuable to leave with a harlot. Then Tamar shifted position in such a way that her glorious cleavage was exposed. Judah's serpent took charge of the situation and he agreed. The rational part of him knew it was a stupid thing to do, but it had been temporarily relieved of its command responsibilities. The part of Judah giving orders now couldn't even spell "rational"!

Two hours later Judah was happier than he had been since Zeruah died. He had forgotten how fabulous wild, uninhibited riding could be. Tamar had participated like a fantasy lover instead of a harlot transacting business. How could he have known that for her it was making love instead of making business? When she allowed his serpent to worship in her Temple of Life, he had been totally unaware of the deep emotional significance it had for her. Not knowing it was Tamar, Judah merely assumed she was a harlot whose job skills were well beyond what a man would expect in a harlot working in the Fork.

He looked over her glorious body, but her head, with the exception of her exquisite mouth, remained veiled. He wanted to see her face, but she stopped him. Her family, she told him, had been reduced to poverty so desperate that her becoming a harlot was their only hope of survival, yet it could be tolerated only if no person ever would be able to recognize her. Judah honored her wish and then let her show how much she appreciated it in all sorts of ways.

When the sun was setting, Judah forced himself to rise. He said, "I must get going. The shearing'll start without me if I don't."

Tamar caressed his serpent as she said temptingly, "It'll get done if you're not like there, I'm sure."

He smiled, his eyes on her lovely parted lips. All his craving was to forget business and kiss her some more, but his sense of duty was still firm enough to reply, "It'll get done, yeah, but a boss on the job is the only way to make sure the job's done right."

"If you're like sick does the job get done like wrong?"

Judah felt himself weakening. "I guess not. Hirah's there. Yeah, my foreman too. He's never let me down because I treat him better than most slaves. Sure, if I was sick, I guess the shearing'd be done right without me."

"So like let the moon move without you tonight."

"I, uh, uh . . ." He looked down at his serpent, which was standing tall to cast its vote on what should be done next.

Tamar said, "I'm like gonna kiss this big serpent while you like make up your mind."

Judah decided to do what he wanted to do instead of what he knew he should do. Two days later he held Tamar in his arms as though she was a lover and suddenly he found it urgent to talk about the tragedies that had ruined his life. Tamar knew all about Er, Onan, and Zeruah, but had not known that Judah's worst fear about Shelah had been confirmed. As expected, Shelah had joined Anath's priesthood, which meant he had ritually castrated himself. The letter from Shelah containing this news had been delivered to him the day before he had departed for Timnah. His son had bluntly stated that he intended to serve in the Temple in Babylon for the rest of his life. Judah's third-born son had added that he would never be coming back home.

"Here's what I can't get. Shelah says he's happy the way he is. How can any guy be happy being like that?"

"Well, don't lots of guys like riding guys and boys? Like lots of Hebrew guys go to Anath's temple and it's like not to worship. And they don't always ride like the priestesses. God Most High doesn't seem to like care about it. Isn't that like, you know, why he hasn't revealed like a law against it?"

"Yes, you're right. The hardcore orthodox want a law against it, but they haven't persuaded enough people yet — and won't if I have anything to do with it. I don't approve of guys like Shelah, but I'm not going to let them and my son be turned into criminals if I can prevent it."

"Well, I'm like let people do whatever makes them like happy, you know?"

Judah frowned, yet he said, "I don't entirely disagree, but most guys who like riding men or boys still like riding women best, or at least enough to do their duty to sire kids. Liking only riding guys, or, even worse, only being ridden by guys, so you never sire kids, that's what I can't understand. That's what I call perversion!"

He felt the irresistible need to tell her what the shame of it was for a Hebrew patriarch. He summed up the real misery of what it meant to him: "My house is dead!" His eyes became wet with tears he was too manly to allow himself to shed.

Tamar said gently, "You can like get a new wife, I'm sure. You can like have more sons."

"No, no," Judah groaned. "What sons have come from my loins! All three together weren't as smart as your average fence post, and two were perverts. None could've inherited my wealth and kept it without a strong, smart wife ruling them. I was convinced I had found that good woman for Er and she proved she was, but now that Er and Onan are dead and Shelah is lost as though he was dead, she won't be the one who will control my wealth because she never conceived a son with Er or Onan and certainly never will with Shelah. Now I have to name a brother or a nephew or one of my daughters' sons to inherit, or, I suppose, divide my wealth up among my daughters' sons. What does it matter anyway? It's hard enough to endure the humiliation of siring Er, Onan, and Shelah, so why would I want to increase my humiliation by siring more like them? There're enough half-brained doofusses in the world already."

"It'd be like different with a different wife, I'm sure. Was Zeruah like real smart?"

Judah sighed, "No, may she rest in peace. She was a wonderful woman and I loved her, but she'd have lost a battle of wits with a box of rocks. She was no smarter than our sons."

"They were more like her than like you, I'm sure. Like a different mother, she'd give you like different sons."

Judah said unhappily, "Don't be silly. A woman is just the field where the seed's planted. I know there're a few women who believe like you do, and I wish I could believe it's not my fault, but I don't, because men know better about these things."

"Didn't you sire like sons with slave girls?"

"Yeah, I probably did. Daughters too. But I wasn't the only one riding my slave girls, so their kids always had many fathers.

Tamar had not thought of that. A woman full of seed from more than one man would produce a mixed-seed child; hence there would be no way to know which father was responsible for the child's intelligence. She didn't want to argue, so gave it up, embraced him, and said, "Like lay there and let me like make you smile again."

When she let his serpent worship in her Temple of Life, Tamar now hoped to conceive a son for her father-in-law. The rest of the week passed. Judah could not bring himself to leave the delightful, loving, incredibly enthusiastic lover he had found in the last place on the earth he would have expected to find such a woman. The amount of money he paid to the innkeeper increased and increased, yet he thought the happy, greedy guy wasn't charging what she was worth.

When finally some men sent by his worried friend found him, Judah's sense of duty asserted itself because

Tamar had thoroughly drained all the horniness in his body. They parted, Judah promising to return as soon as his business in Timnah was completed. She reminded him he owed her a kid for the first ten rides — and so did the innkeeper as Judah was leaving his grungy establishment.

By the time Judah reached Timnah, he was thinking that the wonderful harlot at the Fork needed the kid to feed her destitute family. He told Hirah to take the kid to her because he wanted his Adullamite friend to experience Tamar. When Hirah arrived at the shabby little village, the innkeeper sadly reported that the mysterious harlot had vanished, and a drunk overhearing them added that she was probably disguised as the young man he had seen sneaking out the back of the inn and heading in the direction of Chezib. Hirah, who had been hoping to find out if Judah was telling the truth about how good the harlot was, returned to his friend and bitched, "I didn't find her! She's gone. Two guys said she hit the road. I better never find out this was a practical joke! You don't even want to live through the payback I'd have to get."

Judah jumped up, growling, "Damn hussy has my stuff! My signet, bracelets, and the staff you gave me! Oh, man, suckered by a frigging harlot! She knew she'd get fifty times a kid's price just for the staff or the bracelets and twice that for my signet! Oh man! What's worse is knowing I swallowed all her honey-coated road apples like I had reached puberty last week!"

"Let's go after her buns."

Judah shuddered. "No! We do that, there's no way this doesn't go public. Let her keep what I gave her, for otherwise I'll be a laughingstock. I'll send my most trusted slaves out telling everybody in the land I lost my signet, bracelets, and staff and offer a reward for their return. That way the signet can't be used. Who knows, maybe they'll turn up." Then he had to grin. "I gotta admit, she *earned* whatever she gets for my stuff. Let me tell you, I'll bet Tamar wouldn't've been that good!"

Nobody could find the harlot, and the items Judah had given as a pledge did not turn up despite the offer of a very generous reward. After a few weeks, he accepted his things were lost for good, and he wasn't going to get any payback. He actually didn't care because he had returned to Chezib with a renewed zest for life. He was not willing to sire more sons, but he definitely was interested in riding more slave girls.

Those slave girls got pregnant, but he didn't consider the children his, because his seed in them was mixed with the seed from other men. These men were his guests and usually, but not always, the slave girls' husbands, who were also his slaves. Judah, like all slaveholders, approved of the steady production of new slaves by his slave girls. Some he kept for himself to eventually take the place of aging slaves. The rest he sold, usually at some age between weaning and puberty.

Judah rewarded those male slaves who earned positions of high trust and responsibility by not selling their wives' children until after they became adults. This policy allowed the male slaves to enjoy the privilege of raising a family, although the men had to accept the ego-bruises of raising children who were not entirely sired by them. (Judah didn't realize this bothered his favorite male slaves; like all other slaveholders, he thought slaves should sing hosannas and alleluias if they were allowed to have anything more than basic subsistence.) For this display of kindness and compassion, Judah was greatly admired by most of the Hebrews, who would tell their young people that he was a wonderful role model for them to emulate.

Tamar had hoped to get pregnant with Judah, and that hope was fulfilled. She was filled with happiness, but Zadok was distressed. She was Shelah's wife, and there was no way he could have made her pregnant while in Babylon. She was a Hebrew worshipper of Yahweh, and therefore was subject to her community's peculiar ethnic laws as long as those laws didn't conflict with the government's laws. Unfortunately for Tamar, the Hebrew community's laws about adultery were acceptable to the Canaanite government. She had put herself in danger of being burned to death for adultery because she was married to Shelah according to the new law.

The full meaning of the law was still being debated, but already it was obvious that the hardcore-orthodox position would most likely triumph. Zadok was forced to understand that his orthodoxy meant he would have a large share in his daughter's ghastly punishment. For the first time in his life, he was able to see exactly how ugly extreme orthodoxy was. The repellant insight cracked his theological bigotry. Now he could see the moral superiority of the more humane theology that Judah and those who thought like him preached.

Alas, Zadok's theological epiphany was too late to help Tamar; he would never be able to change Hebrew hearts and minds in time. It was also too late for Tamar to save herself by converting to Anath. If she had converted before committing the crime, the government would have protected her from Hebrew laws and, since all pregnancies were blessings bestowed by the Goddess, her only punishment would have been naming the father or fathers, who then would have to pay a fine to help cover the cost of raising a mixed-seed child (or, in Tamar's case, the whole cost because she had never received seed from her husband). Who would believe her conversion was sincere after committing the crime? Zadok was so terrified for his daughter that he would have welcomed her committing apostasy if it could have saved her.

Tamar was worried, yet also determined. Judah's seed was the only seed deposited in her Temple of Life since the death of Er—her customers at the Fork having worshipped in the Eunuch's Temples—and she was certain all of Er's seed had been washed away by the monthly flows she had had since his death. She knew there was a seemingly endless debate in the Chezib-Timnah Hebrew community about how long a man's seed remained inside a woman's Temple of Life. She hadn't actually paid close attention to it, but what she had heard persuaded her to agree with those who argued that, without replenishing, all of a man's seed would be washed out after a few monthly flows. Believing that, Tamar was absolutely certain the child growing in her was Judah's

She intended to surprise Judah with a beautiful son, if her child proved to be a son, and was determined to do that. She had a plan and convinced her father it would work. When she started showing too much, she would become "ill" as an excuse to stay in the house until she delivered. If her child was a daughter, Tamar would tell Judah nothing about her and protect herself by saying the child was a slave girl's baby. She had some very loyal slave girls who were mothers of infants and would cooperate with that plan. She was sure it would work.

Zadok was not so confident, thus he sent many prayers of supplication up to Yahweh, who was highly amused, as were all the angels enjoying this show. All of them approved of Yahweh's decision to let the show go on without supernatural interference just to see how it would end.

Tamar should have been a lot more worried. Not all her father's slaves were loyal to her and there was no way to keep her pregnancy secret from the slaves. Some would not be able to resist spreading around such delicious gossip. Tamar also did not consider the fact that some of her brothers and sisters were unhappy with her position of power over them. It was entirely possible one of them would become angry enough with her to want some payback, and what better way of getting that than exposing her illegal pregnancy?

Neither of those possibilities led to the undoing of Tamar. She was betrayed by a sister who bitterly resented Tamar's beauty, her status as their father's obvious favorite, and her marriage into Judah's family. This sister was married to an incompetent who had squandered all the riches he had inherited, and who never would understand that fact; he believed he was being punished by Yahweh for being too proud when he had been rich. Now he was a dull, piddling innkeeper who would never again have real money, never again be important in the community, and never again would want to ride her more than he wanted to worship Yahweh.

This hate-filled sister had always believed she should have been married to Er, who had been old enough at the time of her marriage to have been her husband, and then she would have been able to reign as queen of the Hebrew community. She, who had had three sons already and was pregnant with probably a fourth one, would not have been sonless after three years of marriage, and thus would not have had to marry Onan or Shelah! So when she found out Tamar was pregnant, she talked about it where it would do the most harm.

The young priest who received the report was rigid with the cold iron of orthodox righteousness. He knew only one response to any violation of the community's laws: the severest punishment allowed. He was already treated as though he was a prophet among the hardcore-orthodox Hebrews. As soon as Tamar's sister told him about Tamar's illegal pregnancy, the young priest confronted all the priests in the temple and demanded they unite in a judgment that would inflict the harshest punishment, death by burning, on the adulterous wife. A minority of hardcore-orthodox priests sided with him immediately, but the majority wanted to think more carefully about executing the daughter and daughter-in-law of men as wealthy and influential as Zadok and Judah.

The young fanatic despised the tolerant advice of the more humane priests. He knew they did not like him and had been searching for a way to get him and the others like him out of the temple. Well, he didn't like them either, and enjoyed pounding them with the knowledge that a huge majority of the Hebrew community despised adultery done behind a husband's back, and approved of punishing it as harshly as possible. Ah, what sweet pleasure he got as he blistered their ears with volcanic psalms that described Yahweh as a raging psychopath who would punish all Hebrews if they did not ferociously punish Tamar's sin. When he was done, the reluctant priests acknowledged they couldn't win this one and capitulated.

The merciless, triumphant young priest charged off to Judah and declared to his shocked face, "Your daughter-in-law has criminally copulated!"

"How do you know?" Judah demanded hotly. He loathed the young, arrogant, excruciatingly orthodox priest as much as most of the Hebrews in the community, but the heat of his response came from his fear that the horrible shame of Shelah might be exposed by this scandal if it was true.

"The harlot is pregnant! There's no doubt at all."

"Oh, Tamar, Tamar," Judah groaned because he knew this fiercely righteous priest would not make the accusation if he did not know for certain it was true. "Who's the father?"

"The harlot won't reveal the father — or fathers! — not even to save herself."

"Oh, Tamar, what were you thinking?" Judah moaned while the young priest sadistically enjoyed his suffering. The law for the Hebrew community of the Chezib-Timnah region allowed only one way Tamar could avoid death: she had to name the man or men who had fathered the child. Tamar's punishment then would be being literally branded a harlot on the face, having to keep her head shaved, and being banned from the women's area in the temple. The father or fathers of her child would be punished by having to pay Shelah 50 shekels and, if Tamar's husband chose to divorce her, would have to marry her with the loss of the right to divorce her. (If more than one man was involved, which one had to marry her was decided by casting lots.) Judah said to the maliciously righteous priest, "Let me talk to her. I can get her to name the father or fathers."

"She was given the opportunity the law requires and refused. There is now only the sentence to be declared. Shelah isn't here and that makes you her patriarch, so do your duty! Declare the sentence the law demands you must pass!" the priest insisted with vicious joy. "If you force the community to do it, you'll lose your influence as a religious leader; there are few in the community who are willing to forgive adultery behind a husband's back. And surely God Most High expects the leaders of Hebrews to enforce all the laws of the community."

Judah was a respected religious leader even though not a priest, but he knew he hadn't been winning the debate about how harshly the law forbidding adultery behind a husband's back should be punished. (He'd argued for the punishment to be the same as that inflicted by the Canaanite government.) The religious fanatic was right: even the normally tolerant Hebrews in the region dominated by Chezib and Timnah agreed with the hardcore-orthodox minority about the criminal seriousness of adultery behind a husband's back. It was a battle he couldn't win — at least not in time to save Tamar. Even if he told the truth about Shelah and made himself a laughingstock, most likely he could not win. Yahweh's new law made Tamar Shelah's wife without allowing any exception for the kind of man Shelah was. Judah had not yet come up with some exegesis that would liberate

Tamar from the blatantly unjust marriage. But that was not what he was thinking now. He was subdued by his fear of the truth about Shelah becoming public knowledge, and there was just one way to prevent that. Could he be that cowardly?

Yes! Judah's courage failed him. The law required the sinning wife's patriarch to speak the sentence. If the husband was not present to do it, the patriarch or acting patriarch of the husband's family was obligated to do it. If he refused, which would force the community to do it, his status would plummet to depths lower than those inhabited by wastrels and drunkards. Hating himself even as he was protecting himself, Judah said in a whisper, "Take her outside and execute her by burning."

It seemed to him he had spent a long, long time in wretchedness when one of Tamar's adult brothers came galloping up to his tent. He handed over a large package with a message from Tamar in Zadok's handwriting and obviously his phrasing. Tamar was literate, so Judah had to assume she was not allowed to communicate by writing during incarceration. He was not surprised by this additional maliciousness. Judah read the words: "It was the man who owns these who made me pregnant. Please determine whose signet, bracelets, and staff these are." He quickly tore open the package even though he knew what the contents were. He stared at the three items he had given as a marker to the harlot in the Fork.

"Has the sentence been carried out?" Judah demanded.

"I don't know," the anxious young man confessed. "She was being taken away by that merciless maggot who calls himself a Man of God Most High when I left for here."

"Feets, don't fail me now!" Judah exclaimed even though it was his camel that did all the running to Chezib.

Judah arrived at the part of town called Hebrew Square, which was across the street from the temple, and found Tamar tied to a large stake. A pile of dry branches and twigs was all around her up to her knees. Prancing up and down before her was the maliciously happy priest. He was preaching an inspired sermon about sin and the punishment of sin and the wisdom all those watching better learn from the example to be made of the harlot. He had been at it quite a while and seemed determined to go on for quite a while longer. He was obviously enjoying himself and thus didn't realize he was buying time for Tamar.

The kindlier Hebrew priests stood aside, rendered silent by their fear. What would happen to them if they failed to punish the violation of one of their community's strictest laws? The vast majority of the Hebrew community agreed with the hideous punishment about to be inflicted on Tamar. Yet what would happen to their plush lifestyle if they didn't try to prevent the execution of a member of the two richest families in the region dominated by Chezib and Timnah? They were soft men living comfortable lives because of the pious generosity of wealthy men like Zadok and Judah. In fact, no other wealthy men were as generous to the temple as Zadok and Judah.

The liberal priests truly loved Yahweh, but did not believe their love required the kind of extreme, merciless, intolerant righteousness that boiled in the unbending minds of the young priest and the others devoted to hardcore orthodoxy. How they wished they could undo the mistake of letting him into the priesthood! If only they had not been seduced by the generosity of the rich family that had wanted to make their fourth-born son's dream of being a priest come true. But they had taken the money, performed the sacred rites, and now this!

What to do? What to do? Without the support of the majority of the Hebrew community, they couldn't stop the atrocity. All they could do was let the young priest and the other priests he had converted to his fanatic theology dictate events.

The Hebrew community was gathered, all of them beginning to be inspired by the passionate, intolerant preaching of the viciously holy priest, and showing signs of getting into the vindictive, righteous mood for some capital punishment. The majority truly believed adultery behind a husband's back should be harshly punished, but Tamar's adultery was a very strange kind that had not existed before the new law. Since they all knew what kind of man Shelah was, most of them could understand why Tamar had allowed at least one man to ride her (and most of the men in the audience were wishing she had selected them!).

However, the fire-and-brimstone preaching was having the desired effect — and added to the preaching was the excitement caused by who was being punished. Rarely were members of rich families condemned by the priests, and no one could recall the last time one had been severely punished for sinning. Always there was some sly exegesis that revealed a technicality that saved the rich sinner and reduced their punishment to mere embarrassment and a trivial fine. Those who were not rich and thus were corrupted by envy did not need a lot of eloquent, savage preaching to become enthusiastic for Tamar's flaming execution.

Behind them were curious Canaanites, who all looked amazed that any person could get so riled up about the pregnancy of a woman who obviously was not married. Even if she was in some peculiar way married, a child, mixed-seed or not, was the Goddess's blessing, so what was the big deal? Just have the guilty man or men pay the fine and then everybody could go on with everyday life. Even a fool could see how crazy it was to expect men and women to be virtuous all the time, so it was insane to kill a young woman for being merely human.

In the Canaanites' opinion, the Hebrews had a real talent for coming up with freaky ethnic laws. If any of them had doubted the weirdness of the Hebrew cult, this bizarre new law of theirs that forced a widow to become automatically married to her brother-in-law if she had not given birth to a son sired by her dead husband removed those doubts. What made it even weirder was that everybody knew what kind of man Shelah was and thus knew Tamar was condemned to childless celibacy by this loony new law. What kind of barmy deity was their God Most High if he gave them commandments as irrational as the one that forced Tamar into a marriage no sane father would arrange for his daughter? They were glad their goddess was much saner than the Hebrew god. Most of them whispered among themselves the wish that all these loony male-deity cultists would go live somewhere else. However, that did not mean they were going to deny themselves the delights of the horror show. Executions were just about everybody's favorite form of entertainment, as long as they were observers.

Judah went face-to-face with the young priest and declared for all to hear, "I am the father of Tamar's child!"

The angry young priest declared just as loudly, "The law is the law! She is a harlot filled with the vile crop of adulterous seed! And she had her one chance to name the father. The law does not allow another to name him even if he is the guilty man. Only her mouth could have condemned him and saved herself, but she refused and now must suffer the full punishment required by the law."

"What do you know of the law?" Judah demanded, his powerful, eloquent voice full of contempt. "Have you ever received a revelation from God Most High?"

"No. It's true God Most High has not revealed anything to me, but the law is written and what is written is clear."

"Oh, yes, we should all honor what's 'clear' to a man as young as you!" Judah sneered sarcastically. "Hear wisdom, boy, and know why God Most High speaks to *me* and not to *you*." Judah turned to the Hebrew community and spoke with such passion and eloquence that no one could guess his exegesis wasn't even an hour old yet.

"The new law was meant to ensure tragedy does not remove a family from our people. Brothers are to give brothers sons to carry on their families if they die before they sire sons. But what if there are no brothers? What if, as in my family, the brothers die before they can sire sons to carry on their families and the families of their brothers? Who then must give sons to the sonless dead to ensure their families live among us? It falls at last upon the father. Tamar became married to me and thus I went to Tamar to fulfill the will of God Most High to give sons to my sons. This is the wisdom of the law. Tamar received my seed and is now pregnant because she loves God Most High and wanted to do her duty to my sons, who had been her husbands."

It enraged the young priest to see Judah winning the hearts and minds of the Hebrews. He savagely struck back at the one flaw in Judah's argument, "Your son Shelah is not dead! He is Tamar's husband as long as he lives, according to the law!"

Judah replied, his voice full of shame, "This is what I've hidden from you until now. You all know my third-born son liked men riding him as though he was a woman. You all know he turned away from God Most High and converted to the religion of the Goddess Anath. What you don't know is that he went to Babylon to become her priest! He now serves the goddess in her Temple in Babylon as one of her priests, which means he ritually castrated himself to remove his maleness. He has disgraced my family and shall be the shame that haunts me all the rest of my life. I ask you as a Hebrew father, am I wrong when I say that means he is more dead than Er and Onan?"

Judah was pleased to hear many men and women voicing their agreement. He went on, becoming even more persuasive, "Now you understand why Tamar became my wife and why I planted my seed in her. My only mistake was to let my pride prevent me from letting you know why Tamar and I became married when Onan died. If you had known, none of you would have thought her pregnancy is adultery. If anyone should be punished today, it is me, not this good Hebrew girl."

The liberal priests now knew what to do. They all rallied to Judah's exegesis and condemned the young priest, who felt the crushing agony of defeat when he saw that the Hebrew community — even almost all of the hardcore orthodox! — had been persuaded by Judah.

The Hebrews, being as human as all other ethnic populations, followed the example of the liberal priests and heaped condemnation upon the young priest, as though they themselves had not been eager to light Tamar's fire.

He tried to defend himself, but something terrible happened inside him: the vigorous strength his rigid righteousness had given him suffered an awful breaking. He fled from Hebrew Square and then from Chezib. Rumors later circulated about a wild holy man living in a cave in the southern desert of the land of Canaan, and all the Hebrews of the Chezib-Timnah region were certain it was the priest who very nearly pulled off the gruesome execution of Tamar.

"Theology, you have to love it," Yahweh chuckled.

"Are you going let him get away with that unauthorized interpretation of your law, big boss?" Satan asked.

"What the Sheol, why not? He's earned Tamar. Let him have her."

"My, my, aren't we in a good mood today!"

"Yes, we are, smart ass, but don't push your luck. There are lots more lonely sheep down there, if you know what I mean."

Tamar and Judah lived happily ever after. Although it wasn't necessary, they treated themselves to a humongous

wedding ceremony followed by the biggest party the
Hebrew community had ever seen. They invited the entire
community. Canaanites who did business with Hebrews
or had Hebrew friends were also invited. It was said for
decades after the hangovers lasted three days!

Tamar gave birth to twin sons. The one named Perez
was proclaimed to be Er's son and the other, Zerah, to be
Onan's son. Both were as handsome and as intelligent as
Judah and grew up to keep the family's wealth growing
and growing in partnership with Zadok's and Hirah's sons
and grandsons. No son was ever given to Shelah. Nothing
Tamar said could ameliorate her husband's unforgiving
rejection of his third-born son.

That was not the end of pregnancies for Tamar, even
though, unlike her happily fruitful and multiplying sisters,
one experience with giving birth was all Tamar ever
wanted to experience. However, she wanted to give Judah
himself two sons and it took four more pregnancies to
accomplish that. After that, Judah's serpent worshipped
only in Tamar's Eunuch's Temples.

No man was ever happier than Judah. He was so in
love that he rode his slave girls only two or three times
a month. He was doing it mostly so nobody would
think he had become a weirdo monogamist like Zadok.
Tamar approved. She didn't want people laughing at her
husband the way she knew they laughed at her father.

Tamar's joy was perhaps even greater, because Yahweh
returned to blessing Zadok, who regained all his wealth
and then joyously lived to see it doubled. His third wife
lived long and produced children for him almost annually
without her health breaking.

Zadok never stopped believing in the moral supremacy
of monogamy and the other laws concerning sexual
behavior he had always advocated, but he was no longer
intolerantly righteous about it, and lost all of his previous
enthusiasm for harsh punishments. He even began

preaching what became Tamar's favorite proverb: "Don't do to another what is hateful to yourself."

Yahweh blessed all their lives with many decades of good health, increasing wealth, serpents that were always studly when Judah and Zadok wanted to do some riding, and children who did not die before their parents. These wonders were amazing things to witness and inspired the Hebrew community to be more sincerely religious—for a while. Then, because humans are always all too human, they returned to normal and, hard to believe though it may be, did not seem to suffer in any unusual way because of it.

EXODUS SCROLL
(from Cave XIX)

NOW WE COME to perhaps the most theologically revolutionary of my selections. Yes, as you may have guessed, my dear G., it is the scroll concerning the Exodus, the third most important event in world history to that date. Here begins the true glory of the Hebrews as Yahweh proceeds to mold them into the great nation worthy to receive fulfillment of the promises he had made to their great ancestors. Though the Bible seems to tell all about this profoundly important ordeal, much that is vitally important to fully understanding the incredibly important theological issues of the Exodus never made it to the Bible as we know it. Alas, what has this meant to the history of Western civilization? I personally (and who should know better than I?) am certain that the discovery of the New World would have happened sooner and the conquest of it would have been undeniably more humane if what there is to learn from my Exodus Scroll had been known then as it shall be gloriously known, as taught by me, throughout the rest of human history.

Yes, the acclaim I shall reap (and you, as well, for your important, though essentially supporting, rôle in bringing me and the Terminally Ill Sea Scrolls out of the unjust, unfair, unhealthy obscurity that has been our fate so far) will not be in vain. No, celebrity will not spoil me. I will prove that fame and fortune, which I have deserved for so long, will not corrupt me. I eagerly wait for the time when theologians all over the world humbly come to me to learn all the profound and revolutionary truths of the Terminally Ill Sea Scrolls, especially the Exodus Scroll.

Here we are taken to Heaven when the divine laws given to the Hebrews through Moses are being made. Consider how shaken the Pope will be when the enigmatic reference in 1:10 Corinthians, where Paul says of the Hebrews during one of their toughest times that "all drank the same ethereal drink, because they all drank from the ethereal rock that followed them as they went, and the rock was the Christ," is brought into the full light of history. In Exodus the incident is inadequately told in Chapter 17, which merely mentions that Moses struck a rock and from it came water to quench the thirst of his people. Nowhere in Exodus does it mention that the rock followed them to Rephidim, nor does Exodus tell what really took place there. You will notice, and I am sure not be surprised by, the dismal fact that this mystery is not cleared up by the Dud Sea Scrolls! Then there is the great Battle of Midian, which is insufficiently described in Numbers 25–31. This stupendous feat of arms will—finally!—be better understood by discerning minds because of my splendid Terminally Ill Sea Scrolls. My account of this important and instructive battle will serve to train military genius for as long as military genius needs training.

True, the Exodus Scroll gives but fragments of the whole story of the Exodus, but it is my certainty that what survived is stupendous enough to ameliorate the natural grief we must feel when contemplating what we have lost. Nevertheless, I can assert confidently, knowing none of my misguided peers has the authority nor the genius to dispute me, that these mere fragments are more important than all the trash called the Dead Sea Scrolls combined.

◆ ◆ ◆

YAHWEH SAID, "Listen up, troops." When the gathered archangels and all the rest of the angels were paying full attention, he went on. "OK, some things are going to change on the earth. First, the Hebrews are now my special herd. When you take R&R in the flesh, you will not mess with the Hebrews unless I tell you to, and then you'll do it the way I tell you to. There're more than enough peoples on the earth for you to mess with, so I don't want to hear any bitching and moaning."

"Won't be none of my troops doing that, sir," Michael promised sternly, then gave a quick, hard-ass look at the vast formation of angels assembled before them to receive the Word.

"Fine. OK, some new duty assignments. Gabriel, you're going be my messenger when I don't feel like going down there myself."

"Glad to serve, sir," Gabriel replied gung-holy.

"You, smart ass, you're my boy for the petty miracles I'm tired of working to keep the road apples believing in me. Also, I want you to start tempting them to sin."

Satan laughed. "Yeah, like any of them need extra temptation! Sin is about the only thing they've got a natural talent for. Well, add being fruitful and multiplying. They definitely are into obeying *that* commandment!"

"We'll see if we can't get them to obey a few more of them," Yahweh said. "You still have temptation duty."

"No problem, big boss. I like messing with their heads."

"Sir, speaking of being fruitful and multiplying," Raphael said, "I'm about to run out of souls again. I'll need a few million more and in a hurry; the ensoulment detail is running low."

"That's hard to believe with all the wars, famines, plagues, and other disasters culling the herd just about daily."

"Yes sir, they're dying all over the place, but they're still increasing in population, and that means more souls."

"What a pain in the buns! Yeah, OK, I'll whip up another batch ASAP."

"Sir," Raphael continued nervously, "I hate to keep bringing this up, but morale in Limbo's about as low as it can get. Those souls're about bored senseless. We have to give them something to do."

Yahweh growled, "They can sit around and be glad I don't create a lake of fire and brimstone to cook their sorry buns for the rest of eternity. What do they want? Streets paved with gold and harps to play?"

"Well sir, I guess a lot of them would like that, but most of them want their bodies back. They don't think it's fair we angels have bodies and they don't. Also they want bodies so they can be sexually active like they were on the earth. I guess that'd be the number one activity they'd like in Limbo."

"Nope," Yahweh said decisively. "There's no nooky in Heaven and that policy won't be changing. Nooky causes enough problems on the earth. I don't want any of that in Heaven. Tell them they're souls now and that means they don't have bodies because they don't need bodies to live in Heaven. Bodies! They didn't have very high standards of personal hygiene on the earth, so I doubt they'd do better in Heaven."

Satan added, "If you gave the souls bodies and let them have nooky, big boss, you would have a revolt of the angels on your hands if you didn't let *us* have nooky in Heaven, too. That would mean making half of us male and the other half female. Or maybe you could make us both! Double the fun. Just thinking about it makes we want to try it out on my next R&R! Are you sure you won't reconsider, boss?"

"Nobody I command will ever revolt for any reason!" Michael declared harshly before Yahweh could respond.

"Just kidding, Mike," Satan replied, sounding more like he was teasing than apologizing.

"A revolt would be amusing," Yahweh chuckled. "I could uncreate you all in less time than any of you could flap your wings once. It would take one seriously doofus angel to think a revolt against me would stand a chance. Do we have any angels that doofus, Mike?"

"Not in my command, sir!"

"I *know* that's a fact. As for your idea, smart ass, the answer is still no. You all get enough nooky when you're on R&R."

Hoping to get back to the original issue, Raphael asked, "What about the ones that want to assemble before your throne and worship you for the rest of eternity? Would that be OK, sir?"

"No way!" Yahweh declared with awesome, booming finality. "Been there, done that. It sucked."

The harassed archangel looked as unhappy as he felt. Riding herd on the souls was more like eternal damnation than anything he would call Heaven. "Well, sir, there's also the ones who were really sincerely pious and worshipped you as faithfully as humanly possible. These souls're real upset about Hebrew sinners and everybody who never worshipped you or even never heard of you getting the same reward in Heaven they do. They don't feel that's just. They want you to punish them in some way."

Yahweh replied patiently, "All the souls that worshipped all the ding-a-ling gods and goddesses all of you have pretended to be, and the ones that were too rational to believe in any of them, including me, *are* being punished. They'll be embarrassed about being wrong for all eternity and suffer just as long as the souls that worshipped me are gloating about being right. I think that's punishment enough."

Raphael wasn't happy. "What should I tell the souls that don't think that punishment is harsh enough, sir?"

Yahweh gave Raphael an annoyed look. "Tell the maggots this: justice is what I say it is! When do humans stop being so frigging human? If they weren't such pukes, they would realize they all got punished enough just by being human? Don't they make each other miserable enough in Limbo by endlessly telling each other the same stupid stories about themselves that they bored people with when they were alive? Tell them if they don't like being immortal my way, I can uncreate souls as easily as I create them. We'll see how bored and unhappy they are after that!"

"Yes, sir," Raphael said without enthusiasm.

"I've got an idea, boss," Satan said.

"You've always got an idea, smart ass," Yahweh replied irritably.

Satan chuckled, then said, "Look, their problem is simple. They're still all too human even if they're only souls now. They need something to take their minds off the dreariness of being human. So what I've come up with is team sports. You give them bodies again, but no genitals; they won't even care about not having them. After they get bodies, take the most athletic of them and divide them up into teams that play against each other. Everybody else can be spectators. Each team will represent groups of spectators, so they'll all get fired up like they do about war down on earth. I tell you, they'll spend all eternity wrapped up in the games and won't even care about not getting nooky in Heaven. You won't be hearing any bitching and moaning in Limbo. It'll be all prayers for you to help their team to win. Trust me on this one, Big Boss."

"Not a bad idea, smart ass," Yahweh agreed. "What game will they play?"

"I've thought up several. You see, each different sport will have a season so they rotate. That way the groups with a lousy team in one sport can always hope they'll have a champion team in one of the other sports. Each team will have players, coaches, other kinds of supporting personnel, and cheerleaders. There'll be playoffs after the regular seasons and championship games. Think about it. They're just as human, all too human, as they were on the earth and they'll have bodies again that'll let them get physical with each other, so there'll probably be fan riots at almost every game. Boss, if I'm right, Limbo could become as entertaining as the earth!"

"Sounds perfect. You and Raphael work out the details after this meeting."

"Sir, what's with the major change in policy?" Uriel asked to get the conversation off the souls in Limbo. He didn't like the souls being in Heaven even though they were confined to Limbo. When he looked at Limbo, all he saw was a slum that tarnished the glory and purity of Heaven.

"I'm through being Mr. Nice Guy. If the Hebrews want be my chosen people, they're going have to earn the privilege from now on. I'm going to toughen the discipline. I've got laws for them that'll make the laws they've got now look like weak-kneed humanism. If it amuses me more than it amuses them, then they should remember this proverb: 'A wise chosen people love their God's heavy hand, because the human who loves the heavy hand loves the lessons it teaches, therefore only stupid humans who don't want to be my chosen people hate my heavy hand.'"

"Outstanding, sir!" Michael exclaimed. "They've been a bunch of pukes for too long. It's about time they got their heads and buns wired together."

"Yes, I'm going to make them lean and mean, and, if I have to kick buns and take names until they get that way, it'll hurt them more than it hurts me, and that's a promise! And, if that doesn't work, I'll pick another herd to be my chosen people, then woe to the Hebrews."

"Way to go, sir!" Michael cheered.

"I've got a great idea about how to do that if you want to go that way, boss" Satan said immediately.

"OK, let's see if you can give me two good ideas in a row."

Satan grinned wickedly. "This will really mess with their heads, boss. You go down there in the flesh yourself, only you tell them you're actually your son, but you're also your father. It'll blow their minds when they figure out you're telling them you're a two-person deity. Then you say you're not changing the laws you're going to give to the Hebrews, but you do it anyway. You give them new commandments and emphasize certain of the old ones in a way that gives them new importance and new meaning so it's obvious you *are* changing the laws after all. You also tell them the world is going to end soon, but it won't. You say a few mystic things so they can make themselves believe 'soon' doesn't really mean soon. It'll be the funniest damn eschatological show you've ever seen. And, oh yeah, don't exactly say you've dropped the Hebrews as the chosen people, but leave the door open to all races and ethnic groups so anybody who believes the new preaching can become one of the chosen people without being orthodox Hebrew or even Hebrew, which will make the orthodox Hebrews go bonkers. You know how much fun humans are when they're trying to eliminate heresy."

Yahweh grinned. "Not bad, smart ass, not bad."

Gabriel said, "If you want to get them really into this, sir, you'll have to come on like you're three persons, not two. They're really into number mysticism. Three is what you'll need to pretend to be if you want to really sell the multiple-personality product."

"Hmmm, good point. Who should the third person be?"

"Something really freaky like a holy ghost," Satan said immediately. "Most of them already believe their breath is their soul and souls can be ghosts, so it won't be hard to sell them on the third person being a holy ghost. But don't do it in their faces. It'll be more fun if you put it out there in a way that doesn't make it easy to believe, so there'll be a big theological fight about it, which means there's going to be lots of physical fights about it. This thing could entertain us for centuries!"

"I like it!" Yahweh said enthusiastically. "We'll work out all the details if the Hebrews blow it. Hmmm, I'll give them some hints about what could happen if they don't start marching to the beat of my drum. I wouldn't want them bitching and moaning about not getting any fair warnings if we kick off Operation Son of God."

"How about briefing us on the new laws, sir," Michael suggested.

"It's the next subject, Mike."

Yahweh told his angels the new laws would be revealed to Moses after the Exodus was under way. At this time Moses was still living happily as though he really was an authentic Egyptian prince. The pharaoh's sister loved him like a son, and he was a favorite of the pharaoh even though he was a Hebrew. He was beginning to be troubled by the plight of the Hebrews in Egypt, but had not yet reached the point where his conscience would force him to give up his exalted lifestyle among those who exploited his people.

Yahweh said to the assembled angels, "These are the divine laws of the Uniform Code of Hebrew Justice" ......

— Missing Text —

THE ARCHANGELS and the other angels laughed and joked about the ordeal Moses would face when trying to enforce the harsh new laws on the Hebrews, who always could be relied on to behave as though divine laws were really just imprecise advice. With few exceptions, they said all the right things and didn't mind engaging in rituals, but their religion was mostly ceremonial. Only a few had authentic passionate faith, thus it wasn't that hard to seduce them into apostasy, which angels pretending to be deities during R&R in the flesh had long enjoyed doing. They were glad Yahweh did not entirely forbid this most amusing entertainment, though many regretted they could no longer mess with the Hebrews like they could with other ethnic groups. They comforted themselves with this proverb: "If you're still having fun, the change you're bitching about wasn't even close to being as bad as it could have been."

Then one of the angels stepped forward and said, "Sir, permission to speak."

"I'm listening, Lilith."

"Sir, as you know, I am the leader of the Guardians. We Guardians are the angels who are moved by compassion for the humans and want to guide them in the pursuit of happiness. We want to nurture the humans to be the best they can be, not sport among them as do most other angels, who lead them astray to worship bizarre gods and goddesses and encourage their tendency to surrender to lust, greed, gluttony, sloth, and all the other detrimental behaviors that are all too human."

"I know all this, Lilith," Yahweh reminded him. "You make me want to make redundancy a deadly sin."

A smirking Satan added, "If I remember right, you once sported with the best of us, Lilith. You used to like being female down on the earth when you had R&R. Couldn't hardly get enough serpent, if I remember right." He laughed, and was joined by the other archangels, who also recalled what fun Lilith had been in the flesh. Even Yahweh, who had watched it all, grinned. Lilith had definitely been amusing then.

"Yes, and I regret that," Lilith replied humbly. "Now I want all angels to work to make life better on the earth for the humans."

"You're getting way too close to insubordination, Lilith!" Michael declared.

"Let Lilith speak," Yahweh said to his supreme commander of the hosts of Heaven.

"Sir, meaning no disrespect, one uppity smart ass in Heaven's about all we need," Michael replied unhappily.

"I resemble that," Satan chuckled back.

"Sir," Lilith began, "these new laws for the Hebrews will do nothing but breed hate and discontent among them, or worse than that there will be those who cannot obey them and will live covert lives diseased with guilt. They're oppressive, repressive, and suppressive. They'll make it so the worst in them is perceived as righteousness. It'll be the final proof they need to believe being the chosen people means they're the master race. They'll feel liberated to kill as though killing was holy work. They'll persecute their neighbors and believe they're serving *you*. It'll be one long, gory horror show if you give these laws to them."

Yahweh smiled. "What's not to like about *that*? What laws *should* I give them?"

"Sir, laws that promote life, liberty, and the pursuit of happiness. Laws that promote tolerance. Laws that prevent government from being run by priests. They need laws that guarantee them freedom to discuss their ideas, and freedom to meet with those who think like they do. The only law about sex should forbid physical force or coercion to make the unwilling submit to another's lust. The laws should promote justice, not revenge. And the laws should ensure all people are treated as equal—"

"Enough, Lilith!" Yahweh interrupted. "I get your point."

Satan laughed, "My, my, Mike, all this talk about hard-core discipline and here you have a mob of humanists in your command."

Michael rose up, his vast wings flapping furiously, and he roared, "On your face, Lilith! Squat thrusts until *I* get tired!" The terrified angel immediately complied. Michael turned to Yahweh, his eyes wild with rage. "Sorry about that, sir! This *will not* happen again! Buns will be kicked and names will be taken until there isn't a humanist road apple left in my command!"

"Settle down, Michael," Yahweh said soothingly. "Lilith, stop already with the squat thrusts. I'm not bothered by you angels who want to be Guardians. Have at it. It's been amusing watching you try to bring out the best in humans. It should continue to be amusing. However, my new laws are going into effect, so deal with it. Remember who created everything, you included. I created the universe and the humans because it wasn't that interesting in Heaven before I did. In other words, the humans are there to amuse me. Because I'm basically a nice guy, you angels get to have some fun with them too. You and the others who want to be Guardians, do your thing down there. The rest of you, do *your* thing down there. Just remember the Hebrews are mine from now on. You Guardians can try to 'nurture' them, but they're off limits to the rest of you horny jokers, except when I say otherwise. Have you all got that?"

"Sir, yes sir!" the vast hosts of Heaven replied in one thunderous voice. ......

— Missing Text —

THE WHOLE COMMUNITY of the sons of Israel pitched camp at Rephidim, a grim, waterless desert valley in the Sinai range. They erected tents and built fires. There were 600,000 men over the age of 20. With them were women, girls, and the males under 20, for a total population of about 2,500,000 Hebrews who had migrated out of Egypt. Later skeptics wondered whether that number could even fit into the desolate valley, but that such a number was indeed the true number was yet one more miracle during a time when Yahweh showered miracles upon the Hebrews. Woe to the unbeliever.

They were dirty and dressed in robes that looked almost alike for both sexes. Cows, goats, horses, and camels all wandered about in search of food and water that were not there. They created the usual foul-smelling mess of the pre-pooper-scooper era.

Moses moved among the people he had liberated from slavery, hoping for a show of appreciation, but he was not satisfied. He wondered what more he had to do. He had parted the Sea of Reeds, then collapsed it on the awesome army the pharaoh had sent to recapture the Hebrews. The pharaoh's surviving military units would probably be fishing the bodies out of the Sea of Reeds for two months or more.

Where, then, were the hosannas and alleluias that should have been sung in his honor? Moses looked around at his people and did not see many friendly faces smiling back. There were ancient, bent grandfathers; responsible, sober fathers; arrogant, horny bachelors; frisky, prankster boys. There were girls learning distaff; young women who wanted to marry the bachelors; mothers nursing babies and wondering how long it would be before they would be pregnant again; grandmothers wishing the grandfathers had reliably studly serpents now that they were free from the risk of pregnancy.

Did the people heap upon their savior honors and glories and gratitude? Forget about it! The Hebrews were born to bitch and moan.

A group of young mothers groaned to Moses, "There were plenty of graves in Egypt, so why did you bring us to this wilderness to die? What good has come of it? Didn't we tell you in Egypt to leave us alone? So what if we were slaves? We had water in Egypt! It's better being a slave in Egypt than a corpse in the wilderness! But, *no*, you had to liberate us no matter what we wanted! Now we die of thirst and all because of you, road apple!"

Moses replied persuasively, "Be courageous! Hold steady, and Yahweh will save you when he decides to."

Next, a group of fathers seeing their young sons in pain from dehydration bitched to Moses, "Why couldn't we have been killed by Yahweh's fist in the land of Egypt? There we could sit down to jugs of water and drink our fill of it. You've brought us into this desert to kill the whole community by thirst. Oh, Egypt wasn't good enough for you even though you lived like a prince thanks to pharaoh's sister! 'It is better to rule corpses in a gehenna than serve the pharaoh in Egypt.' That's your proverb! Now we will die, and all because of you, maggot!"

Moses replied calmly, "Soon you're going to see Yahweh's magnificence, for he's been listening to your grumbling against him. Why complain against me, for who am I? Your grumbling is not against me but against Yahweh. When your God decides, you'll then see his glory and be given water to drink until you're full."

Then there was a group of grandfathers looking about as near to death as old guys could get and still be alive. They shook gnarled fists at Moses and moaned, "Who's going to give us water to drink? Think of the water we used to get abundantly in Egypt. We also remember the fish we ate freely there, and the cucumbers and the melons and the leeks and the onions and the garlic. Now our breath is dried up. Even if we had good food again, there's no water to cook it or wash the stuff down with! You just had to set us free so you could strut around being the Big Man in Camp. You think we should sing hosannas and alleluias because we're free even though we will die in this wasteland? Well, wrong, Mister Ego-tripper. We're dying here and it's all because of you, puke!"

Moses scowled as he said, "Yahweh told me to free you, and right now I don't know why!"

Before reaching the sanctuary of his tent, a group of sexy young women, who could not remember when last they had been able to wash their hair, glared at Moses and screeched, "We'd rather have like died when our kinsmen died in Yahweh's presence before Yahweh sent you on this mission to save us even though none of us like asked to be saved, you know! Why have you like brought Yahweh's community into this desert, so we and our livestock, which young herders need to like make mohar, can die here? Why did you like force us to leave Egypt and bring us to this wretched place? There's no place for sowing, like no figs, no vines, no pomegranates, not even like water to drink. And, like even worse, there's no way a young man can come up with mohar, so we'll like die as virgins, we're sure. You've messed this exodus like totally up! Were you like thinking you'd score with all us young babes being like this big hero? We're like dying of thirst and it's all your fault, doofus, we're sure."

Moses growled with nasty sarcasm, "Y'all can like bite me, I'm sure!"

Moses entered his campground and did his best to release his anger, muttering, "What can I do about these people? They're on the point of stoning me."

Yahweh never told him he would have to eat this kind of clamjamfry day after day after day! Hadn't they seen enough miracles to know Yahweh was on their side and he was Yahweh's number one boy? Miracles in front of their very faces they had seen! The plagues and the Sea of Reeds parting at his command, then crashing back together to swallow the entire army pharaoh had sent to recapture them. Still they bitched and moaned! Moses almost regretted the day he saw the burning bush that was not consumed by the flames. He didn't feel like the superstar Yahweh had promised he would be. He felt like the victim of a divine practical joke.

His brother Aaron was waiting in front of his tent, spoiling for a fight, yet no voice was more beautiful than his, even when he barked, "Where the Sheol are we?"

"Rephidim, bro," Moses said evenly, but his eyes narrowed and his hands clenched into fists.

"I *know* that, maggot! I mean, *where are we*? Where are we in terms of the Promised Land? Do you even know?"

"I'm sure Yahweh'll let me know when he's ready. We're in his hands, or have you forgotten?"

"Just as I thought! There's a proverb: 'Yahweh punishes the wicked and forgets the stupid.' I said turn *left* after crossing the Sea of Reeds, but noooo, not you. Sure, don't take the advice of a mere man! Now here we are in this waterless desert, dying of thirst, and with no idea where the promised land is. The people are getting ugly, road apple, in case you haven't noticed. We've got to do something and do it now. I mean, we've got to mollify them somehow, and we'd better do it quick."

"You're such a wuss!" Moses sneered. "You want to cave in every time one of the crybabies frowns! Stand up to them like a man. Yahweh's on our side."

"Yeah? Well, look around. There's way over two million of them and just two of us, and right now none of 'em look like they like us too much!"

"Trust in Yahweh," Moses advised, then added, "Oh, and get outta my face! I stand up to Yahweh to cut you in on the deal to save your sorry loser buns from being a disgrace to our family, and this is the thanks I get! Right now I need a ration of clamjamfry from my own brother like I need a golden idol!"

Aaron's rage boiled over and he shouted, "At least I got a Hebrew wife! At least my sons ain't half-breeds!"

Moses, who was quite a bit bigger than Aaron as well as a whole lot handsomer, raised his fist to commence a serious buns-whupping. But at that moment a young Hebrew named Eliab came rushing up to Moses. He was one of the men Moses had sent out to recon the area. Fear was all over his face.

"Moses, Moses," he cried out, "we're in deep road apples. No water's good luck compared to this."

"Cut the dramatics, Eliab. What've you discovered?"

"The Amalekites have an army comin' at us! Thousands of 'em! Armed to the teeth!"

Aaron fell to his knees, lifted his face to the sky, and wailed with self-pity, "I need you, Yahweh, because I'm in deep road apples now. Fear is rotting my guts. Wretchedness ruins my life. My last days will be moaning and groaning. All I hear are threats from everywhere, as my abusers unite to plan my death. But I trust in you, Yahweh. I proudly say, 'Yahweh is my God.' Save me from all who want to harm me. Smile on your humble worshipper and show all the maggots how much you love me!"

Moses looked at Aaron and asked Eliab disgustedly, "You ever seen a bigger wuss, boy?"

Eliab wasn't about to say anything about the number two honcho, at least in his hearing, since the day might come Aaron would be number one. The young man replied, "All I know, sir, is there's one big army headin' this way."

Moses slapped his shoulder and said with manly confidence, "Remember we can put a pretty damn big army in the field ourselves, and we got Yahweh on our side."

Eliab looked around, then asked, "He wouldn't by chance be here now, would he? I don't see the pillar of cloud."

Moses had noticed the same thing. Until then, Yahweh had been constantly with them as a pillar of cloud during the day and a pillar of fire at night (which many Hebrews bitched and moaned spoiled their sleeping). Moses, who had no idea what Yahweh was up to, said, "Don't you worry, son. Yahweh's always where he needs to be when he needs to be there. Keep the faith, but sharpen your sword."

"Yes, sir!" Eliab replied, though not too confidently.

"He's right, he's right," Aaron sobbed, still on his knees. "The pillar of cloud's gone. Yahweh's thrown us to our enemies! We're doomed. Doomed! Who doesn't die of thirst'll be slaughtered by the Amalekites! We'll all die here and it's your fault, road apple!"

"You miserable punk!" Moses growled as he drew his foot back to punt Aaron's head over his tent.

At that moment another member of the recon team trotted up. "Sir! Sir!" he said excitedly.

Moses put his foot down and asked, "What is it, Gamaliel?"

"Sir, there's this big ol' rock rollin' this way!"

"Say what?"

"Yes, sir, a rock. Pretty much round. 'Bout seven cubits in diameter. Kinda ordinary lookin'. But I'll kiss your hairy buns 'til next sabbath if it ain't rollin' towards the camp!"

"A rock!" Moses exclaimed. "You sure you ain't been in the sun too long without water, boy?"

"Sir, I seen it an' pretty soon everybody's gonna see it. I mean it looks like it's been followin' us."

"Then why haven't the pickets spotted it?"

"Can't say, sir. I just know I did an' she's a-comin'."

Aaron jumped up, his unattractive, gaunt face full of hope. "It's gotta be Yahweh! He hasn't forgotten us! It's Yahweh come to save our buns!"

"Could happen," Moses admitted. "He's been a burning bush and the two pillars. He could be anything, since he is who he is. Why not a rock? We better check it out, though. If it's some other god or goddess lookin' for converts, we'll have to do something about it. Some pagan god or goddess comes in here, promisin' 'em they can commit all the debauchery they want if they just drop Yahweh, this mob'll be makin' golden idols all over the place!"

To Gamaliel he said, "You did good, son. Take liberty for the rest of the day."

As the brothers passed by tens of thousands of sons of Israel and their families, the thirst-tormented multitude began bitching and moaning disrespectfully at their deliverer and his number two.

"Give us water so we can drink!"

"What's the point of this exodus? Is it so that I will die of thirst along with my children and my cattle?"

"Where's the pillar? Is Yahweh with us or not?"

"Weren't you happy living the easy life pampered by the pharaoh's sister while we toiled as slaves? Our deaths in this desert, is that going to make you happy, maggot?"

Moses took all he could, tugging on his long beard, but at last lost all restraint. He roared, "You whinin' losers can all go back to Egypt for all I care!" But even at the peak of his wrath, he knew that was not true. He loved his people profoundly and it hurt that they evidently did not know that. He would stand up to Yahweh himself if necessary for his people! A little love back, would that hurt them? A little support during tough times, was that too much to ask?

His show of rage hushed them up for the moment. Moses sighed as he and Aaron headed for the perimeter of the vast, overcrowded camp. If only the quiet would last! But he knew it wouldn't.

They moved beyond the camp to the entrance of the desiccated valley. The brothers were amazed to discover Gamaliel had been right. A large granite boulder was rolling along the trail made by the community of Israel. It wasn't very pleasant looking, covered as it was with mashed-up road apples dropped by the herds and flocks of livestock accompanying the horde of displaced Hebrews.

Moses tensed up. He couldn't help it. The rock could be Yahweh, and Yahweh had tried to kill him on the road to Egypt. Moses still had no idea what his offense had been. Yahweh gave him his mission of liberation and then, when he was en route to do his deity's bidding, the terrifying incident happened. Sometimes he wondered if

Yahweh had done it just to mess with his head. Or maybe to get a laugh when his number one boy dumped and squirted all over himself. What else could explain Yahweh letting Moses live just because his panicked wife got the crazy idea that circumcising their son would appease the furious supreme being? Poor Gershom, now nicknamed Half-Serpent! Zipporah still cried sometimes whenever she thought about it, but mostly she repeated the proverb she had made to comfort herself: "It is better for a mother to have a son with half a serpent than a wife to have no husband!"

Now, Moses always felt very nervous when Yahweh showed up. What man could know what mood the supreme being would be in? Moses sure didn't.

"Do you think it's Yahweh?" Aaron whispered, his beautiful voice full of fear.

"I hope so. We're in deep road apples if Yahweh doesn't show up pretty soon."

The rock rolled up to the two men and stopped five cubits from them. "Hi, guys," the rock said pleasantly.

Not at all surprised by a talking rock, Moses asked cautiously, "Are you Yahweh? If you ain't Yahweh, get your pagan buns movin' on down the road. Nobody wants you here."

"Not to worry, guys," the rock said reassuringly. "I'm Yahweh, but not exactly, you see."

Moses and Aaron exchanged perplexed looks. This definitely was not Yahweh's usual awesome booming style. "No, I don't see," Moses replied suspiciously.

"I'm Jesus Christ."

"What the Sheol? I never heard of no Jesus Christ! You're some damn pagan god tryin' to fake me out, ain't you? It won't work, puke. You best be rollin' your buns on to some other place. My god's the king here and nobody's lookin' for a replacement. There's plenty of pagans around who'll be glad to worship you, whoever you are, not that I want to know. We're Yahweh's chosen people and that settles it as far as you're concerned."

The rock laughed amiably. "Now, take it easy, Moses. I am who I am. Really. Trust me. I'm here to take care of the water problem, and to give you a little hint about what could happen if the Hebrews blow their gig as my chosen people."

Moses looked perplexed. Aaron looked even more confused. Moses said, "Look, if you're Yahweh, then what? We should call you Jesus Christ now? I mean, whatever name you want, that's the name we'll use. Yahweh, Jesus Christ, you name it — uh, I mean, name yourself."

"No, I'm Jesus Christ, the son of Yahweh, meaning myself, but I'm still a distinct person as Jesus Christ and also simultaneously a distinct person as Yahweh, but the sons of Israel will call me Yahweh for as long as they're Hebrews. I don't even really have to be Jesus Christ again, but I will if you make me."

Aaron said, "Huh? If you're Jesus Christ now, why wouldn't you be Jesus Christ always? I mean, you're eternal and all that, right?"

"I know it's confusing, but, trust me, this is how it might be if it has to be, and that depends on you keeping the faith and obeying all the laws I'll be giving you pretty soon."

That confused Aaron even more. He asked, "So, like, you're your son while you're also your father, but not right now, just sometime later?"

The rock chuckled, "Close. Let me explain it again. I'm the Son of God, but I'm also my father, meaning I'm also God the Father. So I'm both Yahweh and Jesus Christ. I'm also the Holy Ghost, but I won't get into that for now. Just keep in mind that I'm one god, not three gods. At the moment, I'm predominantly Jesus Christ, but also simultaneously Yahweh and the Holy Ghost, because in all things I am who I am and the unity of my trinity isn't to be questioned, at least not by my true believers."

Aaron struggled mightily to comprehend, then thought he had it. He grinned as he said, "Of course! Jesus Christ is just an alias!"

"No, doofus, I'm here before you as Jesus Christ, a complete and entire person. Did you not pay attention?" the annoyed deity demanded.

Aaron's mind was blown. He just stared stupidly. Moses wasn't much closer to understanding, even though he was a much better theologian than his brother. Diplomatically he asked, "Could you say it in simpler terms?"

"OK, one more time. This is as simple as it gets. Ready? The Father (that's me when I'm Yahweh, which I always am, but not necessary predominantly) isn't created or begotten. The Son (that's also me, and what I am predominantly now while still being entirely the other two) is begotten without participation by the Holy Ghost, but the Father didn't make or create the Son. The Holy Ghost (the third person I am while simultaneously being only one deity, but I won't be predominantly that person now, since it wouldn't help you figure this out) isn't made or created or begotten by the Father or the Son, but proceeds from both. The Father is one Person, the Son is one Person, and the Holy Ghost is one Person. But the Father, the Son, and the Holy Ghost make only one God. I strongly advise not muddling the Persons, and don't even try to divide the Substance. That means I am who I am no matter who I am predominantly at any given moment. Three Persons are one God and one God is three Persons, all equally eternal, and none is not even the tiniest fraction of a second older than the others. Now, isn't that simple?"

Moses' and Aaron's heads spun wildly. Neither was able to comprehend the plain, clear explanation of the triune glory of the god of the Hebrews, the one true god, who was the Father, the Son, and the Holy Ghost simultaneously and also individually predominantly whenever he felt he had to be predominantly one of the three.

Aaron looked as if he wanted to go to his tent and lie down for a long time. Moses pulled his beard, squinted, mumbled, thought mightily, but finally had to ask, "Uh, you mean you begot yourself without existing before yourself? I mean, you're your father, but you didn't exist before the part of you that sired the other part of you?"

Then his over-extended brain produced a sudden new idea that made much more sense, and he looked at the rock suspiciously as he charged, "You gotta be some damn devious pagan deity tryin' to fool us!"

An awesome voice boomed from the rock, "You fool! You'll never figure it out. Maybe no Hebrew will ever figure it out. Well, I'm here to warn you that, if the Hebrews don't want to have to figure it out, or suffer the consequences of failing to figure it out, they better keep all the laws that I'll be giving to you and they damn sure better never ever convert to other gods or goddesses! If they fail me, I will give them for enemies peoples who haven't even heard of me yet — who aren't even nations yet.

"These peoples will speak languages the Hebrews will have to learn and one day there'll be Hebrews who can't speak Hebrew and don't want to! The worst of the Hebrews' enemies will be seriously mean religious bigots who won't respect the old or pity the young if they don't worship as they do. These enemies will eat the best of the Hebrews' cattle and crops and mercilessly exploit the Hebrews' labor until the Hebrews can't remember when they were prosperous. The peoples I empower will leave the Hebrews with just enough to survive and eventually the enemies will terminate the Hebrew nation. The war will put all the Hebrew towns under siege until the strongest walls collapse. The Promised Land will become the possession of the peoples I now bless. They will own all the towns that I will be giving you at the end of the Exodus. Those who survive will live all their lives wishing the Hebrews had never been liberated from slavery in Egypt.

"If the Hebrews do not obey the laws I'll be giving you to write down, they can forget about the blessings of prosperity and increasing national importance. It will be my delight to inflict ruin and insignificance on them. They will be exiled from the Promised Land and I'll disperse them all over the earth to live as humble minorities in nations they've never heard of yet, and the nations that will be the worst for them will be those that worship me in all my triune glory. They'll live in fear every day from birth to the grave, centuries and centuries of fear, among peoples who believe in my multiple Personhood and despise the Hebrews for clinging to the single-Person monotheism I will have discarded. The laws that will require the Hebrews to despise pagans, heretics, apostates, and humanists, if they wish to serve me and be spared the consequences of making me real peckish, will be interpreted by my Trinity worshippers as commandments that require them to despise the Hebrews. Among these nations there'll be times when the Hebrews will think the worst is over, then I'll lay some more heavy hand on them. Those who manage to survive will go on living night and day in fear. Even if I allow some Hebrews to prosper, never will I give them the comfort of security. Centuries and centuries of the heavy hand, *that* is what's going to happen to your descendants if you make me come again as Jesus Christ. The body count will increase as each new tragedy crushes your descendants like you will crush the pagans when I bring you to the Promised Land.

"But it doesn't have to be that way. This is a warning. I don't have to be a three-person deity on the earth. In fact, when I'm done here you and all Hebrews will continue to experience me as the one-person deity the Hebrews have worshipped for as long as I have been among them. But fail me and humans on the earth will only experience me as a three-person god. I will walk among the Hebrews as Jesus Christ again, except I'll be in a human body instead of a boulder. I'll offer them a new way to find salvation, but it won't be their traditional way and it will be hard for them to accept. Woe to them if they do not! If the day comes when I again let humans experience me as the Trinity, that day will be the beginning of when the Hebrews remember being slaves in Egypt as like having been in a paradise."

That awesomely booming voice removed all his doubts. Moses knew the voice of Yahweh by now! His joy was so tremendous that he paid not the slightest attention to the awful prophecy given to him. He didn't care about what name Yahweh wanted to be called or how many persons Yahweh said he was. He had more pressing problems, and they needed a miracle or two right now. Some other time maybe it would be nice to try to comprehend what this Trinity stuff was all about. At the moment he had a rebellious people dying of thirst and a hostile army approaching. But more than that, he again had the only shoulder he could cry on.

Moses unburdened himself to Yahweh. "Where have you been? Why are you tormenting your slave? Why do you view me so unfavorably that you load the weight of this entire nation on me? Did I conceive these losers and give them birth, entitling you to order me, 'Carry them on your chest like a foster father carrying a suckling infant, to the land I swore to give their ancestors'? I'm more like a wet nurse with a spoiled brat hanging on her nipple like he wants to bite it off!

"I was as good as a prince in Egypt. I had it easy. I could've skated through life and not even got bruised, but no, I had to care about these people. I had to give it all up because I felt guilty I didn't share their ordeals. Then I found peace and happiness in Midian, but you came along. 'I've seen the way the Egyptians oppress my chosen people,' you said, 'so I'm sending you to pharaoh so you can lead my nation the Israelites out of Egypt.' What's my reward? Stranded out here in the middle of nowhere, no water to drink, hostile troops marching on us, and all these bitchin' an' moanin' losers about ready to stone me!

"Where am I to find water for all these crybabies? We're so weakened by thirst I probably couldn't field a thousand men fit for battle. I can't hump this load by myself, you know, and I ain't the one who dreamed up this whole exodus thing! If all you're going to do is dump road apples on me, kill me now and save my people the trouble! I thought I was your number one boy, but you never told me I'd be in misery like this!"

Yahweh said to Moses, "One thing the Hebrews are good at is bitching and moaning."

"Tell me about it!"

"Well, relax, I know your problems and you know I have solutions to them all. First off, don't sweat the Amalekites. You'll kick their buns when the time comes because I'm with you. It'll be good practice for the buns-kicking you'll have to do in Canaan before you actually own the place. The water problem's no problem. Stand by for another reason to worship none other than me. Now, Moses, just whack me with your staff."

Moses did this, and promptly a steam of yellowish water flowed out of the point of impact. At Yahweh's bidding, the brothers drank. The liquid was rather warm, but they were too thirsty to complain.

Aaron praised, "Ahhhh, profoundly delicate, slightly fruity, yet not without solid body, but at the same time decidedly spiritual."

"Yeah, and it tastes good too," Moses added.

"Hey, I am who I am," Yahweh bragged. "My road apples don't stink and my pee tastes like wine."

Aaron immediately turned green and fell to his knees

vomiting. Moses looked on in disgust, saying, "You wuss! I'm ashamed we're related! I can't believe I felt sorry for your sad buns and got you put on as my executive officer!"

Aaron recovered and begged Yahweh to forgive him. Yahweh said, "Forget about it! You're only human. Let's get on into the camp and let everybody drink up until they're feeling fat, dumb, and happy again."

Moses suggested, "Maybe we should let 'em think it's just water."

"I can live with that. It's the miracle they need to appreciate. They don't need to know every detail."

"And the Trinity thing, maybe it's good that's not brought up yet."

"Yes. It's too early for that. And, like I said, it doesn't ever have to be a problem for the sons of Israel if you all keep your heads and buns wired together. If you listen carefully to the voice of your deity and do what is right in my eyes, if you pay attention to my commandments and keep my statutes, I won't inflict any of the evils on you that'll happen if I have to let humans experience me as a three-person deity."

"I'll do my best to keep 'em squared away," Moses promised.

Moses, Aaron, and the rock went into the camp of the miserable Hebrews. All were awed by the miracle they beheld and then overjoyed when Moses again struck the rock so that the warm, yellowish "water" flowed abundantly. There was almost a riot two seconds later, and only terrifying thunder blasting out of a cloudless sky cowered the desperately thirsty people. The brothers organized the sons of Israel into an orderly procession for drinking from the rock, and after them every herd and flock. The delicious "water" kept flowing abundantly. By evening all the Hebrews loved Moses again, and the latest polls had his job performance rating at a record high.

Two days later, Moses sent an army of his toughest men

out to do battle with the Amalekites. Joshua commanded them, and Yahweh was with them in the form of a pillar of cloud to ensure it wasn't a fair fight. "I'm going to annihilate totally all memory of Amalek from under the skies," he confided to Moses. And so it was the Hebrews slaughtered every last single enemy soldier, even the thousands who surrendered and begged for mercy. Yahweh saw the body count and pronounced the battle a job well done. Moses built an altar to hold formal worship service in celebration of the great victory and named it Yahweh-nissi.

A few days later Moses led the Hebrews out of the valley of Rephidim and followed Yahweh to the wilderness of Sinai, where they pitched camp. Yahweh appeared before all the sons of Israel as an active volcano and commenced to give them the new Uniform Code of Hebrew Justice ......

— Missing Text —

SATAN AND GABRIEL came before Yahweh in Heaven and Yahweh said, "Excellent job, smart ass! You certainly give good temptation."

Satan chuckled, "Wasn't any big deal, boss. They're so human that tempting them is as easy as flying."

"You didn't get them all. Phinehas, for instance. He took the best you had and hung tough. He isn't a wuss like his granddaddy Aaron."

"He's definitely a hardcore true believer. Even Gabriel's excellent Baal didn't rattle him."

"Yes, fine work, boy," Yahweh agreed. "You've got a real talent for doing pagan gods and goddesses."

"Yes sir, all that R&R in the flesh really paid off," Gabriel said happily. "But, I have to agree with smart ass; it's not hard getting humans to commit apostasy. I can't believe, after all the miracles you've performed right in front of their faces, they'd fall all over themselves to worship a clown like Baal. I mean, yeah, smart ass's a Sheol of a seductive evangelist, but, come on, get real! What a bunch of gullible chumps!"

Satan said, "You forget the babes of Moab, Gabe. They were the clincher. On a scale of one to ten, they're all Sarais and Tamars. The Hebrews haven't got enough chicks. All those thousands of horny boys with no hope of scoring a wife no matter if they have plenty of mohar to offer, how could they resist girls as hot and as easy as the Moab hussies? I notice you scored your fair share while being Baal."

"Just following your example, smart ass. Best damn time in the flesh I've had since the universe was created."

"Amen, bro!"

Yahweh chuckled, "Well, they seem to wish they hadn't been seduced, either by your sexy preaching or the girls' sexy bodies."

"Yeah, that was a great plague, big boss," Satan exclaimed sincerely. "Twenty-four thousand wiped out—" he snapped his fingers "—just like that. What do you call it?"

"Ebola. I think I'll keep it in the inventory, but maybe save it until the humans discover science and start getting cocky about their ability to cure diseases."

"What's next, sir?" Gabriel asked.

"The Battle of Midian to punish the Midianites for seducing my Hebrews to worship Baal and violate most of the sex laws I gave to them."

"Which they probably wouldn't have done without a little help from me and Gabe," Satan said merrily. "After all the buns the Hebrews have kicked since you delayed their entry into the land of Canaan, the Midianites were dumping and squirting all over themselves when the Hebrew army camped at Shittim. They probably would have agreed to anything not to be the next conquest. But Gabe and I made sure that didn't happen."

"My boys need one more dress rehearsal for the invasion of Canaan, and they need one more lesson about what happens if they break my laws and worship other gods and goddesses. They better start taking their job as chosen people seriously because I can kick buns and take names for all eternity if I have to, and they haven't got all eternity."

"How much time are you going to give them before kicking off Operation Son of God, boss?" Satan asked.

"Not a lot. They'll have twelve hundred years to get their buns and heads wired together and be all I want 'em to be."

Satan laughed. "They couldn't do it in twelve thousand years! You want me to start doing scenarios for Op-SOG?"

"It can wait. Let's get this show on the road."

Yahweh appeared before a naked Moses as flames that didn't consume a pile of dirty robes, and commanded, "Harass the Midianites and strike them down, for they have afflicted the sons of Israel with apostasy and their hussies turned them into perverts."

Moses, who was 120 years old and usually grumpy, complained, "Maybe you could've waited until I was dressed?" He no longer felt anxiety when his deity showed up. Numerous meetings during the long decades of the Exodus had leeched away his fear of the supreme being. Indeed, he had spent so much time with Yahweh that now he hardly felt even awe when in the divine presence.

"Oh, like I haven't seen your naked buns before!"

"That don't mean I like showin' 'em to you."

"Didn't I show you mine once?"

"Oh, sure, and you laughed too, you and all the angels. I ask to see your glory and you moon me. Was that a nice thing to do? Is that being a good role model for young people?"

"Moses, the older you get, the less sense of humor you've got. Well, that won't be a problem much longer.

The grunts of Israel will take vengeance for the Israelites on the Midianites, and after that you'll be joining your ancestors."

"Oh, wonderful. And I suppose you want I should have some sense of humor about it being time to die? You used to let your number one boys live a lot longer. Nine hundred fifty years Noah got. Have I done less than him for you? Was his ordeal worse than mine? One hundred seventy-five years for Abraham and, big deal, he sired Isaac and that's his wonderful contribution. I've slaved for you leading the most obnoxious, difficult people there ever has been or ever could be. You wouldn't have a Hebrew worshipper left if it wasn't for me. I ain't had nothin' but pain in my hands since writin' down all the laws you dictated to me. And what's my reward? A lousy one hundred twenty years!"

"Yes, but your serpent still wakes up when you want it to, doesn't it? Thank me for all the nooky you've had during the decades of old age when studly serpents are just bitter memories for men who live that long — *and* also during the extra decades I've allowed you to live that have made you the envy of old men who know they will never live as long as you have. Really, Moses, how can you complain like you do? You're as bad about that as any other Hebrew!"

Moses sighed. He really was too old to be struggling with Yahweh like he had in the good old days to turn the angry deity's wrath away from the misbehaving Hebrews. "OK, OK, forget about it! You want the Midianites' buns kicked, I'll send the army out."

"Just send one thousand men from each tribe."

"Say what? The Midianites don't want war, but they ain't cowards. Most of them stopped being nomads long ago and now live in fortified towns. Midian's the biggest and its walls are thick. They could put over a hundred thousand men against us, and you want us to send just twelve thousand when we could send about fifty times that? If they decide they'd do better in a siege, twelve thousand piddling troops won't ever take the place. Which of us is getting senile, that's my question?"

"I will work a great miracle in the Battle of Midian. Twelve thousand shall be as twelve million. When the sons of Israel invade the land of Canaan, they'll remember Midian and have no fear like the first time. After Midian falls, the rest of the army can be unleashed on all the rest of Midian's realm. They also shall show no mercy to the enemy."

"OK, OK, whatever you say."

"Give the command to Joshua son of Nun. Caleb son of Jephunneh will be the number two honcho. Say to the sons of Israel it's because they were the only ones who weren't wusses when I first wanted the invasion of the land of Canaan to begin. After your death, Joshua will be supreme commander of the Hebrews."

"Good choice. Joshua's real hardcore. He'll need to be, leadin' this bunch of bitchin' an' moanin' ingrates. Lots of luck, that's what I say."

"So maybe you should cover your wrinkled old buns and get the show on the road?" Yahweh suggested and then the flames vanished.

Moses put on clean robes and passed out of his tent. He paused to watch some of his young slave girls, all cute Hebrew darlings sold to him by poor fathers in desperate need of shekels (proving true the rich man's proverb, which was one of Moses's favorites: "The black cloud of poverty has a delightful silver lining"). The well-trained lovelies stopped their housework and displayed their glories with all the seductive charm they had, which was a lot. They thought he would be selecting one of them for a nooner, unaware that he had more serious work to do. Moses sighed. How many more times could he enjoy the succulent little honeys before Yahweh snuffed out his life?

Again the injustice of being given a piddling 120 years for his long, mostly arduous service stung him, but what could he do?

"Later, sweethearts," he promised the firm, yet soft, exquisitely beautiful slave girls. He went out of his tent thinking that, to be honest, being Yahweh's number one boy did have its perks!

When he had assembled the captains of thousands and the captains of hundreds, Moses announced that Midian was to be their next military objective. The senior officer corps of Israel cheered. They had been conquering cities all over Transjordania since the disgrace at the border of the land of Canaan a few decades ago. They now had a fine empire. No Egypt, true, but no joke either. Like all good empire-builders, they were always ready to build their empire a little bigger. They cheered again when Joshua and Caleb were given the top command assignments for the battle and after Moses died. Both were respected military leaders and it put to rest the worries about the transfer of power. Moses, after all, looked as if he could drop dead any day. It was good it was fixed so there wouldn't be a power struggle after his death. Moses was tempted to tell them his death was near, but thought the timing was wrong.

None of the senior officer corps of Israel cheered when Moses told them the army was going to have only 12,000 men. But Moses told them what Yahweh had said about it, and that was good enough for Joshua and Caleb. When they declared they were eager to go up against Midian, even though they'd be outnumbered ten to one or more, to prove how much they trusted Yahweh, no man was willing to argue. They had just survived the horrible wrath of Yahweh and weren't willing to risk arousing the wrath of their commanders.

"How about the booty?" Joshua asked. "Same deal as always?"

Moses thought for a moment, thinking of the invasion of Canaan and wanting to give his people a strategy that might reduce the carnage and destruction of property, then said, "Here is how the sons of Israel will wage war now and in the land of Canaan. When you advance against a town in order to assault it, first invite it to surrender peacefully. Why should our boys die if it's not necessary? So, give a town a chance to surrender. If it accepts the terms of peace and surrenders to you, then the entrie population of the town is to be reduced to serfdom and forced to do slave labor. But if they reject your peace terms and wage war against you, you're to besiege the town and, as soon as Yahweh has delivered it into your hands, you're to kill every male in the place with the blade of the sword. But the women and children and livestock and everything else in the town, you're to plunder for yourselves. You're to eat your enemies' goods that Yahweh gives you."

The men present all cheered. Caleb asked, "The women, sir, it'll be open season, right? Nothin' like warm nooky after a hot battle, right, boys?"

After the cheering died down, Moses said rather sternly, "What, now we're pagans? No, we'll show the world how civilized Yahweh's troops are. When you go to war against your enemies and Yahweh delivers them into your hands and you take prisoners, and among the prisoners is a hot POW babe whom you lust after and wish to own as your wife, then you're to take her home to your house and she's to shave her head and trim her nails, and discard her prisoner's uniform. She's to remain in your house and mourn her father and mother for a full month, and only after that are you to get into her and thereby become her lord by making her your lady."

One of the commanders of thousands immediately raised this objection: "When grunts storm a town, I don't know any way to keep 'em from rapin' every female in the place. It'd be harder'n stoppin' 'em pillagin' the town."

"Rape and pillage're part of the battle," Moses replied. "I'm givin' rules for *after* the battle, when the booty gets divvied up."

"Yeah, maybe nobody'll bitch 'bout that! Personally, I wouldn't want no wuss in my unit who ain't into rapin' like a hardcore grunt oughta be!"

All the commanders vigorously voiced their agreement about what kind of man made the best grunt, but there was still grumbling about not getting to ride a woman acquired as booty for the first month after taking possession of her. Joshua and Caleb glared at the men, but before they spoke an order to silence them, a commander of hundreds asked, "What if you got a wife or two already?"

"So now you got one more," Moses replied, "except the one who's booty serves your Hebrew wife or wives like a slave, so probably you won't get a ration of clamjamfry about it no matter how young or pretty your new ride is."

"Does that mean we can sell her when we get tired of her?"

"No, that's what a pagan'd do. We're more civilized than that. She's your wife, so no sellin' her like a slave. But she's not like a Hebrew wife, so if riding her turns out to be a disappointment, then you're to free her to go anywhere she chooses. You're not to sell her for cash, re-enslaving her, because you will have destroyed her dignity. Where she goes after that is her problem."

"What about if we've gotten her pregnant an' that's why we wanna dump her so we don't have to deal with another brat?"

"Trust Yahweh to take care of her and the brat she carries accordin' to the mysterious plan he's got for all people, pagans and Hebrews. Besides, there's always a market for slaves, even pregnant ones, so she can sell herself and provide a home for herself and the brat."

"If she sells herself, can the guy who divorced her buy her so he can keep on riding her and sell the brat?"

"Yes. She and her brat will be slaves then and not Hebrew ones, so they won't have many rights and you'll have all the rights that justly belong to a slaveholder. For example, you can sell her at any time and to anybody, Hebrew or pagan, who wants to buy her."

"Can we take more than one?"

"Only after all the troops get a pick. Oh, yeah, the bachelors, they gotta get first pick. This chick shortage's a real problem, so we gotta do the smart thing an' use the POW babes to solve it. Married grunts get to pick next. Anybody wants seconds, they pick from what's left."

"Is it OK to sell our right to pick to another guy?"

Moses chuckled, "Yes, but tell the troops they better never bitch and moan about not having any nooky if they do that."

Joshua stood up and announced, "Enough already with the questions. We got buns to kick. Move it! I want the best for the twelve thousand. Our meanest and leanest grunts. Trust in Yahweh, but be prepared."

"Urrrr-rah!" the senior officer corps of Israel shouted gung-holy, then scrambled to prepare to do great battle against the Midianites. With the swiftness that had been perfected after years and years of waging war all over Transjordania, the army that would go against Midian was on parade before Moses and all the sons of Israel. There was much cheering and ostentatious patriotism because Yahweh hovered nearby as a pillar of cloud, and thus all were confident that their small army would be victorious.

Joshua marched his force to the great walls of Midian. The inhabitants were inclined to surrender even though so small a force was confronting them, because the Hebrews had an awesome reputation as conquerors. The Midianites had celebrated during the brief period when Baal was physically among them and was assisted by the irresistible eloquence of Urbura, the great religious leader with the strange name. Both had arrived in

Midian just when they had needed them most. Then, converting Hebrews seemed easier than breathing, and the way the Hebrew grunts went nuts over the babes in Peor, the Midianite town nearest the Hebrew camp at Shittim, it seemed as though the Hebrews would conquer themselves through assimilation.

Then things changed. Baal and Urbura disappeared at the same time as a ghastly, horrifying plague swept through the Hebrews. Because of the plague, and their belief that Yahweh caused the disappearance of Baal and his prophet, the Hebrews rediscovered their faith in their deity with an enthusiasm that was frightening.

Better to surrender, convert, and live in peace than die for a deity that had deserted them when they needed him most. This was the reasoning of the Midianites when Joshua stepped forward and gave them Moses's terms of surrender. The Midianites declared they would not surrender if it meant slavery for all men, women, and children. Their counter offer was conversion to the worship of Yahweh and their entire army joining in the Hebrews' empire-building campaign. Joshua was adamant with the cold iron of righteousness of those who truly love Yahweh. The Midianites were enraged by such irrationally brutal arrogance, and declared they would rather die fighting than live like cattle.

Against the 12,000 Hebrews came 120,000 angry Midianites. They were not the world's greatest grunts, since Midianites preferred living in peace and pursuing success through trade rather than empire, but they would fight ferociously when backed into a corner. They came on with supreme confidence, assured that 12,000 of the toughest grunts in Transjordania could not whip 120,000 men fighting for their freedom. Alas, they had not reckoned on Yahweh, who blessed the Hebrews with invincibility. Ten minutes after the first swords clashed it was obvious to both sides that no Hebrew soldier could be either wounded or killed in battle. The Midianites threw down their useless weapons and fled.

It did them no good. Utterly fearless because of their invincibility, the Hebrews rushed after the enemy with a wild abandon that had no military discipline in it at all. The slaughter was ghastly as the Hebrews chopped up the hopeless, helpless Midianites while singing alleluias and hosannas to the glory of Yahweh. When all 120,000 enemy soldiers were rendered into bloody chunks, the Hebrew army stormed into Midian.

They met no resistance from the terrified population. Pleas for mercy were like prayers to Baal, as useless as they were worthless. No man escaped death. The old, the crippled, the ones who were so new to puberty that they still looked more like children than men: all of them were chopped down with utter mercilessness because each one was a sacrifice Yahweh wanted. Only the women and children were spared death, but, alas for the women and girls, they were brutalized by a rampage of rape that only Yahweh himself could have stopped so totally out of control were the raging emotions of the savage, triumphant conquerors. Joshua looked at the horror show and grinned grimly as he pronounced it a job well done. To him the terrible wrath of Yahweh was just retribution for the Midianites seducing so many Hebrews to commit apostasy and debauchery. In the end the only girls who had not been raped, often several times, by rampaging Hebrews were the very youngest.

When Joshua sent back word that Midian was captured, Moses unleashed the rest of the army to storm throughout the Midianite realm. Rape, plunder, and slaughter came to every town and encampment of the Midianites. Most of these places were burned to the ground after being gutted of all valuable property and the surviving women and children. It was a horror beyond anything the Midianites could have imagined.

The women and girls of Midian began wishing they were dead as they were driven by their conquerors towards Shittim. Repeatedly grunts would drag them off for more rape, often by joyously vicious gangs of grunts celebrating their great and awful victory. Many thousands of the victims were killed, most of them unintentionally. Thousands more killed themselves. The remaining 32,000 endured and endured and endured, having a stronger instinct for mere biological survival than those who escaped the horror the only way they knew how.

Moses spent the time getting all the nooky he could. When the Midianite campaign was finally over, he would finally be over. The short, atrocity-drenched war had given his lust a vigor that surprised even him. One afternoon, close to the end of the campaign, Moses was cuddling with his newest slave girl, a gorgeous little darling he had bought just that morning. Already he had taken two of her virginities and now he was preparing her for taking her third virginity, the one called the Muddy Road. She lay in his old, weakened, wrinkled arms while he fondled her lovingly and sang about being her "back-door man." Suddenly she became limp and unconscious, as though she had died.

"What the Sheol?" Moses cried out, shocked and disappointed.

An instant later he was startled to find himself being confronted for the second time in his life by a burning bush. Out of the flames came the awesome booming voice of Yahweh, "Moses, why have you spared the women? These women were the ones who perverted the sons of Israel. If not the actual ones, then the moral equivalent of them. You shouldn't have spared them."

"Yahweh, I gave the orders I thought were best," Moses protested. "I just wanted to set policy that would make the conquest of Canaan easier for my people."

"You should've checked with me to see if I wanted it

easier for them. You blew it. When the invasion of Canaan begins, it will be a war of genocide. The Midianite campaign is just the final dress rehearsal for that. When the sons of Israel invade the land of Canaan, they must show no mercy to the inhabitants of the country. They must destroy their stone sculptures, all the cast-metal statues, and all their altars in the high places. They will conquer the Promised Land and stay in it, knowing their God kept his promise to Abraham and Isaac.

"However, if they do not force into exile any surviving Canaanites, if they let any of them live among the sons of Israel, then their mercy will make them miserable like barbs in their eyes and thorns in their sides. These Canaanites will seduce the sons of Israel into apostasy and perversion, and I eventually will deal with the sons of Israel as I promised I would when I came before you as Jesus Christ at Rephidim. Every living thing in Canaan is doomed. Men and women, young and old, even the oxen and sheep and donkeys. Massacre them all. If they show mercy, their descendants shall curse them. Midian is practice for Canaan. As it shall be later in Canaan, so it shall be now in Midian."

Moses was not appalled. He was thinking about the daily realities he faced and how Yahweh's instructions affected them. He saw one glaring problem. As he had done so many times before, he sought to change Yahweh's mind. "Yahweh, wisdom you have," Moses began, "so I ask for some of it about our nooky problem. You know the whole affair at Peor, that was all about nooky in the end. We got more guys than we got chicks, and they're mostly young guys. A guy can't feel manly unless he's gettin' regular nooky, so what's a guy gonna do? Your new laws, they don't let a widower celebrate the Rites of Lot, brothers and sisters can't take the Vows of Abram and Sarai, nobody can have fun with their dogs or sheep, men can't have fun riding boys, and didn't I take a big load of clamjamfry about it? All these years, still I take clamjamfry about it, but one hundred twenty years, that's all the reward for taking all I've taken for all these new laws! Now you want me to take more clamjamfry about the POW babes by putting them under the ban. Yahweh, cut me some slack. I'm too old to take this anymore."

"I mean for my chosen people to have traditional family values, and they better obey if they want to remain chosen!"

"Yahweh, I'm just askin' for a little reality here. My boys got seduced because they had no nooky at home. Once their serpents took charge, what chance did they have to keep your laws? They're mostly young, so that means they're mostly stupid. That's reality. From their point of view, with you they were lonely and horny and with Baal they had all the nooky they could handle. Who's gonna win that one? We gotta face reality, Yahweh, that's all I'm sayin'."

"I am more real than reality. I created reality. The law is the law because I am who I am. The Canaanite women, young and old, virgin or not, are under the ban."

"Yahweh, be reasonable now. I'm not saying change your Canaan policy. You're probably right about the best way to win *Canaan*. It's the *Midian* policy I'm asking for a little slack on. Let us have the women. We need 'em for our bachelors or there'll just be more Peors when the Canaanite campaign gets rolling. You know it, I know it, so let's deal with it rationally, OK? Besides, if I'm gonna die here in a little bit, cut me some slack. Don't make me take the clamjamfry on this one."

"Very well, Moses, here's the final deal on the Midianite POWs. The male children are to be massacred. All the women who've slept with a man, they're dead meat, and I mean ASAP after they're all gathered here. You can keep the young girls who haven't slept with a man and divide them up with the rest of the booty. By the way, the troops don't get to hog it all. The troops get half. The other half goes to the rest of the community."

Moses sighed. He knew when he had gotten the best deal possible from Yahweh. It meant more clamfamfry flying at his old, wrinkled head, but what else was new? He did have one more thing. "Yahweh, about my rules of engagement, let me make some law here, OK? How about lettin' 'em be the rules for when we wage war outside the Promised Land?"

"I can live with that, Moses. When you settle the distribution of the booty, time's up for you. Hope you're ready to go."

Moses was not ready to go, but he made a manly reply: "If you're callin', I'm comin'. Can I make a farewell speech to my people?"

"Have at it," Yahweh replied, then the burning bush stopped burning and the concubine slave girl regained consciousness.

Moses took her third virginity, but his mind was distracted enough to spoil the satisfaction he usually got from introducing young girls to the glories of the Muddy Road. When Joshua reported the next day to let Moses know all the booty and POWs captured during the Midianite campaign were now at Shittim, Moses revealed Yahweh's commands to him. Joshua scowled as he thought about how his men would react to this latest from their god.

"This ain't good," he said. "Killin' all the boys, that'll be seen by the troops as a whole lotta slaves bein' lost, which's like them losin' shekels they earned, but that won't even make 'em as peckish as the booty divvy. The troops won't like givin' noncombatants half the booty, but even that won't be the real problem. The POW babes'll be the real problem."

"I know, but the ban exempts virgins, so that should make it easier to accept."

Joshua laughed harshly. "Forget about it! Moses, are you maybe gettin' senile here? You know how it goes when grunts win. They're all bonkers with bloodlust when they get to pounce on the civilian population. Good grunts ain't humanists an' our grunts're the best in all Transjordania, so what chance was it they'd act like humanists when they finished off Midian and the other towns? Half my share of the booty says there ain't a virgin left over the age of five, which won't leave many out of the thirty-two thousand babes we brought in. I'm sayin' this ain't gonna cut it."

Moses thought for several seconds, then smiled as he said, "Yahweh said to spare the virgins. There's three virginities, right? So it seems to me a babe's a virgin as long as she's got at least one of her virginities left."

"Forget about it. These Midianites are *Moab* sluts, the descendants of Lot's son by his oldest daughter. If there were ten virginities, wouldn't none of 'em be virgins a month after puberty, and I doubt a whole lot of 'em'd reach puberty as virgins. Like it was for us in the good old days before Yahweh gave us the hardcore laws after gettin' out of Egypt, that's what it's been like for all the Moab peoples, only about ten times more'n it ever was for us. They're so sexually liberated they make Tamar and Sarai look like prudes. Besides, even if they all were virgins before we captured their buns, you ever see grunts gangrapin' POW babes? Ain't no virginities gonna be left after that kinda celebratin'!"

Moses grunted and thought and scowled and thought. It was quite a problem, but fortunately he had become a much better theologian than he had been at the start of the Exodus. And because of that, he began to see a solution to their problem. He said, "Yahweh didn't really say 'virgin'. He said 'slept with a man.' Maybe that's the loophole we're lookin' for."

"I don't know. How about 'girl'? Didn't you say he specified 'young girls' who hadn't slept with guys?"

"Oh, no problem. You know how 'girls' is used to refer to just about any woman still young enough to conceive, so 'girls,' or even 'young girls,' is no problem. We got 'slept with a man' as our out. That's gotta be the loophole."

Joshua frowned. "I don't know 'bout that. Just about everybody uses 'slept' to mean gettin' nooky, and the Midianites definitely were into gettin' nooky!"

Moses suddenly grinned. "But the precise term is 'slept,' which means precisely sleeping, not gettin' nooky. I mean, would Yahweh use slang when givin' laws? I don't think so. So, the question is, did they *sleep* with men?"

"I'm still not gettin' your meanin'. Isn't 'girls' an' 'young girls' slang when used with babes who ain't precisely the age when babes're still girls?"

"Oh, no, not at all. Using 'girls' or 'young girls' for all chicks young enough to conceive, that's not slang because it reinforces their inferiority to men, an' I know Yahweh doesn't want chicks to start thinkin' they're equal to men an' oughta have the same rights an' all."

"Yeah, OK, you know this stuff better'n I do, but I still don't see how 'slept with a man,' even if 'slept' really means sleepin' an' not gettin' nooky, solves our problem."

"Answer this: the Midianites had no laws forbidding guys ridin' guys, right?"

"Yeah, right. They were definitely perverts. They had it better than it was for us before the Exodus. All the sexual options were legal in Midian, an' just about every guy an' gal enjoyed 'em."

"Well, only *our* laws're important here an' by our laws, if a man becomes a *woman* for a man, then he's not exactly a *man*, is he? He's a girly-man, isn't he? That's why Yahweh's law states 'You must not ride a man like a woman. That would be detestable.' It's detestable because you stop being a man when you ride a guy like a woman! In other words, any of our POW babes who're still able to conceive are *legally* virgins if they haven't slept with a man, meanin' precisely sleepin' with a guy who ain't never been a woman for another guy. Since all the Midianite males were really girly-men because they became like women with other guys or rode other guys like they were women, the only POW babes who've slept with men would be the ones who did precisely sleep with our troops. Did that happen?"

Joshua laughed happily, "No way! It'd be like askin' to get our throats cut! After ridin' 'em, they get returned to the POW herd where we keep 'em under tight security. Didn't none of 'em sleep with any of our boys."

Moses felt triumphant. "So, there it is. We get the POW babes and Yahweh gets his law obeyed! It doesn't get any better than that."

Up in Heaven Satan laughed, "That doesn't sound much like the commandment you gave, big boss!"

"Do you think I should make exegesis a deadly sin?" Yahweh asked amiably.

"No way. That would take all the fun out of theology."

"There it is."

"You know, boss, I think you created me a lot more like you than you'll ever admit."

Yahweh replied, "I am who I am and you are who I created you to be. Since my ways are mysterious, what you think is probably not what I know."

Back on earth, Joshua said enthusiastically. "Let's divvy up some booty!"

Moses sighed, "You and Eleazar can make the decisions about who gets what. I'll make a ceremonial appearance when you're ready to distribute. I've got a speech to write."

"A victory speech?"

"A farewell speech," Moses replied and then told Joshua about Yahweh retiring him from life after the Midianite campaign.

Joshua was sad even though it meant he would be getting supreme command sooner than he had expected.

"Make it a long speech," he advised mournfully.
"You got that right!" ……

— Missing Text —

Elisha Scroll
(from Cave I)

MY LAST SELECTION, my dar G., is also one of the strangers, dealing as it does with one of the oddest events in the Bible, that being the miracle Elisha worked on the road to Bethel. This was the Miracle of the Bears, which involved the prophet causing two she-bears to slaughter forty-two boys who had teased him. It would seem to be a wholly senseless abuse of the divine power invested in Elisha, particularly to a limited mind working with information no better than that contained in the Old Testament (2 Kings 2:23–25) or the Dung Sea Scrolls, which naturally do little to provide adequate justification for the massacre. My marvelous Terminally Ill Sea Scrolls prove that Elisha had more than sufficient justification to inflict the punishment he inflicted.

Juvenile crime, as you probably know, is a serious as well as seriously escalating problem in all modern cultures. Here at last we find a source of wisdom addressing the problem in a way that shall lead us out of the jungle and into the realm of rationally peaceful law and order. Yes, when correctly interpreted by a brilliant mind such as mine, one, that is, steeped long in the wisdom only to be found in my Terminally Ill Sea Scrolls, the "Elisha Scroll" will be found to be the repository of all the answers we need to deal successfully with juvenile crime.

No less important, of course, are the astonishing revelations the Elisha Scroll makes about the crucial decisions concerning the fourth great event in human history, the one following the Exodus—that is, if you have not guessed it, and you may have not, lacking as you do the level of education necessary for truly sophisticated intellectual analysis the life of Jesus Christ. Yes, theologians will spend decades revising all that has been written about Jesus Christ and his mission on the earth. Their gratitude for the enlightenment that will be given to them once my magnificent Terminally Ill Sea Scrolls are published will be boundless. The glory shall be mine, and not unjustly, as I am sure you will agree, but I assure you I shall be worthy of that glory and will not corrupt the purity of the message of my precious Terminally Ill Sea Scrolls with unreasonable greed, although it would be foolish not to accept the generous rewards given in gratitude for all the glorious benefits my years of long, courageous, unjustly ignored work shall bring to a civilization at a time when its need for it is most desperate.

By the way, perhaps a minor point, but nevertheless one that demonstrates how pathetically wasted is time spent infatuated with the Dupe Sea Scrolls, and that point is that the Elisha Scroll confirms what only the profoundest and most rigorous scholars have long suspected, though until now none of us dared to even hint at it in even the most obscure professional journals, and that is the fact, now conclusively proven, that the Hebrews have the glory of responsibility for humanity's greatest invention! Here we are at one of the pivot points of history, when what might have been is lost by a turn to what came to be. All this is to be found in my Elisha Scroll, but never will be found in all the litter collected by the second-raters who have beguiled an unsuspecting world far too long!

◆ ◆ ◆

ELISHA WAS EN ROUTE to Bethel and feeling fairly pleased with himself. Ever since Elijah had been swept up to Heaven in a whirlwind, he was no longer second banana in the brotherhood of prophets. He was on top, the undisputed Number One! It felt good. Now, instead of kissing Elijah's buns, his were the buns to be obsequiously osculated. Not only that, but being first among the prophets meant he was first in collecting the profits! As the proverb said, "Not even a prophet of Yahweh can eat righteousness!"

He came to a creek issuing from a wood not far from Bethel. It was all of two cubits wide and so shallow that he could have walked through it effortlessly. But having the power to work miracles was still new to Elisha, so he relished trivial as well as spectacular ones. They all proved he was who he was! So, taking Elijah's cloak, which the prophet had dropped in his hurry to get to Heaven, the new superstar flogged the creek, shouting, "Where is Yahweh, the God of Elijah?" The abused creek swiftly divided to the right and left, and Elisha crossed over, chuckling and thinking that Moses had nothing on him. It was a big turn-on to overpower the little creek with the awesome power Yahweh granted to his prophets.

A hundred or so feet away a large group of boys was playing a strange new game that had been invented by a young priest, hoping to give the rowdy boys something to do besides get into trouble. It involved four bags arranged in a square; three were called "bases" and one called "home." At the home bag, a hitter would try to hit a small ball (made of hide and stuffed with straw tightly packed about a small rock in the center) thrown at him by a boy standing in the center of the square. If he could not hit it, another hitter got to take a chance and the failed boy was called "out." If he did hit the ball, he had next to try to get to the bag called "first base" before the ball was delivered to the boy guarding the bag. If the ball was caught before it hit the ground, though, the hitter became automatically out. Three outs caused the group of boys trying to get the hitters out to become hitters themselves, while the other group of boys who had been hitters had to go into the field to try to put the hitters out and thereby regain the privilege of being hitters. Each time the hitters successfully managed to go from bag to bag until they were once again at the home bag, they scored a run. The genius of the game was that it could go on and on and on until the boys grew tired of playing, which meant by then they were too tired to get into trouble.

To ensure the endlessness of the game, the young priest had taught them a new proverb: "It is not about winning or losing, but how long you play the game."

Alas, this marvelous and innovative idea had become darkened by the young priest's terrible sin. He had been caught uncovering the nakedness of the daughter of his father's wife and had been promptly cut off from his people (that is, stoned to death along with his half-sister).

His blackened reputation tarnished the game he had invented and prevented it from becoming popular among the sons of Israel. The rowdy boys, however, did not care about any of that. They loved the game, and none of them wanted the goody-goody boys of their community playing with them anyway.

The forty-four boys were divided up into two equal teams, and all of them were either hitters or fielders as the game went on and on. It was an obviously inefficient way to play the game, but they didn't care because they were having fun. At the moment when Elisha was working his miracle on the tiny, inoffensive creek, the teams were switching over after the fielding team had gotten three of the hitting team out. One of the lads noticed the prophet flogging the creek with the cloak, but was too far away to see the miracle that ensued. Which meant the boy laughed instead of being awed by a demonstration of the power Yahweh gave to his prophets.

"Hey," he called out to the others, "look at the old doofus whomp on the creek!"

The boys looked and laughed, one saying loudly, "I've heard of beating your meat, but never beating a creek!"

After the next roar of laughter died down a bit, another boy suggested, "Hey, let's go give the old doofus the biz."

"You only wanna do that cuz your team's down twenty-nine runs," a boy on the other team accused.

"You pukes maybe got seventy-seven runs, but you only scored three last ten times you was hitters, an' we're smackin' homers now like Samson smackin' Philistines, so we ain't even got a reason to wanna call it a game."

"Oh, yeah? Your momma worships phallic symbols!"

"Ain't so!"

"Is so!"

"Your momma wears combat sandals!"

"Ain't so!"

"Is so!"

Tempers were getting hot when Elisha came up to the boys and, feeling his own magnificence, decided to take charge of the situation. "Here, here!" he said sternly. "You rowdy boys ought to be studying the sacred laws or getting job training to be productive, tithe-giving workers when you're men. What are you doing out here quarreling like a bunch of women bartering in the marketplace?"

The boys resented this interference, not knowing who they were dealing with. To them, Elisha was just a strange old man with at least one screw loose. As little boys will do, they forgot their argument and turned on Elisha with united force.

"Get going, baldy!" one of them sneered, then all forty-four began chanting with merry derisiveness, "Get going, you bald puke!"

Elisha became furious. He was a prophet of Yahweh! These ragged kids were just rabble! "You can't talk to me like that!" he roared in his best fire-and-brimstone voice.

"Sez who?"

"Sez me!"

The boys laughed, which made the prophet more furious. He thundered, "I am Elisha, prophet of Yahweh, leader of the brotherhood of prophets! I inherited a double share of Elijah's spirit!"

"You sound like you've had a double share of spirits!"

"I can part rivers!"

"I can part my hair!"

"I can purify foul water!"

"I can make foul water!"

"I saw Elijah go up to Heaven!"

"I saw Eglah go down on Heber!"

Elisha's anger was so extreme that all he could do was stand there shaking violently as if his head would explode, which it looked as though it might as red as it was. The forty-four small boys jeered him relentlessly. Elisha felt a helplessness he had never expected to feel after becoming the head honcho of the brotherhood of prophets. These little boys had not learned that prophets and priests, the most important pillars upholding the traditional values of society, deserved respect and obedience. They were the ragged offspring of poor families and thus had little respect for traditional values. They had no future, thus were rowdy in the present.

Elisha's fury mounted until his rage was almost as great as his ego. Being unable to defeat his adversaries by himself, he did what Hebrew holy men always did in times of duress. He looked up toward Heaven and, in a voice full of self-pity and hunger for vengeance, cried out, "Hear my voice, Yahweh, when I petition. Protect my life from fear of the enemy. Hide me from the conspiracies of these little boys, from the uprising of the perpetrators of uppityness. They sharpen their tongues like a sword, and bend their arrows like abusive words, so that they can secretly shoot at the head honcho of the brotherhood of your prophets. They shoot at me with no warning and with no trepidation."

He went on and on and on, momentarily impressing the boys with his oratorical skills as he repeatedly oscillated between woe-is-me and fire-and-brimstone. None of the priests in their town could put on a show like this! It was so dramatically different from anything they had seen in their short lives that it was quite entertaining, and they all sang merry alleluias and hosannas whenever Elisha got off a really hot zinger.

Alas, the small boys did not realize that his prayer was ascending to Heaven over the hotline reserved for Hebrew prophets and priests. There it was transcribed by the seraphim on duty, who gave it to one of the seraphim under his command. The seraphim flapped his six wings and flew off to find the archangel Gabriel and give him the message to pass on to Yahweh. He found Gabriel drilling some divisions of the special forces that had become slack in their parade skills.

"Another request to punish enemies!" Gabriel spat out disgustedly. "The Hebrews are the biggest crybabies there ever were or ever could be. Stub their toes and they're launching laments up here, wanting Yahweh to blow up the pebble! Why don't you go to Limbo, snatch up one of those crybabies, and file that where the day never destroys the night."

"Sir, it's from Elisha, the new head honcho of the brotherhood of the prophets."

"Aw, damn! OK, OK, I'll pass it on."

Yahweh sat on his throne and beside him was Satan. They were working on the scenario for Operation Son of God. Satan said, "You know, boss, you haven't taken any R&R in the flesh. You've been a number of burning things down there. You've been a rock a couple times, and an active volcano. You spent a lot of time as pillars of fire and cloud before you gave that duty to me when nothing interesting was going on. But you haven't been in the flesh. You've missed riding some of that fine nooky down there. I don't believe you passed up Tamar, but you did."

"Your point is?"

"Op-SOG's the perfect opportunity for you to get some. You want to show up in the flesh as Jesus Christ. Well, why not get some babe pregnant and start from birth? You could work some miracles as a boy, get the PR ball rolling, dazzle some priests when you're a little older, get the legends started, prepping the masses for when you get going for real. That will be better than showing up as an adult with a fictional bio."

"Hmmm, not a bad idea. I've been wondering about nooky and what I've been missing."

Satan chuckled, "You been missing some good times, big boss!"

"OK, let's consider the scenario."

"Well, here's the way I see it. You want a hot babe, but she needs to be a bimbo so she'll believe you when you tell her she's still a virgin after you've rode what brains she's got out. It's important your birth's believed to be virgin."

"We don't really need a virgin birth for Op-SOG."

"We definitely do, boss. If you do Op-SOG, you're going to let anybody who believes the new theology become the chosen people. Trust me, if you want to sell yourself as the Son of God to the pagans, a Hebrew-style miracle birth won't help you. You need to come like they expect you to or you'll waste too much time persuading them they've been wrong about how sons of gods come into the world. Virgin births are the rage down there right now. Maybe they won't be so hot when you're ready to do Op-SOG, but I doubt that'll happen. Anyway, you should do it just for the fun of it. I've done that gig myself on a couple of my extended R&Rs. It's a trip being born, and afterwards you get all the titty milk you want for a few years. Trust me, you get born once, you're going to want to get born again!"

"Hmmm, 'born again.' Catchy phrase. Could be useful during Op-SOG. I see another selling point for your idea: a virgin-born messiah will mess with the heads of the orthodox Hebrews. They'll never believe it because that isn't the kind of miracle birth I've been using with the Hebrews. Yeah, I can see how amusing that'll be. OK, the mother of god will have to be a bimbo. She's going to have to be married though. No Hebrew girl would survive as an unwed mother if there's any respect for my laws left among the sons of Israel when Op-SOG kicks off. How's she going to be a virgin if she's married?"

"No problem. You get a bimbo babe who's engaged to a doofus who will fall for the virgin birth line and still marry her. If there aren't any hot bimbos engaged to guys doofus enough, take one with a guy who can be intimidated. Send Gabe down there to give him the word it's better to have horns than have a bad case of head-to-toe boils for the rest of his suddenly shortened life. Or you could use that plague you zapped the pharaoh and his aristocrats with, you know, the one that made peeing like squirting boiling oil. I liked that one. You should use it more often. However, I don't think a doofus fiancé will be hard to find; there's no shortage of doofuses on the earth."

"Not bad, not bad."

"Oh, yeah, when you go down in the flesh to ride her, go as the Holy Ghost. That'll prove the Trinity isn't just some silly fantasy."

Yahweh chuckled, "It'll take some serious doofus down there for the humans to believe they're practicing monotheism when they're worshipping a three-person deity!"

"Well, boss, I've got a proverb about that: 'Nothing makes humans more doofus than religion.'"

"You know, the entertainment that Op-SOG will create is too good to miss. Even if the Hebrews get their heads and buns wired together so they're marching to my drum, I'm doing it."

Satan sang, "The word of Yahweh can be trusted, and all his deeds are honest; his virtue and justice are perfect, and his love is a golden shower on his chosen people."

Yahweh grinned in a way that made Satan a little nervous and said, "Always with the uppity. I'm thinking about that little Op-SOG speech about the eunuchs who have made themselves eunuchs for the kingdom of Heaven's sake. I'm thinking you could be in the flesh with me as one of the disciples and demo that for people each time I preach it. It'll have the added value of being a really impressive miracle. Won't they all be impressed by a serpent and stones that always grow back after being sliced off? What do you think about that, smart ass?"

"Well, uh, boss, maybe I could give uppity a rest for a while instead?"

At that moment Gabriel flew up and informed Yahweh about Elisha's prayer. The supreme being radiated annoyance.

"Why do these damn Hebrews always want me to destroy somebody? Do they think I don't have anything better to do than whack people for them?"

Satan was who he was and so couldn't stop himself from laughing, "Well, you made them the chosen people, big boss."

"I'll give them some chosen!" He formed the biggest, mightiest, most destructive lightning bolt omnipotence could produce and prepared to hurl it down at the sons of Israel. "I'll start over again! I did it once! I'll do it again! I don't even need the earth! I have a zillion other planets I can start on again!"

Satan courageously stood and laid a restraining hand on the mighty arm of the enraged Yahweh. "Hey, big boss, come on. If you do that, it's all over for Op-SOG. That'll be more amusing than starting over again. Cut them some slack, boss. You created them all too human, remember? They're like me: they can't help it. That's what makes them so entertaining, right? That's what they're for, right?"

Yahweh glared for a few moments then made the horrifying lightning bolt disappear. "Yeah, you're right." He stared down at Elisha, who was still preaching a fire-and-brimstone sermon at the rowdy boys. "Maybe I designed them to be a little too entertaining! One of these days I'm going to lay an apocalypse on them they'll never forget!"

Satan suggested cheerfully, "Hey, that's part of the Op-SOG scenario anyway. Let's kick around doing it for real and see if it bounces."

"Hmmm, not a bad idea. Except it won't be the end of the world, just the end of the world as they know it. We'll see then how entertaining they are living on the earth after the apocalypse! OK, you take care of this," he handed Elisha's prayer to Satan, "and I'll work on the scenario."

Satan chuckled, "Heavy hand done right, that's my specialty!"

"Make it spectacular, smart ass. I want it to make the history books."

"No sweat, boss."

Satan flew down to the earth and found Elisha had returned to weeping and wailing up to Heaven. He showed no hint of tiring. It was as if he intended to break the record Moses set with his farewell address. The little boys were gathered about the prophet and were enjoying the show.

They did not look as though they were a frightening enemy inflicting intolerable insults on the old man, but that wasn't Satan's concern. The boys had played their final inning because the Big Umpire in the Sky was throwing them out of the game.

Satan looked about for some way to kill the boys that would be as spectacular as Yahweh wanted. He spotted two she-bears in the woods eating nuts and berries. He grinned when the plan popped into his head. It would be art. Performance art. He went over to the two she-bears and said, "OK, girls, duty calls. You see those kids? Go out there and put some serious hurt on them. Leave two alive so they can tell everybody about the miracle worked here today. That ought to get Elisha some respect for all the rest of the days of his life."

The she-bears looked at each other as though wondering what the boys had done to pull Yahweh's tail hard enough so that he'd sent a mighty archangel to whack them. Then they shrugged as if agreeing that it wasn't any of their business, and that orders from the high command were orders from the high command. The two she-bears came out of the wood and savaged forty-two of the boys.

Elisha stood nearby enjoying the spectacle, unaware that Satan hovered over his head to observe the miracle. Limbs and viscera and gore went flying in all directions. The boys tried to run away, but the bears were faster. Heads rolled, geysers of blood gushed from severed necks, and lumps and loops of wet guts rained down upon the executed priest's field of dreams. Elisha cheered them on with one of the victory songs the sons of Israel used to sing after massacring towns during the conquest of the Promised Land.

When the she-bears had slaughtered all but two of the boys, they went back into the woods, going to the small creek to wash the ghastly mess off before resuming peacefully eating nuts and berries.

Satan flapped his mighty wings and returned to Heaven to continue working on Op-SOG.

◆ ◆ ◆

WHAT THE ELISHA SCROLL reveals is that a real tragedy happened at that time. This real tragedy was that baseball was lost to civilization until it was again invented 2,700 years later. Think, dear G., what this has meant to world history as we know it!

Would Alexander the Great have conquered the known world if he could have been a starting pitcher instead of a king? Would Julius Caesar have wanted the tawdry position of Roman dictator if he could have been a major league general manager? Would the Romans have sacked Jerusalem and scattered the Hebrews throughout a hostile world if they'd had a contender for the World Series to root for? Indeed, would the American colonies have revolted if it had meant their minor league teams would no longer be associated with the British European League teams and thus their finest players no longer could play in the Big Show?

We shall certainly know these answers and many more when I have finished my laborious interpretations of the supremely important Terminally Ill Sea Scrolls. However, it is equally certain we never shall know any important answer as long as fools are fascinated by the Dim Sea Scrolls!

All that fame and fortune wasted on worthless scraps! It is so unjust that men who are in every conceivable way my inferiors reap the fame and fortune that ought to be mine and mine alone! (Well, partially yours, though, as I know you will agree, not a part that would be even close to as great as the part due to me.) How can I have ended up in such total obscurity, surviving first on my mediocre professor's salary, now on my wretched pension, and always having to beg for funding for my supremely important research, when my discovering the Terminally Ill Sea Scrolls ought to have been the most important event in world history in the 20th century?

How can the world be so beguiled by the Drab Sea

Scrolls? I can prove, as only a man of my superior qualifications and talents can, that the obsession with those perniciously useless scrolls is directly responsible for the failed American tactics in the Vietnam War, the giveaway of the Panama Canal, the One World Government Movement, and the scandalous cultural analyses by sexual libertarians like that Paglia woman! But these shocking truths I shall withhold, even from you, until all the world recognizes my glorious achievements and is waiting for the enlightenment only I have to offer them.

Thank you, dear G., for all you have done for me and even more for all you will do for me. Put all your heart and every second of your time into getting these selections published. I am still vigorous enough to enjoy the pleasures of fame and fortune and I am impatient to begin enjoying them. Not, of course, that material rewards are important to me, but, since they must naturally come to me once the world possesses these first fruits of my long, struggling years of labor, I see no harm in enjoying them. As superior as I am, I, too, have a touch of the human, all too human!

I now return to working on perfecting the next selections for publication, and you should begin to work on getting these I have given you published. Think of the glory you will be bringing to one who has so justly deserved it for so long and never tire in your efforts! Remember this proverb: "Lucky is the humble man who can serve a great man more like a footnote than a footstool."

Your humble servant,

Dr. Sebaceous Piafraus, Ph.D.

P.S. What the Sheol, you can have six percent!

Bible Quotes in Text

Introduction
Matthew 6:25, 31–32

Creation Scroll
Psalm 13:1–3; Genesis 1:26

Noah Scroll
Genesis 6:13; Psalm 95:1–7

Ham Scroll
Psalm 111:1–5; Psalm 128:1–5; Genesis 9:2; Genesis 9:25–27

Abram Scroll
Genesis 12:1–3; Psalm 26:1–3; Genesis 12:7; Genesis 3:17; Genesis 12:11–13; Genesis 12:18–19

Tamar Scroll
Psalm 102:1–20; Psalm 95:1–2; Job 3:11–13, 17–19, 24–25; Job 7:2; Job 23:2–7; Genesis 38:13; Genesis 38:16–18; Genesis 38:23; Genesis 38:24; Genesis 38:25; Tobit 4:15

Exodus Scroll
1 Corinthians 10:4; Exodus 16:3, 7–8; Numbers 11:4–6; Numbers 20:3–5; Exodus 17:4, 2; Numbers 11:11–12; Exodus 3:9–10; Exodus 17:14; Numbers 25:17; Numbers 31:2; Deuteronomy 20:10–13; Deuteronomy 21:10–14; Numbers 31:15; Numbers 33:52–56; Numbers 31:17–18; Leviticus 18:22

Elisha Scroll
2 Kings 2:23; Psalm 64:1–4; Matthew 19:12